Lincoln Public Library

November 1989

Dollar Road

The Pegasus Prize for Literature

Dollar Road

A Novel by
KJARTAN FLØGSTAD

Translated by Nadia Christensen

LOUISIANA STATE UNIVERSITY PRESS
Baton Rouge and London

Designer: Laura Roubique Gleason
Typeface: Bembo
Typesetter: The Composing Room of Michigan, Inc.
Printer and Binder: Thomson-Shore, Inc.

First Printing
98 97 96 95 94 93 92 91 90 89   5 4 3 2 1

Library of Congress Cataloging-in-Publication Data

Fløgstad, Kjartan, 1944–
    Dollar Road : a novel / by Kjartan Fløgstad ;
    translated by Nadia Christensen. p. cm.

    Translation of: Dalen Portland.
    I. Title
PT9069.F63D313   1989
839.8'3374   89-8244
ISBN 0-8071-1525-8 (alk. paper)

Publisher's Note

The Pegasus Prize for Literature has been established by Mobil Corporation to introduce American readers to distinguished works from countries whose literature is rarely translated into English. *Dollar Road,* by Kjartan Fløgstad, was awarded the Pegasus Prize in Norway in February, 1988, after a committee of distinguished scholars, writers, and editors selected it from among the best Norwegian novels written since 1975. When it was first published in 1977, the novel won the Nordic Council Prize—the most prestigious literary award in Scandinavia. Prior to now, Mr. Fløgstad's novels have been translated into eight languages; this book marks his English language debut.

Chairman of the Pegasus Prize selection committee was Paal-Helge Haugen, himself a prominent poet. Other members of the jury were Arild Linneberg, a critic and professor of literature at the University of Bergen; Liv Sæteren, managing director of the Deichman Library in Oslo; Simen Skjønsberg, a poet and former cultural editor of *Dagbladet;* and Thorild Viken, editor-in-chief of Den Norske Bokklubben.

Dollar Road covers about forty years of modern Norwegian history, from the 1930s to the 1970s, as the country moves from a traditional agricultural society to an industrialized economy. Work in this new economy, and duty to it, are central to the lives of the novel's main characters, the Høysand family. In the end, however, Rasmus Høysand breaks the family pattern, going to sea and landing in Latin America. There, as Rasmus questions his identity, the novel becomes a rich blend of reality and fantasy, myth and even verse.

In selecting the novel, the Pegasus Prize jury wrote that it is "a kaleidoscope, a carnival, part *bildungsroman,* part alternative history of a Social-Democratic society, Scandinavian style, and the blend of caustic social satire and poetry is unique."

Dollar Road is the second Pegasus Prize-winning novel to be translated by Nadia Christensen. In 1980, she earned praise for her translation from Danish of Kirsten Thorup's *Baby.* She is also noted for her work with Norwegian texts, as will be evident from a reading of this book.

On behalf of the author, we wish to express our appreciation to Mobil Corporation, which established the Pegasus Prize and introduced it in Norway. We also thank William Jay Smith for his assistance in translating three of the poems: "Lullaby," "Shipping Out," and "Far-Out Ode."

Contents

The Parliamentary action hereby proposed is based on the experiences of industrial communities with regard to difficulties that arise because large industrial firms believe they have the right to take actions that cause destructive harm to the area and its inhabitants. With no certainty as to whether a factory will keep its operation within reasonable limits, one "lives on a volcano" here in the district. This becomes even more true in view of the fact that only a few of the factory workers have their roots here, whereas all the rest have no ties to the district other than those connected with their work in the industry.

—Appeal to the Government and the Parliament from the four townships of Tinn, Sauda, Odda and Kyrkjebø to pass a law that would protect Norwegian communities against the consequences of arbitrary actions by industrial companies (Rjukan Newspaper and Book Publishers, 1939)

Let all People ponder this nonetheless within themselves. A Person born of honest Folk who in foreign Lands doth wander, findeth that his Travel oft doth take him among Enemies, oft among Friends and Foes, and many a time against his own Will is he beset by unforeseen Hardship and Misfortune and doth require Money and other Necessities of Life, and so he desireth, and in Truth he hath but this Choice, to set out upon Land and Sea. What shall he then do? He doth consider his Honor and his clear Conscience, and he fleeth the Multitude who roam the Land and rob and steal. He is a Person of Esteem that God hath also given Decency and other good Qualities; and so he doth wander and beg his Way through the Land. To stay in one Place is not his Lot in Life, for then on moral Grounds would he be nabbed and imprisoned as well; and what shall he then do? The Truth doth not suffice for him in any Way, for if he telleth the Truth in a Tavern, to wit that he hath no Coin, he receiveth no Food, nor Drink, nor Lodging, but must lie with a hungry Stomach under the open Sky; and if he telleth the Truth to the Postmaster he is given no Horse, but must travel on Foot; and if he hath fine Garments whereon he would borrow, he doth rarely receive the half their fair Worth; and if he selleth the Garments outright, it is only the worse for him, for no one in any Place doth show him Respect if he arriveth like a slovenly Dog. Discreet Folk and such Men as perceive the true Qualities of a Person, are not found in every Village, and a Peasant doth not give better Bread for a hundred Words of Latin. There never yet hath been any Person who did always tell the Truth and survived well in the World. Did he possess half of Fortune's Purse, yet would he still fear lest someone take his Life for the Sake of the Purse. A Person of high Standing oft must make himself appear more lowly than his Position warranteth, and a Peasant oft must put on the Clothing of a Gentleman would he survive. Oh, dulce bellum in expertis, *they that have tried both Good and Evil hold not in contempt a poor Fellow that falleth due to Need and youthful Carelessness. The old Proverb sayeth that One can lie, but never steal, one's Way through a Country. Need breaketh Iron, and Need forceth a Dog to run with a Pack when it much rather would run free. . . . I say nothing, I know well what I think. God alone knoweth best what I, a poor Fellow, have had to endure from Time to Time in foreign Lands ere I arrived where I could learn and see somewhat in the World, and God knoweth that I, nonetheless, against great and grievous Sins have guarded myself, as much as is humanly possible; but this I do confess, that I have had to be sometimes a Gentleman, sometimes a poor Devil.*

—Laurentius Wivallius, "Open Letter," Kristianstad, 1630
(National Archives of Sweden)

Dollar Road

Full Force

CHILDREN AND DRUNKEN FOLKS

She plants her feet on the concrete and stands. She stands and bends forward, throws out her arms as if beginning a racing dive, takes hold of the handles on each side of the full zinc tub, and lifts. The older woman beside her throws a last wet garment onto the pile of clothes in the tub. She shakes her hands in the air. Then she wipes them over the apron on her stomach, dries both sides of her hands.

Well, she says. That's a big enough pile. You can go and hang it up now.

The young woman waddles heavily across the floor, with broad hips and a stiff back and the tub in her outstretched arms. She is dressed in a long skirt and has a white kerchief on her head and wooden shoes on her feet. At the cellar door she pauses, standing utterly calm against the sunlight outside, like a dark, symmetrical, one-dimensional figure cut out of history and laid on a bright rectangular background for contrast.

Now what can it be? she says half aloud, out into the light.

Behind her, there is an abrupt silence. The older woman leaves her work at the scrubbing board and wooden tub inside the cellar. Then she comes clattering across the floor and stops beside the woman in the doorway. Blue fjord, green mountain slopes, blue sky. She knits her brows and stands squinting at the sun. Then she, too, sees something moving.

Ain't that Samel Høysand's son?

Why's he runnin' like that, do you s'pose?

The old woman shades her eyes with her right hand in order to see better.

Don't know, she says. But if it's right what they say, that it's from children and drunken folks you hear the truth, then it looks like the path away from what ain't true, well, it ain't exactly straight and easy. Just try and follow the tracks of that little guy there, and you'll find out there's lots of roundabout ways to go.

That's so.

Sure is.

I see.

The old woman does not say anything more. She turns abruptly and clatters back into the semidarkness. The daughter shifts her grip on the handles of the zinc tub and waddles on across the farmyard, erect under her burden. She hears the noise from the wooden washtub and vat begin again inside the cellar.

IN DUE TIME

The boy they have been watching follows the borders of the fields at the edge of the forest on the opposite mountain slope and runs swiftly toward the gate of the outlying pasture. He is perhaps ten years old, tall and gangling for his age, with large blue eyes in a thin face that can look sad or sorrowful or simply stupid. On the few occasions he smiles, the smile rises in his face like a new moon from the dark crest of a ridge, and yet it can light up November days, tropical nights, or hardened black hearts, the grownups think, depending upon the nature of their own experiences. Now he is so taken up with what he is doing that he almost forgets to shut the gate behind him, but he catches himself, stops briefly, and fastens it to the gatepost with a loop of rope. Then he runs on, with long legs under the thin boy's body, white-blond hair, bare feet, his trousers rolled up and wide suspenders outside his shirt. He runs over the stone bridge, across the brook that turns white in wild swirling and is captured in a wooden trough, plunges toward the waterwheel, drives the millstone, grinds the grain. But he is busy, does not stand very long looking at the stream, the trough, the water-

2

wheel, the mill before he rouses himself and starts running again. The first slope is steep and rocky, but he does not notice, runs the entire way. You're such a spry fellow, his mother had said, can't you run up with the message? Then I'm sure Grandfather will carve you a hiking stick. Oh, yes! He can, he can bring the message! He runs up the slope, barefooted and empty-handed. It is late summer, they have had rain, the sun is shining, and now it is warm and fresh under the soles of his feet. He runs along the *stølsveg*—the road between mountain farms—sending up small showers of mud and dust. He can bring the message, he knows the road. Nedsta Kvednakleiv, Øvsta Bogemyr, Hilradn. He knows the names, all of them, he knows the stones he treads, he knows nearly all the trails along the *stølsveg*, out from the cultivated meadows, through the pastureland enriched with artificial fertilizers and up through the forest with its mixture of ash and alder and pine and clumps of hazel and fir and a few great oaks. He hurries past Beinhola, where the bones of a man or a calf lie, and runs past Den øde Ø, Gamleleiren. He comes to Stemmen, where two dun-colored horses stand with their rumps toward each other, red poll cattle brush away flies and gadflies with their tails, and sheep, which Papa calls meadow thieves, lie in the shadows ruminating. He runs across Spirele, up the logging path, to the bogs down near Ganske Creek. He runs in fits and starts, the way a young boy does. There are so many wonderful things to stop for. Above him, white horses of fair-weather clouds rear toward the midday sun. He takes tight hold of their reins, gets their front hooves down again, and gallops away toward the bloody battle that will be fought far out in the Svandal Mountains when the sun goes down in the west. He sees all the enemies. There they are! An army of men from outer space steal through the grass on the other side of the creek. It's easy to see they came from another planet. He must stand quite still so they don't discover him. And don't take him prisoner! But maybe it's a bear instead? Then it wouldn't help much to stand still! Where could I go if it's a bear? His eyes search the trunks of pine trees and find a branch where he could sit. No, best to run away! He starts off again, leaps over the stones in Ganske Creek and hurries with his eyes closed past the big rock where the woman from Sunday school once saw the Devil him-self. In the shape of a dog! Remember that, children, you're never safe from the Evil One! Wherever you go, he's after you! The boyish feet pound like drumsticks on a lively drum in an Independence Day parade, and his blood makes drumbeats in his ears. Has he gone far enough? He doesn't feel a cold hand on his shoulder, no jaws with sharp teeth snap at his leg. Carefully, he opens his eyes, takes a sidelong peek. No. No Devil! No dog! He runs across the high, dry, flat stretches of forest land on a path that snakes its way around sun-warmed rocks and across creek beds, roots that rain and hooves and feet have dug out at angles to the road, the tufts of bulrushes, the large licorice drops of fresh sheep dung. It's easy to run here, his eyes do not search for the next spot to set down his foot, they see two steps ahead, and his feet follow, find the places his eyes have picked out for them. But there he has to make a long leap over a mud puddle, and just barely clears it, does not even stop to look for tadpoles. Up Springbakken, where the sheep always broke into a run with swinging udders and tinkling bells and lambs on stiff legs, the bear pit at the top, and then down the hill a short way to Stikleiva. Ha! That branch could have made a fine bat! Another time! He runs along the *stølsveg*. He has a message. He has something he must say. A few sentences which his mother made him repeat over and over again until he knows them by heart, a few simple sentences that will resound from his lips like thunder between Vorenuten and Nonskiljene peaks, pour down into the fertile mountain canyons, and destroy the crops he lives from, the language he lives in, the silence through which he runs, the words themselves. He suddenly feels so tired, so tired, and dawdles on the long Stikleiva climb, but soon he can see the whole distance ahead, he can look out from Øvste Stien and all the way over to Drivane, where they are mowing hay for the third day. The flocks of sheep bleat, the birds sing, his heart thumps in his chest. What if I met a stagecoach robber now! What if he had a shotgun! He runs easily across the meadows belonging to Jespersen the Dane, but here they have gathered up the haystacks, and nobody is down by the barn. The mown bogs are damp on the soles of his feet, the hay sheds full of hay. He has

4

to go over and put his hand inside and pull out a handful. He holds it under his nose and drinks in the smell. Dry hay. The best smell in the world. The air is still, it smells of dry hay and warm pine forest and flowers and heather and grass. And at one place, farther on, when fair weather turns the wind to a southeaster, it also smells of something else—bitter, unfamiliar, foreign. He is so tired, so tired. Progress is slow as he continues on his way. He leans down to run his hand through the heather and strips off blueberries growing along the road, in a landscape that has changed only like this: spring, summer, autumn, winter; and has been used only for this: grazing, mowing, felling, shaving bark. It's still summer, warm, he can really feel now how warm it is, the showers yesterday did only good, no damage, the hay from the fields nearest home is under cover, at Drivane his grandfather and his uncles are cocking the hay. He runs downhill again now, which goes very fast, and he is so off in another world that he does not notice the stone in the middle of the path. He stumbles and falls forward on his knees and stomach. Head first onto the path. He tumbles head over heels, and how it hurts! But no one will hear him if he cries. And his trousers didn't tear. He does not cry. He pushes his trousers up over the knee. No blood, no wound, take it easy now, easy. He stands up, and the trousers fall down into place again. He starts running. Yes, his knee is all right. He's not going to let himself be stopped by a little fall and a sore foot, not him, on an early afternoon when the sun has crossed Kvitaberåsen and meets him on Skarslihaugen! He begins the last ascent, up toward Sirikleiv. Down in Skarsli the people from Espeland have finished their haying, but they are still mowing on Sirikleiv and out toward Barlønnskåra. He has to take a drink at the springhead below Sirikleiv, thrust his head far into the cool darkness under the big stone, purse his lips and suck in, one time, five times. It's a good spring, always water there, and it's fresh, and there's one sheep turd to add some taste—that protects against everything. Suddenly he is not tired anymore. He walks up the steep, bracken-covered hills below Drivane looking at the red blossoms on the foxglove, and the thought comes to him that among these flowers you can capture bumblebees for making radios: you put them in a tobacco carton, poke holes in it with Mama's knitting needle, and on the front of it you draw buttons and knobs and the tuning dial with Hilversum and Motala stations. Then you hear the buzz of the bumblebees inside, just like in a radio. But not today. Today, later today, he'll pick some foxglove blossoms and play with them in the cave, because now he sees that what they resemble most is a secret clergy as they stand like scarlet-clad cardinals nodding to each other in deep meditation. He looks up. Has he stopped again? He mustn't dawdle too much now. What if Grandpa's watch has been running and running, faster than he has been running himself, the minute hand running across the final swathe? But now he sees the grass on the barn roof! He's all the way up now, just a short field yet to go. And there is the small hay barn, built of logs, with a roof of birch bark and sod. It stands high and free, at the edge of the mountainside, with a view toward the green ridges through which he has run, the blue fjord that stretches out to Stavanger, and the brown smoke from the factory far back in the fjord. The barn is already half filled with hay, and over by the stone-gray wooden wall four men and a young woman sit looking at him. They are having a meal and watching him. They eat and look, stop chewing and just stare at him, wipe their mouths with the backs of their hands. Three of the men and the young woman are in their prime, somewhere between twenty and thirty. They squint at the sun and the boy with wrinkled foreheads under black, curly mops of hair. The fourth man is perhaps in his sixties. He is wearing a striped shirt that is open at the neck, dark trousers made from the wool of his own sheep, and a vest with a gold watch chain on it. The watch chain goes down into the vest pocket, this the boy knows, down to a shiny tombac watch with an engraving of a peacock, which is now almost completely worn off, on the cover and the name of the watchmaking company, N. D. Allen, Cooperstown, North Dakota, on the face. This the boy knows as well, because often he has been allowed to pull out the chain, open the watch-case, and look at the watch. No one has said anything. On a flat rock inside the barn lies a black homespun jacket, neatly folded, with a stiff black hat on top of it. The three young men are dressed alike, in rolled-up homespun trousers and gray wool

6

undershirts with long sleeves. The young woman is sitting slightly behind them with the coffeepot. They have drunk sour, strong-tasting curdled milk and eaten thin cold porridge. Now all five stare at the boy who stands in front of them trying to catch his breath. He is panting heavily but is neither sweaty nor flushed; he is still pale and cold as quartz. One of the young men has stopped short with his spoon in his mouth. Another wipes his spoon silvery clean in the grass next to him. On the bogs behind them, new-mown hay is spread out to dry. It is still a fresh green color, which means they turned it just before they ate. Three-pronged rakes lean against the barn, from its rafters hang several long-handled scythes, hip-holders for whetstones and water, a rope for carrying hay on one's back; naked feet in the mountain grass. Silence, silence, since the beginning, since always. The boy gasps for breath and the words that will break this silence for always, for good, that will tear up the peaceful picture as easily as if it were a defenseless, useless photograph or daguerreotype that no one cares to keep any longer. Over on Øvst Drivane he sees the bent backs of the Jahans brothers as they walk beside each other mowing with scythes. *Langkjerra!* The word for long two-wheeled carts flashes into his mind. We've got the longest *langkjerra*! And not the Jahan brothers! And the best manure-spreading cart! Then he feels the others looking at him and tries again to get out the words. What *were* they now? He *must* remember them, he's going to say them soon. But it's not he, it's the oldest man, it's Grandfather, with his watch chain and dark, solemn dress suit for Sunday, church, weekend, who breaks the silence. He is about to say something, but his eyes are not fixed on the breathless boy; they are faraway and unfocused and full of Liaset, Brekkeheia, a glimpse of Nevrålen, Breikvam, Botnane, Børkjelandsnuten, Reinfoss, Tempreinuten, Napen, Reinsnuten, and Skaudel, with the white glacier farthest back that embraces everything and turns its back to the east and the distant Suldal Mountains. Strong and wild and mighty. And so vulnerable and defenseless that it is all no more than a photograph the boy can hold in his hand and tear to pieces. The old man fills his gaze one last time, as if he knows that what he sees will soon fade. Then he draws his watch out of

7

his pocket, clicks open the clasp, looks down at the face: the historic moment, the precise time and place.

Well, well, so it's you! he says, looking up again. You're a spry one, all right. Set yourself down here now, and have some food, along with us men.

The boy has finally caught his breath. He does not sit down. His voice is shrill. The words come in a torrent.

I'm to tell you, he says. I'm to tell you from Mama that I'm to tell Uncle Selmer he could get a shift at the factory. And I'm to tell you that it could probably be more, too, and that he should hurry, because he should be there this afternoon at three o'clock.

KRONER AND ØRE

There are many ways of explaining how the world functions and why things happen as they do. Selmer Høysand, who had already risen to his feet, and looked tall and slim and serious beside the small gray barn, could be a credulous man in many ways, and he was kind and trusting, as are most Norwegians from the west-coast area of Vestland. But when his brother Sylfest's boy came rushing far into the wild heaths and gasped some breathless words that would change his destiny and point out the direction his life would follow for all the rest of his days, there were several things Selmer Høysand did *not* believe. He did not believe, for example, that his fate was determined by the constellation of the stars on the day and at the hour of his birth, or by the results of the local election the previous year, or the lines in his palm, the sequence of playing cards in a pack, the parliamentary elections coming up in two years, the Almighty God, the pattern of coffee grounds (which were boiled twice) in the bottom of his cup, which he now emptied out in the grass and cleaned with a tuft of hay. In a plain, indisputable way, Selmer Høysand sensed the mysterious power that finds its statistical expression in the capitalistic logic of daily stock-market prices and its dynamic expression in the equally impenetrable Marxist dialectic, and when he set off at a run, after a few brief words of goodbye and after his father had pulled out the tombac watch yet one more time and clicked open the clasp and said,

You'll just make it, Selmer, if you hurry, he thought clearly and coherently about the powers that ruled his life. He made his way down the steep fern-covered hills, tramped on slate rock, sloshed through bogs, shuffled through grass, stumbled in the buckthorn bushes, hopped over stones, and thought about money. Pure and simple. Kroner and øre. About the facts that last year he had earned forty-five kroner working for the summer as a farmhand, that he was twenty years old and this year worked at home for his room and board. Now he envisioned yellow wage envelopes containing coins and wage statements and fluttering bills that drifted down onto the counters of the tradesmen in town and paid for one fine thing after another—ready-made suits, leather shoes, store-bought bread, a bicycle perhaps, pastries, a white shirt worn with the collar outside his suit coat, a cap, a radio. A radio! The mere thought made him take an extra long stride and quicken his pace. A radio—music, ski meets, skating competitions, brought right into the room! Grøttumsbråten, Ballangrud, Sigmund Ruud, the Olympics in Garmisch and Berlin, Blaupunkt radio. He sees it before his eyes as he lopes down the gentle ridges where, twenty years earlier, far-sighted and fast-talking Norwegian businessmen had persuaded the farmers to give up their water rights, and where American investments laid the foundation for a large industrial plant down where the rivers run together and out into the fjord. When the terrain becomes more open, he also sees the smoke, which curls its way up in the clear air until it is caught by a sea breeze and laid lovingly over the green mountainsides. The smoke rises. In Europe and the United States, the sensitive noses of the stock markets have begun to register small upward gains. Cautiously, cautiously! But Germany is rearming, of that there can be no doubt, and weapons are made of steel. Steelworks and weapons factories in England, France, Sweden, the USA do not lie dark and cold, either. To say nothing of Japan. Yes, the most important stock markets around the world show a rise in steel. Cautiously as yet, cautiously, but indisputably. No bull market so far. Upward movement. Manganese is a major ingredient in steel for weapons. In New York City, the board members of a corporation in the organic-chemistry industry discuss, and fi-

9

nally agree to, an increase in production. It is midsummer, and in the streets thirty stories below the boardroom the asphalt melts and bubbles in the heat. A uniformed policeman holds a large-caliber Ruger pistol in both hands and shoots down a man who has stolen a loaf of bread. The man throws up his arms and falls forward on the sidewalk. Casual passers-by crowd around him. The police officer sticks his pistol back in its holster. Manganese removes undesirable qualities in steel used for weapons, makes it hard outside and resistant inside. Upon receiving a telegram from the United States, a Norwegian board meeting in Oslo blindly endorses a resolution to start operating a manganese-smelting furnace at one of the company's Norwegian plants. The furnace will produce standard silicomanganese. When those in charge at the factory find out about the resolution that same day, they quickly evaluate the situation from many perspectives. The Number 3 and Number 4 furnaces are being repaired, Number 21 will be rebuilt, assuming the board in the United States appropriates the necessary money. The factory directors review the situation together and decide to put Number 32 into operation following a report from the production engineer that the start-up can begin more or less immediately. The power company connected to the factory reports that the water reservoirs are full and overflowing. In consultation with the personnel office, the directors look at the employee situation. Thirty new men must be hired, they conclude, three on the tap floor and three up in stoking on the operating floor on each shift in the furnace room, plus one in Receiving, besides extra men in departments such as Electrode Assembly, Packing, Cleaning, Raw Materials. And what about the Cooling Department? The personnel office looks at its endless waiting lists, crosses off names, and the bosses finally have good news—for a few—when they pass the clusters of unemployed men waiting for them or passing them on Storelv Bridge as they head home for lunch or dinner. Others hear it from relatives or neighbors, who leave their shift even more eagerly than usual and carry home messages to brothers, sons, brothers-in-law, lodgers—men whose bodies jolt upright and whose faces liven as their limbs relax again and they look around for

10

somebody to grip tightly or hug very hard. Work? Me? Work! There's work! Paradise! Work. Or less direct. For example, a tired, breathless little boy who runs through a pastoral fjord landscape in western Norway to tell his father's brother that he is going to be torn out of the natural household and integrated into the national and international social economy, and that his future, his work, love, loyalty, development of talents and strength and class consciousness and political understanding will be tied to the expansion of, or crises in, the capitalistic economic system. No, Selmer Høysand does not believe in horoscopes or in palm reading or in coffee grounds or parliamentarianism or seriously in any god. He keeps on running downward, beyond Barlønnskåra, Sirikleiv, Skarsli, Øvste Stien, along Forekammen, through the precise names of places in a production process that collapses and becomes overgrown with weeds and disappears in silence in the wake of his long strides. Selmer Høysand runs for all he is worth, sweaty and flushed and flustered, and wonders what time it is, runs across gurgling bogs that are no longer mowed, through clumps of woods that are no longer foraged for firewood, under pine trees that are no longer cut for timber, takes hold of ash saplings whose bark is no longer scraped for fodder, slips on steep ledges that are no longer used for pasture, knows where he is by names which no longer refer to his means of livelihood, names that soon will lose all meaning, be forgotten and replaced with: Little Cliff, Big Cliff, Little Mountain, The Knoll, The Mound, Big Rock, The Ridge, Factory Hill, The Pond, The Lookout.

STARTING TO ROLL

Selmer works out in the factory yard for just one day. He stands under the locomotive shed waiting. The regular workers are laughing and cracking jokes, the new ones don't know anything, not even where to focus their eyes. Finally the foreman comes. You guys can come with me and take a look at the salmon, he says in passing, and walks agilely from sleeper to sleeper along the railroad tracks. Selmer, his body still covered with congealed sweat from his trip down the mountain, ends up in Loading where, using his bare hands, he fills huge steel skips with sharp chunks of standard silico-manganese, and doesn't see salmon anywhere. Maybe they call this the salmon? But he doesn't dare to ask. They thrust an iron hook into the heap of manganese and make it slide so the dust flies. Selmer doesn't understand anything. Suddenly, when they've finished loading, the crane's huge shackle hangs above them, dangling two hooks that are to be attached to the ears of the skip; then a locomotive comes creeping down the tracks pushing a long boxcar. But the work itself he understands. Selmer pays full attention to everything going on around him and sees what the others are doing. It's not so difficult when you watch those who know how. After three skips, he and his partner, a boy from Suldal who seems even a little younger than himself, are able to keep up the tempo and build walls of the finest stones in the front of the skip so that the chunks don't slide out when it comes on the scale and make the crane operator—whom Selmer finally discovers far up in the shadows beneath the roof like a wrathful Old Testament Jehovah—go completely crazy, swearing and cursing in Swedish and Finnish and English and Russian, pointing and shouting, Dumb farmer! and Fuckin' idiot! and Holy shit! and totally unintelligible things down through the thick gray dust. Uzheli mal bila gorya nam? After each skip, they get a five-minute break. When at last they too come out into the fresh air, Selmer and the boy from Suldal sit down and look with wide eyes at the other workers, who are pinching snuff or chewing tobacco or smoking cigarettes or pipes and spitting through their front teeth down into the railroad tracks and laughing and lying about things that Selmer and the boy from Suldal barely sense the meaning of. Selmer has been away from the farm before, he had three months of military training after all, mostly together with other farm boys. That was something else. This is something else! Selmer sits watching intently, following everything that happens. He's a slim, round-shouldered fellow with thin wrists and ankles, and he walks with a light, loose-jointed gait. His features are delicate and irregular under curly dark hair. He is wearing the same clothes he wore for mowing hay, plus a jacket and shoes. Shoes. Not on his life would he have dared to come in his farmer's clogs and risk being called a Wooden-Shoe Jesus. Wooden-Shoe Jesus, Wooden-Shoe Jesus! Still, his clothing clearly indicates that he belongs to other times and other places than beside the skips, the heaps of manganese, the boxcars, and the gondolas. He realizes this himself, too, and does not try to pretend to be other than he is. That night, he stands with a sore back and cuts on his hands waiting for the whistle and for permission to go home, and he feels frightened. Is this what it's like to work at the factory? Then the foreman comes out of the office and tells him to show up at the furnace room tomorrow. At seven o'clock in the morning.

ON TOP OF THINGS

Selmer Høysand becomes a good furnaceman, moves from one job to the next in the furnace room. His hands heal. The work looks easy when he does it. He has the knack for it. After a few days, his back and arms are no longer stiff from the unaccustomed movements. He learns faster than most, is on the alert for new tasks, and if another worker needs a hand, Selmer rushes in to help all he can. So he becomes well-liked, even if he is also quick to follow the foreman's slightest suggestion, because for him it is all part of the same feeling of solidarity. Selmer rents a room in town; it gets to be too far to go home to the farm each evening. A room of his own no less, on the second floor. He has to tiptoe through the darkened room of the son in the house, who they say has tuberculosis, and over to his own door. He closes it carefully behind him. The boy coughs in the other room. Selmer has heard about the dangers of TB and lies awake with his eyes wide open. Smoke kills! he has seen in the Sauda newspaper. But it's the Socialists who say that. Victims turn blue-black in the face and die within a few days. Sauda pneumonia. Selmer manages to get a few hours sleep before trudging off to work again. The streets he walks through remind him of what he has read about the Klondike and the Western Front, with large trenches where they are laying sewer pipes, tripods above the largest stones, dilapidated old houses, painted houses and unpainted houses, new clapboard houses and houses built of rough planks. Selmer takes food with him from the farm, enough to last an entire week. It is at least a month before he ventures into the café. Good food, well prepared. Radio music each evening. Selmer hesitantly surveys the half-empty room, discovers the radio, and reverently sits down right in front of it. No music. No sports. Victor Mogens' commentary, flatbread and yellow pea soup. On weekends and during his free shifts, Selmer goes home. He sits in the light of the kerosene lamp in the living room or, in good weather, out in the farmyard, or he helps tend the cattle, and gives no direct answers but merely repeats, How do I like it? Well, I'd say I'm beginning to earn my pay over there now. And he's right. He is earning his pay, very well in fact, and taking care of whatever falls into his hands as though it were his own. He's a good worker, say the bosses. He's a good worker, that Høysand. Selmer gets so much on top of things that he's about to burn up as he stands on top of the furnace pot to clean out the runner or open the skimmer. But Selmer is no longer afraid. He knows when the shop truck will come and what's needed when it does, and when the crane's hooks will dangle above his head, and what to do with them. With his first three pay envelopes in his pocket, Selmer goes to a store. He does not buy a radio, or a bicycle, or just one little pastry. Selmer Høysand goes into town and buys overalls. Overalls made of stiff, dark blue denim. America. The U.S. of A. Those who did well over there, the successful ones, came home wearing overalls. That was one of Selmer Høysand's earliest clear memories. They came home along the road to the Høysand farm in faded blue denim overalls. There were two of them, both brothers of his mother. They had herded sheep in the hills of Montana and accomplished the most incredible, heroic deeds. They had survived Indians with tomahawks and Buffalo Bill's revolvers and landing at Ellis Island and had lived through sandstorms and snowstorms on the prairie by slaughtering the horse they rode on, cutting it open, ripping out the bowels and stomach and creeping in where the intestines had been. But how did they manage to breathe? Ve yust breathed through his asshole! Later they got jobs as coachmen or rod men at the plant and impressed people with their English by saying

14

"Yes very well" and "I love you" to the horses, and "Giddap!" to the American engineers in puttees who drove in phaetons and directed the expansion of the carbide factory. Now the brothers were home for the first time and had traveled across the bounding main and gone ashore in Stavanger in faded blue overalls and thrown away their money in a bank that went bankrupt two days later, and came home to the Høysand farm with ten dollars and pocket watches made of gold or tombac and fine shiny buckles all over their overalls. They talk to Selmer's parents. High, strange, unfamiliar voices far up in the bright summer air. It feels like the mountains are going to fall down on top of me, they say. They couldn't possibly have been so high before. Have they been added onto while we were away? Or: Is this really what they call Big Meadow? This tiny little patch here? And this is Big Field? They look at each other in disbelief and smile. Spit tobacco in opposite directions. Big Meadow, ho ho. The other grownups look angry, the Americans keep laughing. Then they grab hold of Selmer and throw his light body high up into the empty air, amid the laughter and all the faded blue, and there's the smell of snuff or chewing tobacco and Selmer is frightened and wants to be put down again. The boy is frightened and wants to be put down! Selmer Høysand is unwillingly set down, finds firm ground under his feet again, and runs as fast as he can out of the keen, sun-filled childhood memory. Selmer Høysand proudly carries the new overalls home from the store and goes to work that evening in a new outfit. They have two sizes, says the furnace operator: Too Large and Too Small. Selmer must have gotten a Too Large. But Selmer just laughs. He is a grown man. The overalls are the visible sign. In far shorter time than usual, Selmer has discovered what a blow is and how to stoke in the blow, and when they need to take mix from the chute to the furnace in a wheelbarrow, and when the electrodes must be lowered and raised. On the tap floor, it does not take him long to figure out the secret of the skimmer, how to slip the electrode with a short, precise little rap of the sledgehammer, pat the red sand with his glove, coat the slag chills and sample cups, smooth the shell sand in the metal chills with a spade, protect his face from the heat when they hook up and unhook. And if there is a rough furnace that has to be stoked, he's quick to put his weight behind a burning bar and rod the fuckin' taphole (which he never says himself but undoubtedly thinks when the men around him sometimes say it), and he's right where he is supposed to be when it's time to pull the slag and one man stands on each side of the chills while the crane operator (with his sloppy hat and booming voice!) wriggles the hooks down in place, and he is thankful, like everyone else, when the crane operator is careful and accurate and gets the ingots up in one piece and over into the sand truck. Selmer is not one to say more than he intends. When they sit in the lunchroom between tap and pulling the slag and between pulling the slag and tap, he doesn't talk much, but he chuckles and joins in the laughter when the other men keep going on and on and on about festivities that he, Selmer Høysand, has only heard rumors of until now: So I'm lyin' here, bangin' her hard, and the other blacksmith apprentice, he's lyin' in the bunk under me, bangin' another one just as hard. In the bunk right under me, goddammit! And me in the top bunk! Bangin'! The both of us! Finally, we get in the same rhythm! And then, no shit, we come at the fuckin' same time, both me and the other apprentice! And Selmer listens and works, and learns, and stays on in the furnace room. Oh, he's a crafty one, all right, say the others on the tap floor.—That Høysand, he's sort of a funny guy.—No, he don't exactly say too much, Høysand don't.—But if you just joke with him a bit, he comes around, too.—Still water runs deep, you know.

A MATTER OF CLASS

Selmer Høysand has become the second man on the Number 3 tap floor, and has substituted for the head tapper. An additional furnace, Number 32, is put into operation. Selmer keeps earning seniority, becomes more confident in his work, more on top of things. The boom trends increase slowly, absolutely, surely. Manchuria. Ethiopia. Soldiers fall to the ground, their rifles left lying to rust; the cannons of Mussolini, Chiang Kai-shek, and the Emperor of Japan shoot each other to bits and have to be replaced; Hitler stockpiles weapons; smoke lies more and more

16

thickly over the Ruhr; a North Sea boat unloads semiprocessed metal in Duisburg. On the tap floor in the furnace room, Selmer Høysand stands watching through his safety glasses how the manganese twists from the tap hole down through the runner, is separated from the slag in the skimmer, and hardens in the metal chills. The Labor party wins the parliamentary elections and forms a government after the Farmers' party gives its support to resolve the crisis. The next day, Selmer Høysand goes to work as before, with the same companions there, the same bosses, the same engineers, the same director, the same job, the same room in town, the same bed in the loft at home, the same amount in his wage envelope. No little barefoot boy comes rushing into the furnace room to give Selmer and the others on the tap floor the message that Nygaardsvold has formed a government. No shrill child's words thunder among the Ryfylke Mountains. No, Selmer Høysand has no use for horoscopes. He has use for work, and he knows where he has received it. He really thinks he has "received" work, and he is deeply impressed by those who give it to him. "Those" who transport brown topsoil all the way from Africa, melt it in many-thousand-degree heat, using power from the Handeland Mountains and dolomite and limestone from Årnes Limestone Quarry. And earn money by it! And employ all those people! And analyze what's in coal and dust! This is what Selmer Høysand thinks. But he joins Norwegian Chemical Industry Workers Union, Local 31, and he pays his membership dues faithfully. Often he attends union meetings, sitting preferably far back in the room, and enjoys the debates, in which the main actors are people like Jakob Pettersen, a northerner and staunch Social Democrat, later a member of Norwegian Chemical's national board, and Artur Fridstad, a Communist and former editor of the Rjukan *Labor News*. Pettersen defended reformism with an erect spine, doubt, honesty, and words such as level-headedness, long-range view, solidarity on wage policies, safe workplaces, confidence in the Labor government. It all had an irresolute tone, and Selmer thought it was more fun to listen to Fridstad, who tore apart Social Democracy and class cooperation with a cutting voice, keen irony, and strange (to Selmer Høysand) and dangerous words such as genuflection, infamous acts, black lies, filthy enterprises, mobilize, revisionist, attack, small–business deals with class interests, reformist rich union bosses, labor union traitors and lackeys of big capital, liquidationist line, saboteurs of a revolutionary Socialist Workers party, coat-tail politics. Selmer Høysand glanced at the man sitting next to him, who was from Svandal and the second man on the Number 3 tap floor on the Lien shift, and they both shook their heads and laughed quietly when Fridstad finished talking and left the platform to loud applause. Selmer and the man from Svandal clapped too, and they agreed, for example, on their way home or when they met at the time clock the next day, that Fridstad was actually pretty good. He's a real hard–liner, but it's okay to have tough guys like that who can give the leaders a punch in the nose when they need it. Then they walked out the factory gate with buoyant strides and, whenever possible, went home to work a double shift on the farm, gratis, purely out of solidarity with the family and the past. At planting and harvesting seasons, it turned into twenty-hour workdays. Sleep at the factory between pull the slag and tap, tap and pull the slag, rake up after the mowing machine, hang the hay on drying racks, take it down and hang up more hay, drive the hay wagon, leave again at night, tap at a quarter after eleven. For the first time, Selmer Høysand realized how little gain resulted from all the hard work on the farm. How did we manage to live from it? How did they manage to raise children on it? Things weren't this hard for us back then, were they? Fridstad's harangues suddenly became as strange and impressive as books and poetry written in Dano–Norwegian Riksmål, poets like Olaf Bull and Arnulf Øverland. And Russia. Another world. The Labor party, yes, but in fact quite a lot of fanaticism there, too, and who could be sure they wouldn't take the farms away from people and run them as collectives, like in Russia. Høysand farm run as a collective! That would be something, all right! Instead, Selmer Høysand went to the Youth Club, the one that was liberal and nationalistic and geared to farmers, and he found a world in which he thought he felt at home, and he often remembered an old farm and read New Norwegian poets—Aasen, Vinje, Garborg, Sivle, Halvor

Floden, and Hans Seland—and heard talks at meetings and parties by Klaus Sletten, Anders Hovden, Sven Moren, countless Eskelands. And Professor Nikolaus Gjelsvik:

When lower-class people
use alcohol, it can harm social advancement in three ways:

1. The *will* for social advancement diminishes or disappears.

2. The spiritual and physical *ability* to achieve social advancement is weakened or completely destroyed.

3. The outer *conditions* for advancement become more difficult.

Think about this some more, now. And I expect you will come to see that alcohol is clearly a very important factor in social outdistancing.

And Professor Gustav Indrebø:

"What are the major, most active ideas in the New Norwegian language movement? They are the concept of national revolt and self-assertion, and the concept of allegiance. There is one thing we cannot get through Dano-Norwegian Riksmål, but only through New Norwegian—namely, a true Norwegian language. To achieve that, New Norwegian is an absolute, essential requirement. And as surely as there is a desire within Norwegians to be one separate people, the national argument about these two languages will remain an element of unrest as long as the current language situation does not change."

Fritjof Nansen was the greatest Norwegian, the Greenland question was the greatest national issue, Prime Minister Hundseid ran a farm out in Vikedal. Norwegianness and forefathers' heritage and mother tongue. Then came coffee and pastry around a nicely laid table with lighted candles, Per Sivle's humorous stories about people from Voss, songs, and then folk dancing and games, the Faeroese circle-dance step, the alternate-your-feet step, the "princess sat in the hayloft with her hand under her chin" dance, and then the other dances, waltz, rhinelander, polka, and march. And at the end, everyone held hands and sang songs such as "To Live Is to Love." The day after, the days after, the days before, the day before, Selmer stood on the tap floor and got things to jibe, got things to hang together, the Youth Club and the furnace room. But strangely enough, it was not at the Youth Club that Selmer Høysand found the girl who would be his wife. No, they met for the first time in the middle of one of the darkest and coldest war winters in the Socialists' People's House at a carnival that had a wheel of fortune, a lottery, a stall where you could test your skill pitching balls at stacks of tin cans. Selmer, who occasionally could be rather funny, almost jovial, began by saying that there was nothing more festive than a sad tune played on an accordion, and then he told the large girl standing beside him, a girl from Sandeid named Alvhild, who worked as a housemaid in one of the engineers' homes and had every other Wednesday afternoon free, about how they slowed down over at the factory in order to produce as little as possible for the Germans, and about the strange places where they hid when the air-raid sirens blew, and about old Froen who had hidden up in a slag car in Cooling and could not get down again and had to shout for help when the "All Clear" siren blew: when the alarm ended, old Froen lying up in the slag car sounded his own loud alarm! Selmer had two balls and only one tin can left, but both pitches went way off the mark. Alvhild wanted him anyway. The next day they went to the movies and saw a Norwegian comedy starring Eva Sletto and Leif Enger. The next year they were married, two years later they had a row house in Factory Housing, and they followed the same daily routine, year in and year out, with Selmer's rotating shifts and movable holidays the fixed points of their existence, until a great sorrow cut through them both, dividing their life into a merciless before and after. From then on, they spent their time being much too protective (no one, neither relatives nor neighbors, thought it strange at all, knowing what Alvhild and Selmer had been through) and utterly spoiling a boy they had baptized with the name of Arnold and who slowly, and apparently unwillingly, grew up to be a strong, curly-haired, chubby, perpetually well-groomed, frightened little boy. Selmer's hair is still just as thick, his body just as dexterous, his face just as fine-featured. Perhaps his head has emerged a bit further from his body, and he can seem slightly stoop-shouldered when you see him standing, for example, up in the tapping ramp in denim overalls with flecks of lime on the legs and on his cap and safety glasses, lit up by the flowing metal that crackles and creaks down in the white sand chills as shadows of the building's framework tremble against the walls. This is Selmer Høysand's world, these are his words—the deadly heat behind the bulging sheets of corrugated iron; no rubber soles in the tap, the soles melt: wooden clogs, but never stand still in them or your legs will catch fire! drink from the hose that's always running in the barrel at the end of the tapping ramp; hear the foreman shout in your ear: Pull the slag at five! Huh? Pull the slag at five!! The hard wooden bench down in the control room (and where it now regularly happened that Selmer said something besides what the head tapper *had* to say); helpless workers who substituted during vacations and kept him from sleeping on the night shifts; stupid engineers fresh out of Norwegian Technical College; sample cups; books he tries to read in the afternoon, *On a Cruise with a Chinese Wife, Death of a Democrat*; mornings down in the new showers after the night shift; the new day, which he is leaving as those who come in the morning are entering, each from his own direction; the magic last two or three minutes on the time clock, when the hour hand becomes the minute hand and the minute hand becomes eternity; the covered soup container, which was soon replaced by a lunchbox with sandwiches and a large bottle of coffee with a cork in it; the wage envelope for 267–Høysand Selmer, 4673 kroner in 1950, gross. "Norway" joined NATO. It was as close and real as the Korean War. Foreign Minister Lange in Washington and General MacArthur in Seoul. Or was it the other way around? Lange was in Seoul. Both were in the newspapers. Seoul was Oslo. Selmer, who had voted for the Labor party in one election before the war and in the first election after the war, voted for the Farmers' party. He was a farmer at heart! He hadn't known that for certain before. Now he was sure. A farmer. Farmers and children of farmers. On long weekends and on his free shifts, he nearly always went off to Høysand farm, walked slowly and not quite as light on his feet up the mountain slopes. Yes, he still remembered many of the names. Here he had roamed as a boy, here his ancestors had toiled for hundreds of years. A large wet knot inside told him that. Selmer sat alone on the bus going back along Dollar Road (whose construction the factory had financed) and knew within himself that he was a farmer. Darkness began to fall. A sprinkling of lights on the other side of the fjord. The driver wriggled the bus around the sharp curves. Selmer sat right behind him, saw the lights of the furnace room come closer, and felt sure. At ten-thirty he sauntered through the factory gate, and knew it. He carried burner bars up to the tapping ramp before the shift began, and knew it. He opened his wage envelope the next Thursday, and knew it. He sat in the row house in Factory Housing looking out at the small garden and the gravel walk and the green picket fence, and knew it. Absolutely for sure. He is a farmer. Selmer goes back and forth to work, makes a trip up to Høysand farm once a week, talks with the neighbor over the garden fence about the thrush that ate up the strawberries this year too, while behind him Arnold peeks out through the crack of the slightly open door until he is sure the neighbor has seen him, and then scampers away and sticks his head up in the hall window like an ermine. Vacation? Selmer repeats in amazement. No, guess I'd better help out with the haying up at the farm. Movies, no; entertainment, no; back and forth to work, bicycle until the snow comes, then go on foot. Selmer Høysand was seen on the streets around seven in the morning, three in the afternoon, and eleven at night, unknown to anyone but relatives and neighbors and the men with whom he worked, never attracting any attention, except from some of the young rascals in Factory Housing who began to notice this man because every day he bought a loaf of coarse molasses bread that he either clamped on the back of his bicycle or carried under his arm in a very unusual way, about the way a British army sergeant would carry his swagger stick, a habit that seemed increasingly ridiculous the more the boys saw him repeat it. But they never dared to make fun of him openly; they just laughed among themselves and at a good distance behind the back of the figure in the white windbreaker who at the end of the shift hurried through Factory Housing with a purposeful stride. There was something, sorrow or some other mysterious thing, that clung to Selmer Høysand and at the same time made him invulnerable, made any attack on him perverse and unforgivable, like a sin against the Holy Spirit. And Selmer, deep in his own thoughts, came home to his prepared dinner without noticing that anyone made fun of him. He walked without looking backward or to either side, his eyes stiffly focused straight ahead, ready to meet any kind of trouble and sorrow and misfortune if only it came from that direction and not from behind, from secret forces he did not understand, and would never want to know about, either.

HELLUVA FACT

All his instincts, and his entire background and milieu, gave Selmer Høysand a deep and constant fascination with facts. The people he knew through his family and upbringing were all dependable, loyal, level-headed, and absolutely trustworthy working people, who would also have been dependable, loyal, level-headed, and absolutely trustworthy even if they had not happened to help build Social Democracy's modern Norwegian industrial society but had worked instead in the nobility's feudal Norway, in the People's Republic of China, in the party bureaucracy's Soviet Union, or in the heart of the North American Capital Empire. Selmer did not hope for anything, but on the other side of the river the factory sailed like a huge vessel, smoke coming from the stacks, traveling through time. And Selmer went aboard. The best praise a man could get was to be called a good worker, and for Selmer, as for the others with his background, a sense of self-respect and pride in work well done clashed with any kind of thoughts about revolt; active protest was more a defect in the work already completed than a joint action that gave strength and identity. And freedom. As things stood now, they looked back without sentimentality at the poverty of the old peasant society, which still was the only one with which they could identify; they looked with both disdain and admiration at the Money Yankees, and with amazement and distrust on Marxism's distant, shining fictions. Everyone will be equal, ha-ha. Theory is what you believe, but practice is what I know. And: We're best off as we are, and I don't think they're better off anywhere else than we are here. And: He who all he sees would keep / When others laugh, he will weep. Even when

23

they stood year in and year out in the slag dump, and some-times, in good weather, saw the sharp particles of quartz in the air reflecting the sunbeams after each load: Take a deep breath, it's good for your health! Or when they heard, without any agitation, that there were gas pockets under the casting area: Well, a good worker should be able to stand a little arsenic! No protest, no. Best not to get mixed up in anything. Arnold Høy-sand has only one explicit memory of doubt or desperation, which perhaps stands out so clearly in his mind because it is such an isolated instance. Selmer and Johan Jørgensen sit together one December evening letting the stiff pages of the Christmas issue of the company magazine glide through their fingers. In between, they drink coffee. Selmer tried beer in Stavanger in 1957 but did not like it. It's good when the weather's hot and when you're thirsty, he generally says. But he never drinks it when the weather is hot, and he never feels thirsty. They drink coffee. Alvhild is not at home. The company magazine lies on the coffee table, on the cover a color photograph of the factory taken in the dark, in the evening or at night. The main tone of the picture is brown, but yellow gleams out from the furnace building, red from the smokestacks on the roof, and yellow again from the unloading cranes, while the gas is mixed with carbon dioxide and burns with high flickering flames. Do you recognize this? asks Johan Jørgensen, pointing at the picture. Do you know where this is? Well, says Selmer, drawing out the word as he has a habit of doing, I ain't really the right person to say nothing about such things, but that hell-fire-and-damnation preacher, Hallesby, in Oslo, he sure wouldn't have no doubt about where it is. This happened about the same time Arnold was sent off to a New Norwegian school. New Norwegian. When lower-class people do not use alcohol, New Norwegian need not harm social advancement. The school also taught Riksmål, which was, moreover, the language of the class strug-gle, the language of the minutes of the union meetings, the language of notices from the factory managers, the language of the Salvation Army, the language of news about soccer and skating. In Riksmål class, the daughter of the factory director sat next to the son of the Communist chairman of the labor union, the child of the class-conscious proletarian and the child of the class-conscious bourgeois. But most of those who went to New Norwegian schools were sons and daughters of workers, newly proletarian working people who felt less like workers than like farmers and only by chance had been placed inside the fence of the large factory, where they now worked just as hard in order to cover expenses as they had toiled to make ends meet on the small farms from which they came. Are you going to work? Yes, I'm going over to help them for a few hours again. Them? At the New Norwegian schools, the children studied with teachers who had a two-month summer vacation, potato-planting vacation in the fall, a three-week Christmas vacation, a winter vacation, a two-week Easter vacation, a Pentecost vacation, a monthly holiday, and I don't even know what they're called—all those vacations of theirs, and they went to work at eight-thirty and finished at two and had entire hours free in between. Yes, the teachers were the ones who were hated and despised more than anybody else, more than the Communists, the managers, the time clerks, the office people, the sluggards (loafers, lazybones, idlers). The teachers were the ones who did not know where their livelihood came from, did not understand who worked the money up their asses, the ones who walked around in bow ties and slipknotted ties thinking they were so important, who talked to grown-up people as if they were first-graders about high goals and unrealistic ideals, and who were absolutely the biggest traitors against facts. If necessary, Selmer Høysand could listen to them for an hour at the Youth Club, when he was dressed up in a suit and tie and knew there would be dance music afterward. For the speeches and the dance tunes were equally a matter of poetry and tricks and fun. When he wanted to hear the bitter truth, Selmer Høysand went elsewhere.

THE BITTER TRUTH

He still went to union meetings and heard Jakob Pettersen, who was just as staunchly Social Democrat, and Fridstad, who was just as bitingly sarcastic: Mobilize! he cried far into the fifties.

Sectarian line from the Norwegian *Labor* party, as it still calls itself with shameless impudence, and from the leaders of the National *Labor* Union! Wild attacks against class interests! Who causes disunity? Those who swallow the reformist brew will throw up the filth later! This imbecilic idea of peace between the classes! And perhaps old Fridstad knew what he was talking about. One item on the agenda for the meeting, besides the minutes and a report by Rikardsen on the vacation-housing issue, was the question: What is the point in increasing production during an economic slump? The current chairman of the Local, an active young Social Democrat, had been at a seminar arranged by the National Labor Union and conducted by the editor of the Vestfold *Labor News*, Håkon Hoff, and the secretary of Norwegian Chemical, Sverre Enger. Now the chairman of Local 31 had the pleasure of coming back with the following summary: In normal times, he said, and of course even more so in times of economic decline, it is vitally important that workers cooperate fully with reorganization for greater efficiency and efforts to increase production, because this will enable the factory to compete better and thereby make their own jobs more secure! The chairman paused dramatically and looked up from his manuscript, then he continued: If one does not successfully compete in the world market, there are immediate effects that have tragic consequences at the workplace. In periods when trade is flourishing, metal is usually sold long before it is produced. If there are signs of a downward trend in the trade outlook, then only through good management and the individual effort of every person, each in his own sphere, will it be possible to win against the ever-increasing competition!

Jakob Pettersen thought this was going too far. Fridstad could not find words at first. When he stepped up to the speaker's platform, he was the color of a boiled lobster, both outside on his face and inside. If he'd had claws as well, Selmer would not have wanted to get near them. Comrades! was all Fridstad said. Comrades! Comrades! And then it all thundered out. Johan Jørgensen sat next to Selmer and listened. He put his index finger to his lips and whispered Shhhh to Selmer as Fridstad's voice distributed his gift of eloquence: Filthy enterprises are expanding! Genuflection is turning into snot-and-spit licking!

Peaceful work is peace in the grave of the workers' movement! Class cooperation is class coitus! Social Democracy is the whore of the working class, selling her body to the rich libertines in exchange for tariff ducats!

Everyone clapped, some laughed, the pounding of the chairman's gavel quieted things down. Fridstad looked out over the audience for a long moment, and then slowly and with great dignity left the platform. Selmer sat with his mouth open and swallowed, his ears wide as saucers.

There was no substantive vote on "reorganization" for greater efficiency and increasing production in an economic crisis. On the vacation-housing issue, the group abandoned its principle of providing vacation buildings that would be available to everyone and voted instead to ask the company to consider giving individual contributions to union members who wanted to build their own private summer cabins. The leaders of the Local were given complete authority to find an acceptable arrangement. Fridstad and others, among them Johan Jørgensen, voted against the motion. A Communist tried to argue for the principle of vacation buildings based on ideas of collective class consciousness, but he got entangled in long sentences about how individualistic relationships were the completely overshadowing dominant in any justification of building these private cabins and did not manage to change anyone's opinion at all.

There was no further discussion of this issue, or of "reorganization" in an economic slump, as Johan Jørgensen and Selmer Høysand walked home from the meeting together. Down at Forbruken stood a little boy looking at the comic books in the window of the Magazine Center: Fiinbeck and Fia, Butterball, the Katzenjammer Kids, the Hawk Patrol, the Vang Boys and Larris, new adventures of Engineer Knut Berg, Tarzan, Spoof and Suspense, Wild West, Gnome and Troll, Texas, the Ash Lad, Cocktail, with a naked woman on the cover—but that's not as filthy as when a man and a woman are both naked at the same time, is it?

Say, ain't that your boy? said Selmer Høysand, and Johan Jørgensen nodded and smiled. Yep, that's Rasmus, all right!

But does he get to be out so late? Selmer wondered.

Oh, not exactly, but that little guy don't always pay much attention to what we say he gets to do and don't get to.

Well, he'll get to learn to listen someday, I bet, said Selmer Høysand. But now I'd better be getting on home and see if the house is standing and the wife is lying in bed.

Then he walked on through town alone, thin and a bit stoop-shouldered, but in good shape for his age, as everyone remarks on the rare times they talk about Selmer. That Selmer Høysand, he's a real steady fellow, all right! Learn to listen! Yes, Selmer Høysand was a man with his feet on the ground. At least four, said Johan Jørgensen, as he took the hand of little Rasmus and led him across the bridge and up into Factory Housing.

Afloat

PRESSURE POINT

Rasmus Høysand took the floor. After five hundred long years he raised his voice. After five hundred wet, silent, dark years in the deeps, rough and overgrown and blurred with mussels and shells and seaweed, he surfaced from the bottom of a sea of forgetfulness with the most modern means of assistance—a salvage vessel with ballast tanks to reduce the roll angle, metaphor and the logic of capital, modules to take the bearings of jackets, doxies, traveling gantry cranes with a lifting capacity of 1800 shipping tons, ressentiment, iambus, simile, satire, and hydraulics. He was lifted slowly and majestically up through the silent sea, which became less and less black and more and more light green, until the green exploded in foam and was transformed into blue and he broke through the ocean's surface with the water washing over the deck, rose up into the cloudless day, and lay bobbing on the surface, where he could simply fill his lungs and speak out about the enormous cargo holds filled with gold and silver and costly spices and bronze bracelets and diamond rings and brooches and silver pins and Arabian and Spanish coins and bracteates and magic figures with dull, green emerald eyes, and then hoist the sails and let them fill with the wind's huge breath. Rasmus Høysand let out a storm of words and stood at the helm himself. He raised his voice and said:

The way to *the truth*, as the Austrian Doctor Wittgenstein also points out in his profound *Philosophical Investigations*, is as diverse and winding as paths in a landscape. A landscape that is

29

continually changing, I would add, with dams and houses and roads and factories and cut-away mountains and jet trails in the sky. Thus, you can ramble along a path for a while and then, just afterward, quite unexpectedly find yourself on another path going in the completely opposite direction, while both twist and turn forward toward the truth with equal certainty. In any case, this is how it has appeared to me on my countless, arduous wanderings, whether they have been high and free on Norwegian uplands with a clear view out over the hills and heaths, or through jungles so thick you needed to hack your way through them with newly sharpened knives to travel perhaps one miserable kilometer per day, or on German highways where you could drive 180 kilometers in a single hour.

But if it's true that life is a journey, then I believe I could say, from my own bitter experience, that all journeys are no more than the transportation of prisoners. We sit pressed close together in the dark, body against body, without knowing each other, without seeing even the features of the person next to us, bound in handcuffs and leg chains, with blindfolds on our eyes and gags in our mouths. Around us the walls are thick and cold, the doors closed and locked, and there are bars at the windows, which are brightly lit and have dreams of happiness and freedom fastened up one next to the other on the crossbars, glittering with colors and life, like the magazines that hang from the ropes stretched across the window at the Magazine Center or a Narvesen kiosk.

There we sit, mumbling what we have to say about strange forms of freedom, until the guards come and separate us for good, without our ever having seen each other. Our eyes have become accustomed to the dark, but night vision does not help. I see as little as ever. I hear just the sounds of my fellow prisoners sleeping around me in the dark room, and sense the sour breath and the thin skeleton arm of Åge Holte, whom I grab hold of tightly and cling to like a marvelously expensive, indispensable piece of reality as I open my mouth and begin to speak.

I was born in September, I say, the morning after the first frost of the year. By birth, baptism, and dialect, I'm a Harding, as good as any other, but I often regard myself more as a Ryfylking (here I had to go into a mile-long explanation of the difference between Hardanger and Ryfylke), primarily because of my mother, and because of all the other people I admire who also came from that beautiful part of the country (not least, all the great authors who have found inspiration there for their excellent books). Besides, I've always preferred Sauda, and not Odda, for example, to say nothing of Ålvik. There was, somehow, something special about Sauda. At the People's House dances, four generations always took part, until electronic music came and ruined that, and chased home the three oldest generations with electric guitars and amplifiers and synthesizers and boys with girls' hair and songs with English words. And the Sauda girls were always so straightforward and full of life, never any nonsense with them when we came across the mountain on Saturday night or finished our shift at three o'clock when we'd gotten jobs at Electric Furnace. This is what it was like:

COCKCROW

The red sky sinks into the West
    The wind holds its breath a while
The evening's dressed in party-best
    In deep dark August style
And at the People's House tonight
    I'm waltzing with a girl
My arm entwines her waist so tight
    As like a storm we whirl

I whisper to my girl, you see
    I drive a crane, and tell
That all this weekend I have free
    To celebrate like hell
They give us lousy wages there
    And say that we are rabble
We never, damn it all, I swear
    Give in without a battle

So, dancing smoothly you and I
    Like tongue-and-groove we glide
In smells of a cheap-liquor high
    You're warm and at my side

Your body lithe in flowered dress
Your laugh a hearty one
As hard against my chest you press
And cry, Oh, that was fun!

But this is no mere schoolboy who
Now leads you by the hand
And walks out to the floor with you
This is a working man
Who'll dance against big industry
While Ewald pulls the bellows
It's Westin-shift that's here, you see
Next weekend, Lien fellows

The fiddle strikes another tune
You call out, Thanks a lot!
I'm back to booze and banter soon
The air round me is hot
And then you come across the floor
I straighten coat and tie
When all the clocks strike midnight, your
"Ladies' Choice" am I!

The night still stretches out, extends
Its body, morning-white
With fjord and woods and river glens
And peaks where day flames bright
The strong sun rises, the cock crows
And struts with its red comb
You slowly come, at the dance's close
And together, we go home.

CEMENT

Or just take the scenery. It's not a black hole down in a fjord like
Odda or Ålvik, but a beautiful, open town. When I close my
eyes, I still see the fjord by Ramsnes, the Birkeland Mountains
behind, with Napen and Reinsnuten peaks and, on the other
side, the Nordstøl Valley over to Etne, with Kvamen and Rust-
ølsnuten rising up from the luxuriant green valley fertilized by
manganese dust from the old open furnaces. This is what I see,
and not the mountains where I was born. They, too, must have

stood silent and majestic when the construction workers, who had been awakened early by the commotion and screams of childbirth from the cookhouse, came out after breakfast into the high, clean, unnaturally blue and shining autumn morning that formed above their own proud constructions of reinforcing steel, water, sand, and cement, and saw that during the night snow had fallen far down in Onen on the other side of the fjord. The thought that a new human being had been born, here, among their sleeping bodies, made them solemn and silent, and they saw that same solemnity in the view out over the impressive landscape. For a long time they stood quietly outside the barracks door, saying nothing, amazed by the season, which lay transparent and shining after having taken an unexpected turn, until one of them said, Well, *that's* the end of summer for this year, and another said he was cold, and a third went inside again and put on an extra sweater under his working clothes before they began walking slowly up the path toward the high scaffolding for the dam, past yellowed parsley ferns and bulrushes and waving foxglove that had finished blooming. Farther up, the empty gray fifty-kilo cement sacks from the previous day lay scattered about, concrete forms were stacked up, cement spades leaned against an electric cement mixer, the wind sang through a sand-screen, a bolt cutter was fastened above the cut-off pieces of reinforcing steel. The men could still hear an infant's cry coming through the thin wooden walls of the barracks. Then they picked up the pointed spades and dug into the first Portland Valley cement sacks, and the cement blended with wind and air into nothing, or with water and sand and reinforcing steel into a thick crust over all that was, or became dizzying new constructions over all that had been.

Inside the walls of the barracks, an exhausted young woman, really just a girl, lay looking up at the silvery branch-wood ceiling with wide, incredulous eyes, and heard the child's crying much closer, and felt numb in her whole body when she tried to move or wondered about how things would go. What will happen to me now? She was Durdei Steine from Høysand farm in Ryfylke, who came to Lovra in Hardanger as a cook's helper at the age of only seventeen, and when barely eighteen, brought me into the western Norwegian mountain world in the Barracks III cookhouse at Grøvvatn, just below where the rivers meet on the Lovre I tunnel-and-dam construction. She is shown with the barracks crew from this time on a picture printed in a local history yearbook (*Lovra in Sight and Memory*, by Bellest M. Stag), but unfortunately, just at the moment the picture was taken, she turned and shook her fist, and her head just looks like a big, blurred light spot. The man she is turning toward has his visor cap on backwards and is waving to the photographer with both hands and a thumb in each ear. He is laughing. The text under the picture tells that the man is Lars Ossian Frihäth, the Swede who recited poetry by Gunnar Ekelöf—

> Queen of the hearth, go
> to your working men with liquor in your basket!
> Give peace to their strength
> as they wait to bathe in the river of death!

—walked out of the barracks, lit an explosive fuse, put his arms around the boss, sat down on the salvo, and said in Swedish, "Now we're going home."

The midwife, a cook on the same barracks crew, was the widow of a well-known agitator named Julussen who played an important role as a Chemical Union spokesman both locally and at national conventions in the years between the world wars, until he got caught stealing from the pot (as the foreman put it when they discovered Julussen had embezzled money from the union treasury. Why did you do it? the foreman asked. Don't know. What have you done with the money? Drank it up, I guess). Julussen was stripped of all his responsibilities and ended his days working as a furnace operator at the Carbide plant in Odda and having long, querulous debates (which also exhibited his great eloquence and his botanical ideas about pine trees) at the meetings of Local 5. His wife, Big Maria—who outlived him by twenty years, during the last ten of which she ran a small hotel up where the new stadium in Odda is now and took walks (big, buxom, and friendly) to the town center each day with a shopping cart on wheels and a fat, unhappy shepherd dog on a leash—was the one who cut the umbilical cord and slapped my rump and told Durdei, who was still almost unconscious after the birth, that it was a boy, a big healthy boy weighing four kilos. On a stormy Sunday almost five weeks later, I was baptized Rasmus by old Pastor Ancher in Øyste Church (a wooden church built in 1868), and my godparents—Nip, Sigurd, construction worker, Helland district, and wife Malena née Froen; Skarslie, Anders, farmer and factory worker, Saudasjøen, and wife Ragnhild née Aam; Stødle, Gullbjørg, shop girl, Bergen; and Friberg, Sivert, construction worker, Ålvik—stood along the rows of pews down in the nave in prewar dresses and navy-blue suits with scrubbed red hands protruding from the jacket sleeves and freshly shaved necks sticking up from the white collars, and solemnly promised to raise the child in the Christian renunciation and faith. Broad, stiff fingers struggled with the pages of the New Norwegian hymnal, and eyes with Elias Blix's words. The organ pealed over them, and then, Hm-hmmmmm:

> Children of the Earth are sly,
> Shrewder than the Sons of Light
> Earth its Corpses doth require
> Ever gaining Friends thereby.

This was during the third year of the great European war against Fascism, and the Lovre plant was run by German overseers, aging and corrupt guards from the Wehrmacht ("Nix mehr Pus"), Norwegian workers (quite a few were Nazis and collaborators, but not all), and Russian slave laborers. To which of these groups my father belonged was a subject never talked about, so far as I know.

The Lovre plant was ready for aluminum production in May, 1945, with dock facilities for ships up to 20,000 tons gross, an internal rail transport system (with sidetracks totaling 17,830 kilometers), scales and switches, slag cars with side tips, gondolas and boxcars, warehouses for raw materials, an ingenious system of conveyor belts, gates and chutes, several production rooms with closed furnaces and Søderberg electrodes arranged in a triangle, furnace pots with water-cooled covers and gas off-takes to the rotating Buffalo gas scrubbers, and a large combined storeroom and packing area—all of which was shown to countless impressed delegations from the authorities, trade unions, and private industry during the intoxicating summer of liberation (and drought) in 1945. But the factory was never put into operation, the modern closed furnaces were never started up and tapped, and the warehouses were just as empty when the last government-appointed delegation (with representatives from both sides of industrial life) left Lovra late in the fall of 1945. The plant stood there with factory buildings and administration offices and private homes for the managers and row houses for the workers, and slowly but surely became deserted, so that when Parliament finally voted to sell to the Germans at Chemische Industrie in Duisburg in 1948, there remained only a staff of engineers and other office workers, and a few maintenance workers with much patience or much seniority.

FATEFUL GAME

One of the latter was Johan Jørgensen from Skien in Grenland, who had played on a regional soccer team before the war and had a reputation for being a little wild, who had worked at the Lovre plant since '44 (first on construction of the power station in Osen, and later building the factory itself). He fell in love with Durdei Steine and married her in Lovre Annex Church in the fall of 1948, just before I turned seven, in front of an ill-tempered perpetual curate. By that time, the demolition of the Lovre factories had been going on for several months, and that is one of the pictures I still have of Johan Jørgensen, of him in a light-colored windbreaker and a black broad-brimmed hat sitting inside the two-meter-high wire fence at the factory chipping mortar off bricks with a mallet that disappeared in his large hand so that we thought Johan Jørgensen sat chipping bricks with just his bare fingers. My father can chip bricks with his fingers, yes he can! He's so strong he breaks off mortar with just his nails. Here's how he does it: I crook my index finger a little in front of the other fingers of my right hand and hit it against the palm of my left hand. Just listen to him! What a dummy! He really believes it! But all the rest of them believed it, too, after a short visit outside the two-meter fence. Johan Jørgensen looked up at us, tipped his hat, and said something funny. I alluz gits d'woist jobs, as that good guy in the comics says, or something like that. The bricks were later loaded onto boxcars and pushed by locomotive down the four-hundred-meter-long narrow-gauge railway to the wharf to be shipped to Germany. Johan Jørgensen's large hands and wrists (which his fellow workers said were hollow and empty and weak when they wanted to tease him) had also been good to have (as he said when he was in a good humor and wanted to stand up for himself) in 1928 when, as a sixteen-year-old deckhand on the old *Kristianiafjord*, his team won the lifeboat races in New York harbor. And there was 137 teams in the race! That sure was somethin', my boy! I also have a second mental picture of him (the third, of Johan Jørgensen big and heavy and drunk and quarrelsome, appears in different twisted versions in my dreams), from the spring of '49, after half an unhappy year in Sauda, when the Lovra Sports Club played its last game in the Second Division (in the old championship series system) and got beaten 3–2 by Fonna from Tyssedal, despite the fact that Johan Jørgensen, who played center-forward, scored twice for Lovra, the last time with his head. And that is the second picture I remember: he is high in the air and meets a ball while the center-half is still just leaping up, he tosses his head with its graying, slicked-down hair and makes a precise nod toward the right corner of the goal and runs toward center field with his right hand raised in a fist while the left struggles to slick down his hair again. I went around the whole rest of that Sunday, and on Monday and Tuesday, basking in that score, and during recess at the half-empty Lovraneset School I told my few classmates that Johan (I said then) had made the first goal by hanging onto the shirt of the young center-half from Tyssedal (who was much faster than he) on one of the few long passes that was scooped out from the Lovra defense, and he shouted, I've got it! and managed to steer the ball into the goal when the center-half and the Fonna goalie collided.

Without the referee seeing it! repeated the Lovra youngsters on their way to the next class hour. Little did we know then, neither they nor I, that these two scores marked the end of

Lovra's great days. On Wednesday when the *Grenda News* in Rosendal came out, it had this to say about the big game: "No one was seriously hurt when Fonna from Tyssedal beat the home team 3–2 in a Second Division game at Lovra last Sunday." In the fall following this defeat, the last ship carrying production equipment sailed out of the still-unfrozen Lovra Fjord to Germany. Power from Lovre I and Lovre II was transmitted across the mountains in high-tension wires and combined with A/S Bjølvefossen in Ålvik (Lovre III was first expanded in the sixties, and power from there sent right into the coordinated distribution system). Most Lovre factory employees (office staff and laborers) were fired, only a very few remaining as line inspectors and machinists at the stations in Osen and Grøvvatn (the latter left as well about 1960, when all the power stations were automated and could be operated by remote control, first from Ålvik and then, a decade later, from the distribution center for West Coast Electric Works in Sauda). We ourselves followed the power over to Ålvik in August, and just a few days later Johan Jørgensen read aloud from the *Hardanger News*, in his peculiar East Coast dialect that always reminds me of Communists, the Salvation Army, or engineers (I didn't understand at the time that what these groups have in common is that they represent a higher level of organization than the individualistic peasant society into which they were, more or less accidentally, placed by capitalistic expansion), that the Lovra Sports Club was not able to furnish a team for the Third Division and so withdrew from the series, which meant that Ny Von Sports Club from Løvfallsstrand had no contest in the first game of the series (and it was probably necessary to set up a whole new playing schedule). The same day, Johan walked with me to school in Ulvik, patted my shoulder, and said in a voice that smelled strongly of denatured alcohol, Now don't you get too smart in there, and that was the last I saw of my first childhood hero. He went on the afternoon shift at three o'clock, and after it was over at eleven o'clock nobody in Ulvik saw Johan Jørgensen again, and Durdei Jørgensen, who was alone once more with an eight-year-old schoolboy, did not have even a soccer memory to comfort her, only an unclear goodbye letter, mailed in Lillestrøm without a return address, and her new long surname with which to console herself. Johan Jørgensen *was* gone, and he knew, as the poet says, and as I myself later experienced all too well, there is no ready-made path. The steps you take / Your path doth make.

ACE OF SPADES

That was my childhood. The most important years in a person's life. What comes now is not as important. I went to elementary school and junior high in Ålvik, and then to high school and junior college in Øystese, and learned what all other Norwegians in the postwar years had to learn, in the words of the English motto: Twenty years of Schoolin', and they put you on the day shift. But before we got to English classes, we learned the Latin alphabet, and the New Norwegian literary language, and I came up with the answer that is still repeated at parties and around coffee tables and in workers' barracks and other places where people gather throughout Hardanger, Indre Ryfylke, Sunnhordland, and large parts of West Telemark, although it often happens that I become little Lars from Hamrabø in Suldal in order to make the story even better. But I was the one who said it first. It's the first day of school at Lovraneset School. The teacher opens a huge book on his desk and studies it with a wrinkled brow for a long time before turning his back to us and writing a large *A* on the blackboard. Then he turns around again and looks searchingly out over the classroom. You, little Rasmus, back in the corner there, he says, pointing at the letter on the board behind him, can you tell me what this is? I think about the question both long and carefully, without saying anything, because there are four things it could be. Then I say, Well, I wouldn't quite swear to it, but it looks to me like the ace of *spades*.

Later we learned how the world was created and how it functioned in the postwar years. High up in heaven sat God the Almighty, Who ruled heaven and earth. I believed in a holy Christian church, a communion of saints, the resurrection of the body, and the life everlasting. The Labor party had the power in

Norway and in the township of Kvam, a power limited only by the courts, the Opposition in Parliament, and the press, which was the fourth national power. Rapid development in research and technology (which was especially advanced in the United States) was founded on the theories in Brun and Devik's *Physics and Chemistry for Junior College*, and on the theorems in Tambs Lyche's *Mathematics for Higher Education* (particularly the analytical plane geometry), and now only a couple of insignificant details were still lacking in order for the research to be complete, to prove once and for all Euclid's theorem that parallel lines will never meet, and to explain not only all natural phenomena but also all social and psychic conditions forever (social statistics— the opposite of the natural dialectic?). Those who presented these theories were phlegmatic, resigned men (and a few women) who, day after day, year in and year out, armed with pointers, patrolled the small platform between the knowledge and culture on the blackboard and the raw, ignorant, totally thankless groups of youngsters who slept on the desktops in front of them. Back and forth, back and forth, marched these last outposts of civilization, with speaking patterns, facial expressions, gestures, odd habits, which still today—ten, twenty, thirty, forty, fifty years later—we see just as clearly before us and can mimic and parody just as we did in the break before religion class or between the daydreams about women during the awkward parties in college-student rooms: Monsieur Høysand, voulez-vous lire?

In an incredibly short time, I became a master at integrating and deriving equations, and at finding the hypotenuse in a right triangle when the cathetus was known. Square roots were no problem, hyperbolas and parabolas approached the asymptotes in a threatening manner but cut into them only after hair-raising calculation errors. I learned to pronounce English with a rising or descending intonation, depending upon whether it was a question or an answer, and to write long German sentences with the verb at the end. I drew cones and pyramids projected both toward the vertical plane and the horizontal plane. I wrote essays arguing both for and against the proposition that ideologies were dead, and came to my own conclusion at the end. I learned that modern, enlightened people with junior college degrees and *duskelue* graduation caps looked down on, for example, the weekly radio Request Hour, cheap kiosk publications, the encroaching materialism of our times, Russia's Lenin (pronounced with the accent on the last syllable to make it sound as diabolical as possible), and that it was not proper to use phrases such as "looks like a pigsty" (change to "looks like a dog house") and certain common forms of New Norwegian verbs and pronouns. If you signed a letter to an educated person, Yours, Rasmus Høysand, using the New Norwegian *dykkar*, which can also mean *diver*, you got into very deep water, as they say, and received a reply to Dear dykkar Rasmus Høysand. Before industry came, Ålvik was an isolated, backward farming community far in on the Hardanger Fjord. The dumbest farmers got the biggest potatoes. From the surrounding mountaintops, there was no other sign of civilization to be seen. The most popular songs had first lines like this: When Norway in her silver cape glistens. They stood at Stiklestad in battle array. At night a great pounding was heard at the door. I see you outside the small window. Alexander conquers India. King Harald Hardråde fell at Stamford Bridge. Moscow knows no tears. I Chose Freedom. Tell about cows and why. Mama! Mama! They call me Hayseed! They call me Hayseed! Don't pay no attention to them, Rasmus! Petition against prophylactics in the Norwegian Brigade. Did parents have a sex life? Had they ever had one? Durdei remarried but never forgot Johan Jørgensen. Her new flame came in the evening and gave me a Lohengrin chocolate bar before I went to bed, and left again in the morning. He was a big, heavy, silent, and very lonely man who could stand for a long time shoving the door between the living room and the kitchen back and forth, back and forth, with a thoughtful expression on his face before he went on into the kitchen to get a cream pitcher (he was the only one who took anything in his coffee), and Durdei came to her senses and said, Oh, I completely forgot that you take cream. They drank coffee for a long time in silence, except for the small sips when the hot liquid met their lips, and then he set down his cup a little more abruptly than usual (it clinked against the saucer), cleared his throat, and asked if she had some sewing-machine oil anywhere in the house. When she came back and handed him the small can, he smiled happily and got up, went over to the door again, moved it solemnly back and forth a few times, looked at us expectantly, and we heard (for the first time) that it was true, the door did squeak once in a while, when it closed slowly or someone leaned on the handle, and so he put some oil on the two top hinges and everything was silent. Silent, silent, tidied, mended and complete and everything copacetic. Or he would lay the palm of his hand on the wallpaper above the sofa, look at me sternly (when Durdei was not at home), and say, They cheated by putting an extra strip on here, those slobs.

Or when John came and asked, Can I play with Høysand? he stood watching us play with paper men at the kitchen table. It was a Sunday in November, with slush in the streets and sleet in the air. Why do kids talk Riksmål when they play? he asked. Now it's time to use this marshall's star I stole, I said in Riksmål, and then switched to New Norwegian. They always talk that way, girls, too, when they play with their dolls. What brings you here, Marshall? said John in Riksmål. I'm on the trail of the bandit who robbed the Greenville bank. The big lonely man shrugged, took his lunchbox and coffee bottle, and tramped out the door to go to work. Felow is a quiet guy, said John in Riksmål. He's going to get blamed for the robbery! I hesitate a moment, with the villain in my hand. The Sheriff of Tucson wants a prisoner, continued John, but it's not going to be Felow! I dropped the villain on his back on the table. I give up! I said in Riksmål. I know when the battle's lost. You kids clean up after yourselves, said Durdei, and when John had gone, she took me on her lap and sang:

LULLABY
(BEFORE THE 1950'S)

Bye-bye Daddy works all day
Operates the crane's big claw
Scoops up manganese below
Till belly-full it rides away

High up Daddy there you are
Dumping with a steady hand
Loads of rough grain and fine sand
In a waiting cable car

Daddy's working part-time now
Badly paid but working hard
For this piecework his reward
Is some lousy barracks chow

Daddy goes on working late
Mommy at the radio
Sees dreams flicker to and fro
While ashes settle in the grate

He gets a stiff neck way up there
Driving that enormous toy
Thinking of his little boy
Half-asleep in chill night air

Driving through the snow and rain
Daddy's bones are aching, too
He rubs his hand but can't see through
The engine's icy frosted pane

Daddy now attends a meeting
In the drafty union hall
Drowsy Baby Mommy lulls
With the click-click of her knitting

Daddy's on the night shift now
Working steadily till seven
Will he find our little haven
Tramping off across the snow

Daddy's boss one Sunday comes
A ship's unloading at the dock
And though he works around the clock
Daddy's paid for overtime

Daddy barely gets there when
The clam-chain's iced up at the top
No grease in the machinist shop
The boss has blundered once again

Daddy does as he is told
Work wears out a worn-out man

Starts the blade-wheel when he can
Then empties out the vessel's hold

The ship has come across the sea
With comilog and amapa
Now sails off for America
When Daddy sets the hawser free

Daddy slaves for a few kroner
All that will improve some year
When Baby is an engineer
So hush now Baby cry no longer

What promises can Daddy keep
The answer Baby is not one
Daddy's night-shift has begun
Perhaps tomorrow he can sleep

NEITHER IN NOR OUT

By then I had slept through the last six verses. Things started to roll. I left for school at 11:25 and crept carefully along the edge of the houses keeping my head to one side so the wind would not rumple my water-slicked hair before I arrived. On the other side of the schoolyard stood the girls. Some wore skirts and some wore trousers like us. The fifth-grade boys had climbed up at the back of the building and peeked into the bathrooms when the girls were taking showers. Eva Havet had boobs. Somebody who knew somebody I knew went to sea and came home in the late fall before he turned sixteen, and he walked through the snowdrifts in town wearing an ice-blue tropical suit and a black shirt and a white tie and yellow socks and he had tasted an aphrodisiac called Spanish fly in Kingston, Jamaica. You put it in your coffee. That's how you drink it. Somebody who knew the guy I knew got hold of rubbers in Stavanger. Two fingers on the barbershop counter, then the barber goes behind the dividing curtain into the back room. In Takoradi in Africa there was a woman who had Norwegian beer labels tattooed all over her body. On the other side of the schoolyard stood the girls. They were far away. Things started to roll. After the last class hour was over, that is. Then we rowed out in an old flat-bottomed boat and begged for cigarettes from the cargo boats that lay at anchor in the harbor waiting for a mooring. The wide world rained down on us and was called Camels, Chesterfield, Players, and Salem. Everything seemed unchangeable, even the pop-music hits. For over a year, Joe "Mr. Piano" Henderson played the song "Trudy" up to Number 1 on Radio Luxembourg's Top Twenty. Then they stopped figuring on the basis of sheet-music sales and switched over to record sales, and things started to happen. The crane operator was as slow as molasses in January, but he kept coming, and each time he brought a Lohengrin candy bar for me. It was a regular custom. He took correspondence courses in bookkeeping and business correspondence during his spare time and became the time clerk in Electrode Assembly and stopped going to work and began going to the office. One of the short letters Durdei wrote after I moved into a rainy room with a view over the cemetery in Øystese told that Harald Festeskaar, as the ex-crane operator and time clerk was named, had been promoted to the main office, where he now worked with wage specifications, to use his words, the letter said. P.S. Very soon you will have a little sister. Won't that be fun? It was a little brother, Jan (who nineteen years later was featured in the *Bergen Times*, with both a picture and an article, when he passed his junior college exams with a major in English and straight A's in every subject, which made him the class valedictorian and the pride of the school). Not until two years later did there come a sister, Kjellfrid, who, after finishing school, worked in a shop in Bergen (luggage, gloves, and umbrellas) and then one summer in the restaurant at the Brakenes Hotel in Ulvik, and then at the Merino Textile Mill, and at Dale Textile Factories (which gave her the undeserved nickname Dale Bedding). I completed my basic education with an essay about how I beat the bow-legged Russian sports fanatic, Dimitrov, in a final spurt up to the finish line and became the unexpected Olympic skiing champion in the fifty-kilometer event (and also created a big scandal when I did not attend the award ceremony two days later).

PATHS OF FREEDOM

The school path. It was a path that led onward and upward in life. Academic honors, student living, engineer or something else ending in -er—hairdresser, manager, outpost idler, book-keeper, hypnotizer. But were there other paths? Soccer was one. In Stavanger, I was a fan of the Jarl team and of Peder Svendsen, a goalkeeper who threw out his arms and legs and yelled, I've got it! when the ball came over the center line on the Jarl field in Hillevåg; in Bergen, it was the Ny Kronborg and Varegg teams; in Oslo, it had to be the Vålerengen, despite everything (and I was strongly anti-Skeid!); in Sweden, Hammarby; in Germany, the Schalke 04; and in England, the Wolves, Aston Villa, and Notts County (Milwall did not come until later). But what about the Sports Club, which played at the Sletta field and fought with Trio and Etne at the bottom of the Second Division (in the old series system) against the specter of failure? I was afraid of the specter of failure, too. But weren't there other paths to success? I had read that in Andalucia in Spain the only way poor boys could advance in life was through bullfighting; out in the burning sun, cape in one hand and sword in the other, alone against the five-hundred-kilo mass of muscle storming toward you with two sharp horns protruding in front; blood, dry sand, triumph or die, jubilation and shouts of *Olé!* Flowers from the richest and most beautiful women, thrown kisses, a deep bow in return, the way out of Andalucia. Yes! In the dense forests of Norway, the heroes of the poor Norwegian districts struggled to qualify for Garmisch, Cortina d'Ampezzo, Squaw Valley, Seefeld. Norway! Through Squire Løvenskiold's great forests north of Oslo they stormed, the champion cross-country skiers, Gjermund Muruåsen, Kåre Hatten, Marinius Øverland, Sigurd Vestad, Lars Bergendahl, Arne Rustadstuen. From fir trunk to fir truck, battle against the seconds with heavy burdens of Nor-wegian dreams on your back. Thorleif Vangen, Mikal Kirkholt, Martin Stokken, Einar Østby, Erling Steineeidet, Halfdan Kluften. Yes, that was the path away from poverty and toil—faster and faster, a last push now, the skis fitting well in the tracks, gliding smoothly downhill, a fine rhythm in the gently rolling Nordmark terrain. It's toward the goal for the bull-fighters from Trysil, Fåberg, from Hellandsbygd and Hernes, toward the goal, from Rindal, Jaren, and Heidal, toward the goal, toward the goal! The seconds rushing toward them, sharp and dangerous as the horns on the bull, toward the goal, the last double-poling, and, There, There! they made it! The Moment of Truth, the bull of time dropping powerless, dead. They made it, reached the goal, arrived. Race out of Sørke Valley, down toward Portland Valley—Ski Tracks Cross the World, My Life's Race, With Track Shoes and Skis—to brief fame after the fifty-kilometer event, adulation from the shipbrokers in the Ski Association, firm answers to the foolish questions of newspaper journalists from the *Evening Post* and *Sign of the Times* and *Way of the World* and the *Daily News*—How did you feel when Tiainen began to slack off? and finally race back into the forest again, without the public, without a number and a timekeeper. But not all the way back: training consultant, auto-equipment salesman, ski advertisements, recreation camps, short-course instructor, waxing expert, service station attendant. I tighten my stomach muscles, throw out my chest, and stretch out my ankles. Bjarne Iversen talks about training methods in the Big Hall at the People's House. A gathering on snowless ground. Muscle strength first and foremost. Long strides on the hill near the pond, with poles, without skis, arm training. We go out into the rain again. The miserable winters at the end of the fifties. Bjarne Iversen, who had eighty-two seconds on Kalle Jalkanen when he got the baton from Oddbjørn Hagen, Olaf Hoffsbakken, Sverre Brodahl. And then the Finn overtook him again and reached the finish line for the gold. Silver for Norway. We said goodbye at the corner of Lindekleiv's house. A poorer Norway. The black Romika boots were slippery underfoot, the speed-skating Hjallis caps did not hold their color in the rain—red, white, and blue ran down over the forehead. If only it would snow, so we could have proper training conditions.

And then there was the sea. The sea was another path. The broadest. The school of life. It led down the gangway, across the railway tracks on the pier, past a bar and a cloth door-hanging, and into a room where the light made everyone's face look like a green reflector piece, back to the ship again, to snakeskin belts, overweight, Romeo card games, American cigarettes, tax-free beer sold by the steward at low prices, Pernambuco, sticks of chewing gum, the woman in Kingston, Jamaica. And then, all the way back. To the furnace room, the four-shift plan, the bicycle parked in the cellar, twins, two rooms in the Factory Housing. Back.

QUALITY CULTIVATION

Durdei substituted as an office cleaning woman. But one spring that work came to an end—lay-offs. We took the bus to Ølen and then went on to the home of her brother, who worked part of the Høysand farm alone. A few crooked hills where he grew grass for twenty sheep, two cows, a horse, and potatoes for himself. The last part of the trip was on the boat from Sand. He stuck the dung fork into the ground beside the manure-spreading cart and wiped his right hand on his trousers when he saw us coming up the hill. Well, well, so it's them folks. This was before he quit farming and started at the steelworks in Jørpeland. This was in the spring, and he was fertilizing his meadows, and the dung smelled worse than the manganese in the factory yard in Ålvik. No, I never liked that work, but I found out how people cultivated the soil. Later in life I learned it's possible to cultivate other things besides soil—for instance, at schools and at the university or in the Oslo newspapers, where you can cultivate this theory or that theory or the opposite point of view—but to me it always reeked of dung, and in my mind I see Sylfest Høysand trudging behind his manure-spreading cart (when someone cultivates this or that opinion) and tossing manure down a steep West Coast hill with a firm grip on the dung fork. Or the piss dripping out of the liquid-manure cart. That's what it means to cultivate, and quality cultivation means spreading especially soft, good manure over something you are especially fond of and want to bear rich fruits.

A monk once asked Bodhidharma: What is Buddha?

The master replied: Dried manure.

No, I never liked that work. But when I got a job at the factory, that was something else. Because I liked that work.

48

Hurray! Mother, Mother! I got a job at the lab, hurray! Well, well, see to it you don't get to be the overboss there. That was the year I turned sixteen. I went around picking up samples, on the pier, in Packing, and in the furnace room; quartered and crushed and mortared the samples from the tap floor and from the lots and put them into bags marked Std Si Mn and Fe Cr and Reg Fe Mn and brought them in to the pigeonholes and test tubes so the men in lab coats could find out whether the samples were high in coal and low in sulphur. The ones from the furnace room were small round cookies, taken with coated sample cups while the tap was flowing. We put them right in the mortar and under the electric air hammer until they went through the sieve. The lot samples were bigger, to say nothing of the raw material samples, a bucket or a whole wheelbarrow full, which we dumped onto the floor. Then we quartered the heap many times (divided it into four quarters and took away two at opposite angles from each other) until what remained could be put through a crusher. Afterward, we sat around with our feet propped up on a steel stool with a back support that we had pulled close to the chair we were sitting on, and waited for the crane operators and the extras to come and throw sample cups or boxes of shift analyses onto the table so we'd have more work to do. In the meantime, a guy I worked with on the shift (who belonged to a male chorus and had a bad back from operating the old wharf cranes) sang the slave chorus from *Nebuchadnezzar*, verse after verse, night after night, until we turned on the exhaust fans and the air hammers and put on ear muffs. Or I would go out and take samples, or paint lot numbers and tap numbers and gross weight and tare on the barrel heads with black paint and a stencil. Yes, a factory worker was what I was cut out to be, because that was work I liked.

WORDS TO TAKE TO HEART

But no, it was the school path for me, first to Øystese and then to Bergen. The day before I left for Øystese to start the state high school there, Durdei said to me:
Rasmus.
Yes.

Tomorrow you go away to school. You'll get out of touch with a lot of things here at home. In some ways, you won't have no home or roots the rest of your life. If you'd have been born a little later, you'd have had to go away to school even sooner, to a junior high school where they let you choose your main subjects. And this is how we want it, do you understand? We went seven years to a real poor country school where we didn't have no choice about what we wanted to study. You probably didn't even know there's a difference in what they teach country kids at school and what they teach in town; kids in the country didn't have to learn much, just a few hymns and some catechism went a long ways. And we want our kids to go to school for as long as they want, at a school that's as good as the best town school, and that's divided up into classes with thirty kids all the same age, and that's got physics labs and gyms and media tech., or whatever it's going to be called, and where the teachers learned grammar and trigonometry and French at the university and ain't just students at a teachers' college who talk a blue streak about back when King Olav Tryggvason walked out onto the oars of his ship, or who get lost in some fantasy about the Empire of Norway that includes Dublin and Vinland and the Isle of Man. This is how we want it, and that's why they've got to build central schools that you go away to when you're fifteen years old. Do you understand?

Yes.

And this fall, Uncle Sylfest is going to stop running his part of Høysand farm and move to Jørpeland and get a job at the steel mill. And I don't want you going around feeling bad about either him or me because of that. I won't allow it, you hear? Anyway, it's all for the best. I want the leaky old buildings at Høysand to fall down before the end of winter and the stones from the farm to be used to make a new four-lane highway where the newest cars can drive ninety kilometers an hour away from all the poverty, and I want the Høysand ground to be covered with weeds and thistles and nettles that are black with exhaust and dust from the road and grow so thick over the meadows that no one will see that people had to live there once. And I want all of old Høysand's descendants to live in

Odda or in Fylling Valley or in Grorud and have their own apartment or row house with hot and cold running water and a bathroom and a TV and a washing machine and a mixmaster and inlaid floors that don't have to be scrubbed, and to drive to the factory in their own cars, and find a good, wide, asphalted parking place and walk through the factory gate along with other well-dressed workers that are organized in the labor union on a solidarity basis and have just filled up their stomachs with healthy food from the supermarket. And I want them who raise the food to live on Jæren or in Denmark or America, or in Russia for that matter, on farms that are a whole lot bigger, where they drive around with hay tedders and mowing machines and horse-rakes and combines, and don't never have to work with just one scythe up under the tallest mountain peaks or roll the hay home in a hay net in the wintertime so they can feed one sheep. Do you understand?

Yes.

And in a few days I'm going into the hospital to have one breast operated away. I'm going to Bergen and lie in a white, fresh-made bed in a nice, light room at Haukeland Hospital with laboratories that have got all the newest equipment and body engineers in white coats who'll stand around my bed with X-rays and EKGs and intravenous tubes and nod their wise heads and look down at my body as if it was a Stang or Mohr or Vogt or Christie or Heuch or Sibbern or Selmer or Hagerup, and not Durdei Høysand they're making a diagnosis about. And I'm going to have the best treatment and the best care and real good food and be bowed out through the door when I'm well and I've got my strength back, and I ain't going to pay one single øre, because all my life I paid my taxes and my public health insurance. And there ain't no "barefoot doctor" going to be allowed to come near me with his first-aid kit while all the rich people in town get operated on by doctors with expensive Italian leather shoes at special hospitals. That's why we've got to have health centers and big central hospitals. Do you understand?

Yes.

Everybody who'll be young in the seventies ain't going to understand this. And there's lots of things in the seventies we ain't going to understand neither, all of us who'll be old then. But this is what we think, and this is how we want it until we die anyway, and we want the Labor party to do it for us. And I want you to promise me one thing when you turn Communist, which you'll do, because all smart young people in the seventies are going to turn Communist, and that is, that no matter what you do, you'll never travel around making a name for yourself by talking about the Social Democratic hell. Do you understand?

Yes, I said, and swallowed. I understand. I promise.

Then you can leave.

All of this lay two or three years behind me that August evening when I sat alone, among the mail sacks (containing letters and packages for people from Hardanger who had moved away) and crates of Foss and Seftahom apples, riding the bus through Kvam Woods with my cardboard suitcase and plastic raincoat and wearing a white nylon shirt and a tie, on my way to Bergen Business College, which had accepted me. In the administration office there at the school, a government student loan for 4,000 kroner (divided into 2,000 kroner per semester) was waiting for me, because now people no longer needed to ask wealthy people in the community to "guarantee" a loan when one of the sons (from a family of up to fourteen children) was going off to professional school. No, the state invested directly in me, risked money on me. But I felt the responsibility just as heavily. This is what it was like to leave:

SHIPPING OUT

The bus has now arrived and I
Know all will change I leave today
My lips have tried to say Good-bye
My eyes have turned the other way

Lunch in hand in Sunday best
Diploma from my junior high
Which may well be my first and last
I'm on the pier to say good-bye

And ticket then to Ølen show
The driver takes it with a smile
And throws my luggage in below
I like his looks I like his style

To Bergen College Sir I say
And with those words my life uproot
For him who's off to school one day
A new world quickly opens out

The mountains now truck-loads evoke
And ore that's fired to molten mass
In furnaces whose gas and smoke
Engulf the struggling working class

The heart alas has cut its strings
The radio booms a lively air
Gonna loop the loop the whole bus sings
As we pull out and leave the pier

I'm off to books and lecture halls
Away from cranes that have confined
And scooped up those materials
Once stored within my quiet mind

Hands have waved me on my way
To Dollar Road to life and sorrow
A tearless weird good-bye I say
Life that nag is bone tomorrow

THE LITTLEST IN THE WORLD

I lived in a room on Nordnes and read *Manager in the International Economy* by Raymond Vernon until Christmas, and each morning I walked down to Vågen Harbor to take the Lønborg buses or the small ferry over to Bryggen, the old Hanseatic pier. I didn't know anybody. Everyone was smarter and more well-bred than I, and wore clothes that went well with their hair color and with what they thought. Where did they buy such clothes? At Sundt? No. Kløverhuset? No! Storjohann? Impossible. So where did they come from then? A secret! The secret student uniform for people initiated into everything. Inside the large glass doors was the Reading Room. Should I walk in? Maybe that wasn't the way it was done? Maybe they did it in a special way? Maybe I wasn't allowed to go in there? Maybe they all would look up from their books when I walked in the door? Maybe I was supposed to say something for everyone to hear? Maybe all the others knew each other? It looked that way. I went to meetings and heard Progressives with the same names as old Platt-Deutsch officials take me (and all the others who held their tongues) to task sharply, just as their local-magistrate ancestors had reprimanded the farmers from whom I descended (at least on my mother's side). Like them, I stood with bowed head, cap in hand, and looked down and said nothing. (Or: Yes, of course! Right! Yes, I see! Exactly! That's true!) In my room down from the Navigation School on Hauge Road, I said to the wall (not even to the mirror!) and to the dark when I had crawled into bed and turned off the light and heard the rain beating against the windowpanes and gushing out of the drainpipe from the gutter, It doesn't matter to me whether those people are in charge of the Bergen Private Bank or of the revolution (I said it several times, because I thought it was a good sentence). Then I pounded the down quilt, so as not to make noise and get thrown out of my room (the landlords were Christian people who originally came from the east coast of Norway and had pictures of Jesus and his man in politics, Erling Wikborg, on the wall), and slept late the next morning. I was to take my examinations at Christmas, but I never got that far. I never got that far because the exams were set up in such a way (in the auditorium at Bergen Technical School on Nygård Point) that I had to walk past Café Børs on my way from Hauge Road. (Well, had to or had to, but anyway I walked past it, though I could just as well have walked past old Café Vågen.) I went into the Børs and fortified myself with a half-liter of beer and some steak with fried onions, and then another half-liter (I had plenty of time), and was thrown out (pleasantly and firmly) when they closed the café at ten minutes to midnight. Standing down on the Strand Quay, I shouted over to Vågen and Bryggen and the fjord boats and anyone who would listen in the rain that I'm the naughtiest and littlest boy in the whole wide world. Nobody loves me. Mineworker in Sulis, and in my free time, alone in the barracks or alone over a half-liter at

54

the café, enigmatic. Svalbard coal mines, money for food; Packing department at the Carbide plant in Odda, masks, it's dusty, can't breathe; into the lunchroom at Magnesium on Herøy Island, no mask, money for food; don't freeze, pawn a watch in a shop in Dubai, stroll along the streets of Buenos Aires in the blazing sun with a drawn face, the white tropical suit wrinkled and faded, calls from the native sidewalk merchants, nearing the end, look here, fine things, beautiful things, sell, sell, cast a backward glance, buy, buy, they're still following, right hand in the jacket pocket, buy, sell. I staggered down Sundt Street out toward Nordnes. What will become of me? How will things go for me now? In my mind I saw Georg Fant in the Swedish film *Thy Soul Shall Bear Witness*, which Durdei had told me about. He had a scholarship at the university and studied there, but took up wild ways and became a good-for-nothing who slept under the open sky and laughed at everything in the world. I wept. The next day I got a job on a boat at the hiring office on Murallmenning Street, and three days later (after one night on a coastal boat, still with the cardboard suitcase and the plastic raincoat) I left the *Alden* and went ashore at Årdal Point, and after two cups of coffee in the Centrum Cafeteria at the Samvirkelag Co-op, I signed on an Arendal boat that was unloading bauxite from Jamaica at the aluminum factory pier.

HØYSAND

Three days later we sailed out of the English Channel and headed for the Bay of Biscay. The waves were six to eight meters high, and the weather was clear. I was no longer seasick.

Høysand? said the machinist, slapping me on the shoulder as we stood by the rail.

Yes.

Do you see over there? He pointed.

Yes.

Do you know what that is?

France.

Yes, it's an island beyond Finisterre in France named Høysand. In French, it's Ile d'Ouessant, but sailors all call it just by the

Norwegian name, Høysand. The coast around Høysand is one of the most dangerous in the Atlantic, and there's even a saying in French that he who sees Høysand, sees his own blood. On Høysand there's a famous lighthouse called Phare de Creac'h, which marks the end of the English Channel for those sailing south. There, the globe heels over, the ocean stretches out, nothing but blue on blue, endless circles of sea, high heavens, whitecapped waves, storm and stillness, shipwreck and rescue, loyalty and deceit, joy and sorrow, a world that opens before you with trade winds, doldrums, flood tides, primeval forests, forgotten and discovered cities, poetry, ecstasy, the sun in the north, bottomless intoxications, shining splendor, carnival, to this very day, deep orgasms, suffering, and death. Behind you, far behind you, behind the North Sea and Færder Lighthouse, lies the November fog, lies Kristiania—where fine Norwegian folks sit in the Theater Café, and Kåre Willoch sits at the leader's desk in Conservative party headquarters and the Libertas lobby and the *Daily News* and *Evening Post* count their money—and the Oslo New Theater and publishing houses and Norwegian Broadcasting and Baerum. You see the lighthouse on Høysand sink in the north, feel the Bay of Biscay heave with whitecaps, and you are free. Free! FREE!

Escapism's lighthouse in Europe?

No, your name, Høysand! And for those sailing north it signals the entrance to the English Channel, to the North Sea, to the narrow strip of land that grows and grows, and becomes your fatherland, your mother tongue, that stretches across thirteen degrees of latitude, from the 58th to the 71st, becomes seaweed and tang, sand and stone and reeds and cliffs and grass and bogs and barren earth and fields and pastures and meadows and birch forests in May, becomes mountains that fade into blue in the sun and are named Nevrolnuten and Veranibbedn and Temprei and Nonskiljenuten, becomes construction work and roads and dams, high-tension wires, pipelines, summer pastures and bleating flocks, becomes people who work on the land, in the factories, in the schools, who sing together at the top of their voices in their free time and who usually look up from their work when you come back and greet you saying, Wel-

come, welcome, you've been away a long time! That's Høysand!
Then we went in again to the mess.

THE MINE ZONE

I worked on banana boats for many years, the Caribbean, Central America and the east coast of the U.S., the Great Lakes, the Pacific, and the Far East during the last years before I went ashore in Genoa without a Thai wife or a Chinese walnut chest or Arabian camel saddles, but with just the same cardboard suitcase, which I set down equally half-empty on the tracks for one of the large unloading cranes while I waited for the shipping agent's car. It was a pale morning just before the dockworkers' forenoon shift, with thin blue smoke rising from the chimneys, a smell of sulphur in the air, and sea gulls shrieking above the garbage cans aft. In the crane above me, an older man in a red shirt walked from the cab into the machinery room with an oilcan in one hand and a paperback book in the other. At the bow rail near the Number 2 hatch, the first mate stood in a white shirt thinking about his wife and about the fact that after the next voyage he was going to leave August Kjerland's shipping company to become a pilot on the Verdens Ende–Jomfruland stretch and live in a prefab house near Vrengen Bridge. He stood there watching the unloading crew that came slowly along the pier and up the gangplank below him. Then he threw his cigarette down between the side of the ship and the pier fenders made out of old tires, and disappeared into the superstructure midships. The crane operator returned from the machinery room, the oilcan still in his hand. A little later, I heard the chains rattle and a hard slam against the clam shell, and spill being shaken down from the silo coaming. I moved my suitcase and sat down on a bollard. Two longshoremen disconnected the ship's water hose, dragged it behind them along the pier with squishing steps, and screwed it tightly to the next hydrant. Ready to shift berth. The dockmaster foreman came aboard and stood at the railing talking with the signalman. They pointed and looked up toward the cab of the unloading crane. The dockmaster gave the signal to start things up. Then the agent arrived. The station wagon swayed heavily over the crane tracks and stopped at the bottom of the gangplank. He let me off in an underground parking ramp in town. Aren't you supposed to drive me to the Consulate? It's only thirty-six blocks to walk from here. Damn it, you've got to drive me to the Consulate! Get out! I took a taxi the rest of the way and asked it to wait outside. The hotel was on the fourth floor, above a bar. My roommate lay asleep on his cot when I came in. He looked up at me with muddled blue eyes when I opened my suitcase and changed into other clothes. Later I bought him a drink and told him about the good weather on the last voyage, and he said, Call me Johnny Bird, bo'sun from Baltimore, and I know a better place just down the street. Lots better. That's the last I remember. I let myself in for it. I can still feel the lump.

Things started to roll. During the Cuba crisis we were at sea between Tampico and Colón, on the east side of the Panama Canal. The telegraph operator, a big, bearded fellow from southern Norway, came down into the mess at the ten o'clock coffee break and threw a long telegram on the table and said, All hell's breaking loose, boys, right over our heads. And we left the mess and went over to the rail and looked out across the sea as if it were eternity that lay ahead, gray and endless except for us, just a couple of sea gulls high up to starboard (they must have come out from the Mosquito Coast or the San Andrés Islands). Then we sat down in the mess and played cards, and it was Stavanger's deal. Eighteen hours later, we entered the first locks and saw the fully mobilized bases in the Canal Zone, Fort Sherman, Fort Gulick ("School of the Americas," one of the six international headquarters that President Kennedy set up to coordinate antisubversive warfare), Albrook Air Force Base ("Tropical Survival School"), Quarry Heights, Fort Clayton ("American Geodetic Survey"), and heard that the Russian vessels had turned around and were on their way back over the North Atlantic. When Kennedy died, I was sitting in the middle of the mine zone in Santos (the mine zone is what the Norwegians call a string of sailors' dives in Santos) drinking a sugar brandy called cachaza. I was far away from home, but not as far away as at Business College. The radio was playing "Bocage," the most popular samba at the time. Right in the middle of it, the music suddenly stopped, and not for a commercial, because right afterward came "The Star Spangled Banner," and then everything was silent, both on the radio and in the bar, only the flies still buzzed around, until they settled, undisturbed, on the freshly cut papaya and mangos and passion fruits, and then they were silent, too. The bartender put the glass he was drying back into the dishpan with chlorophyll dissolved in it and walked over to turn up the volume, and a voice on the radio began to talk, slowly and very solemnly at first, and then faster and faster and more and more excitedly, and people around us began to hug each other and smile, and some laughed, and a guy right behind us (between us and the bar) hiccuped and laughed without stopping while he tried to say Alliance for Progress, A-ha-ha-ha-ha-ha! When we came aboard the ship again, we found out that Kennedy had been shot in Dallas by Lee Harvey Oswald. It was on the same voyage I got tattooed in Rio, stone cold sober. *LOVE*, one letter on each finger except for my thumb. *L* on my second finger, *O* on my middle finger, *V* on my ring finger, *E* on my pinky, all on the inner joint. It was a caste mark that never disappeared. Love—the sudden gestures in the crew's mess and the bars in Alexandria and Takoradi, always ready to put up their fists, nobody cares what you say anyway, nobody cares about you, give them a whack so they understand or are touched. For there are many ways to be touched. Caressed on the cheek, held closely, having the shit beaten out of you, being kicked, hissed at, flogged. Touched. I don't know whether it was before or afterward, but anyway it was on a cross street of Broadway in New York City (must have been 43rd or 44th Street) with two of the men from the boat (we were looking for Jack Dempsey's Broadway Bar) where I once saw Marlon Brando come out the stage door of a theater along with four or five others, all of them soused. (There was a line of people outside waiting to get his autograph.) He stopped on the sidewalk and stood there swaying while the others pulled and tugged at him, and he yelled and screamed: Przybyszewski! Przybyszewski! Przybyszewski! And rolled around on the sidewalk in his suit and all, until the others finally managed to drag him into a taxi and they drove off toward Fifth Avenue. We didn't find Jack Dempsey's Broadway Bar. Maybe it no longer existed? Instead, we stopped at a hamburger place on 42nd Street on the way back to the ship. Two days later, all our cargo had been unloaded and we sailed to Morocco with machine parts. The world lay at my feet, the sea stretched blue and boundless, with the sky above. The good earth. The seven seas. The seventh heaven.

Sorrow and Death

FROM THE DEPTHS

For Arnold Høysand, sudden death and despair and sorrow were associated with labels on sardine cans. And colored marbles and large shiny balls from ball bearings that sailed through the air in a heavy, majestic curve and rolled in a straight line toward the little hole in the ground. They were associated with holes in red soil, cold fingers, the narrow strip of snow-free ground between the fire station and the town hall, where an underground cable or water pipe made the snow melt faster. Sudden death was associated with labels on sardine cans. Arnold Høysand kneeled in front of the hole and with a flick of his finger knocked the marble belonging to a boy from Åstrand down into the hole with his own. For this feat he won a label that had a picture of a yellow-haired boy in short trousers standing with a fish in his hand against a background of pale blue ocean with whitecaps and the mesh of a fishing net or seine and white and red life belts. Arnold Høysand is too young to read what is written on the bottom of the label, yellow letters on a red background that give the product's name and place of manufacture. But he remembers the picture, that valuable and colorful (blue and white in addition to the yellow and red) piece of paper in his hand, as one of the first clear glimpses of himself, the paper, the cold fingers, the weight and the round smooth shape of the marble, the melting snow, the cold wet earth. He remembers all these raw physical things, along with the label, like an innocent warning of disaster, of loud voices around him, of movements

61

that become abrupt and ambiguous and brutal for a few bewildering minutes before they slowly dissolve into a long wet shadow of unmoving bodies, silence, prohibition. The label and the soccer ball and the lacing needle. Because the big boys come down from the field behind the fire station with a soccer ball and a bladder and a pump and say that one of the little kids has to run over to Halvorsen's place and borrow a needle so they can put air in the ball and lace it up and start playing, because the field is dry enough now. And Arnold wonders why Hadle, his brother, isn't with them, but he doesn't ask, just stuffs the sardine label in his pocket and starts running, across the bank property, behind Mrs. Sivertsen's, and up the stairs to Halvorsen's place. It smells of varnish and lubricating oil and ropes and tar, and there is a woman already standing inside. She says they had evidently gone out on the ice floes down near Russia Bridge, jumping from one to the next as each ice floe began to sink under them. Halvorsen is wearing a blue workman's coat with many pencils sticking out of the breast pocket, and a fine net of purple veins covers his entire face and bald head, and under his coat is something like an old bicycle horn that he presses and makes say tuuut or baaeert far down in his chest instead of words when he is going to answer. The woman hurries out the door with three long scythe handles wrapped in a newspaper, and the door says klingeling after her, and Halvorsen looks at Arnold with eyes that barely have life in them, like white and blue fish that have been in a purple net for a long time. He says tu-uut when Arnold asks if he can borrow a needle to lace up a soccer ball and goes back into the store among the scythes, the clamps, the band saws, the pliers, the hammers, the planes, the compass saws, the hacksaws, the crowbars, the paint buckets, the wisps and glues and pails and shoelaces and shoe-plugs to fasten loose soles, the broom handles, the rakes, the sacks of tar, the packages of nails and the brads sold by the pound. The smooth round wooden handle of the needle is placed in Arnold's hand, and he completely forgets to say thank you or to listen when Halvorsen says baert baert baert, which means, Now don't you forget to bring the needle back. All Arnold is thinking about is, if I run as fast as I can, and I get back in a hurry, maybe they'll let me play soccer with them, at least be a back. And he runs like a wing player across the bank property, past the bakery, where the smell makes his mouth water for muffins, behind Mrs. Sivertsen's, and all the way to the fire station without even resting, and without dribbling or feinting. But there aren't any big boys pumping up the ball by the fire station; there aren't even any little boys. Arnold stops, and turns and looks all around, but nobody is there, not one person. The ball is gone along with the boys, the marbles are gone, the labels are gone. All that's left is a little hole in the ground whose edges are about to collapse and into which melted snow is running. Arnold dashes around to the back of the fire station, stands at the corner with the needle in his hand looking over at the field. Nobody there either, not a soul. It's when he turns around and thinks, I'd better go back to Halvorsen's again with this needle, that he sees them. They're running down by the Methodist church. The smaller ones are all he can see, and only their heels, but that's where they're running, down there, and now the last boy disappears around the corner of a house. The big boys are probably already far away. Arnold starts running, too, down past the Methodist church and the BP gas station and the old stable. High snowbanks still rise up on either side of the road, but out in the middle the snow has melted and water flows and splatters as he runs. He does not stop until he gets all the way down to the pier and sees how many people are there. Grownups and boys, and everyone is standing close together in a big cluster, the harbor policeman, a couple of guests from the hotel, a diver in a diving suit, the crew on the diver's boat, the shipping agent, factory workers who have a free shift, the big boys who were going to play soccer. A large grownup man leaves the cluster and runs in the opposite direction from Arnold, but many people shout, and the big man almost stops, turns around to listen, running backward as he looks at the people shouting from the pier, then answers by raising one arm before he starts running ahead full speed again. At the far end of the pier, the old warehouses lean out over the fjord with their rattling winches, and the black water is full of white ice floes. The bare branches of the forest on the other side of the fjord also look black against the spring snow. The cranes on the factory pier stretch their trim booms out over the black prow of a boat, and the factory drones like a huge generator for the entire scene. But Arnold Høysand sees only high hip boots, low-heeled shoes, diver's boots, and trouser legs, and he notices that it's quiet, nobody is saying anything. There must be something lying out on the pier in the midst of the cluster of people. Then Arnold meets Njål, and Njål thinks that someone fell in while jumping on the ice floes, and that it was a boy from Saunes with a funny name. And no sooner has he said this, than someone in the group begins shouting and pointing up the street, than Arnold sees Papa tearing down the road on his bicycle. He shouts, Papa, Papa, Papa! but the shout does not force itself out of his mouth across the black pier and into his father's ear, and Selmer Høysand does not notice him as he slams on the brakes and leaps off the bicycle, which skids in the gravel and falls down with the front wheel still whirling round and round. Selmer Høysand still does not pay any attention to Arnold, who has never before seen his father with such a look on his face and senses, *knows*, why Papa does not turn around when he calls him. With a couple of giant steps, Selmer Høysand leaves the bicycle and the cluster opens for him, but not fast enough. He pushes at people on both sides and plows a way for himself, as if they were tall, malevolent weeds he must tear out at the roots and clear away. Suddenly, he stops; Arnold can see his narrow back jerk erect, and then Selmer Høysand falls onto his knees. Something is lying on the ground in front of him, and Arnold sees what he has known for a while. He sees who is lying there. He sees it is Hadle lying there, and he has been in the sea because he is soaking wet, but otherwise he looks just like he always does. Selmer puts his head against Hadle's chest, and Arnold sees the profile of a familiar face he has never seen before, and then his father calls, Hadle, Hadle, Hadle! and lifts him up halfway and shakes him so the white face swings from side to side, and Arnold notices how all of those standing around instinctively move back a step. Then Arnold hears a car drive up behind him, and when he turns around he sees that it's a taxi and that the driver is already out of his seat and is pulling open the back door and that the man who rushed off a little while ago is getting out of the other front seat. The driver stops beside the open back door. He is wearing a chauffeur's cap and a gray jacket over a knitted woolen jacket which is buttoned up to the neck. When Arnold looks back at his father, Selmer Høysand has picked up nine-year-old Hadle and is carrying him in his arms toward the taxi. Arnold hears him talking but not what he says. Hadle has on high boots, which dangle down and bump against Selmer Høysand's thigh as he walks. His face is as white as an angel's. Selmer edges himself into the back seat of the taxi with Hadle in his arms and slams the door, without having seen Arnold, and he doesn't see him either as the driver hops in behind the wheel and speeds off into town. The cluster of people slowly breaks up, the grownups talking together in low voices as they walk in groups of threes and fours in the same direction the taxi drove. The diver stands for a long while, stock-still, then he walks heavily out along the pier in the other direction, puts on his helmet, and slowly descends into the depths at the bottom of the fjord, and it flashes through Arnold's mind that now he's going down to bring back another dead boy. But the fjord remains black and silent. The boys surround Arnold, who suddenly stands all alone in the middle of the old steamboat pier with a label from a sardine can in one hand and a lacing needle in the other, ostracized, infected by death, while the other boys whisper among themselves, Look, that's the brother of Hadle, who fell in out there, and maybe he's completely drowned. Poor, poor Arnold! The same pity as for the dead. Then they start running back into town, and only Arnold is left on the pier, so alone and so afraid, as if all the darkness in the world had found its way to a stocky, curly-haired little boy and were closing tight around him.

HERE TODAY AND GONE TOMORROW

Hadle is no longer there, but death is something different. Hadle no longer comes home from school and gobbles a sandwich and rushes out again to play soccer or whatever boys find to do and needs to be called in when it gets dark. Hadle is no longer there. But life has to go on, says Selmer Høysand one day as he stands in the doorway dressed to go to work on the afternoon shift, with his hand on the doorknob. He is aware of the question in the words as well. Must life go on? Alvhild stands at the stove making waffles while, at her side, Arnold gradually eats them up. This is how life goes on. The butter sizzles in the waffle iron, someone in the apartment below shuffles around in slippers, the radios throughout the land of Norway are silent now—and will be for some years to come—between the Midday Concert and the Wednesday Book, waiting for Eivind Groven's melody that signals a program is about to begin. Alvhild does not answer. She pours a ladle of batter into the six-heart-shaped form and closes the waffle iron, but Selmer sees her nod—or maybe it's a sob that tugs and tears at the large body upon which age and childbearing have clearly set their mark, as if they had tried to pull her body from her, downward and to all sides. Selmer lets go of the doorknob, crosses the floor with the expression of a laborer who has entered a big, brightly lit, unfamiliar room, and tries, in a somewhat clumsy and helpless way, to embrace the heavy body standing at the stove and concentrating on other, more practical tasks, such as turning the iron before the waffles begin to burn. The daylight and the steam from the iron filter into each other. Selmer puts his arms around her shoulders and buries his face in the blond hair with its 1940s permanent. Perhaps he says something, whispers words that comfort or ask for comfort into her ear. Arnold, his mouth full of waffle hearts, looks up at the two big people, his parents, with wide, wondering eyes. He stops chewing. There is a faint smell of something burning. Selmer becomes aware of the boy and abruptly lets go of the stiff, reluctant body he is pressing to his own, as if he had been caught indulging in a revealing, secret vice. He casts a confused and guilty look at Arnold, who returns the bewildered gaze until Selmer turns on his heels, walks over to the door again, and resumes his position with his hand on the doorknob, secure once more about the situation and the consequences, on the right road, like a comet that has returned to its path after being on a dangerous collision course with the Earth. Life has to go on, he says firmly, and closes the door quickly behind him. His steps are clearly audible as he walks through the entry decorated with American commercial romanticism from *Life* magazine—the Grand Canyon; the Rocky Mountains crowned with violet snow, with a cowboy in boots and a big white Stetson hat on a rail fence in the foreground; cactus and a lava-colored sunset in the Arizona desert; sequoia trees; the Napa Valley. Then the front door of the apartment slams, and his footsteps go down the stairs two by two, ending with a long leap onto the gravel in the courtyard. Later, on the shift, Selmer Høysand strains with rod and stoking bar to get the tap to flow properly, bathed in sweat, with the entire weight of his body and all his well-spliced-wire power behind him. He feels as if he were poling a heavy, awkward craft out from a remote backwater and onto the river of life. Afterward, he drinks water, lances the taphole with oxygen, downs some salt tablets, drinks some more water, and finally, through the tinted glass in his safety glasses, sees the swirling, white-hot metal cascade down into the chills, where it must cool and slowly stiffen, become hard and cold, and then be crushed with sledgehammers, the genuine separated from the false. That night, after he has eaten and they have gone to bed, Selmer says to Alvhild, a couple of centimeters away under the down quilt in the darkness, that this is the way life goes, this is how it is. We float down the stream, too; I work my shifts and you do the housework and the shopping and take care of Arnold and see to it that we've got food and clothes, and someday we'll capsize, or we'll just float out through the mouth of the river into an endless ocean; or else it'll all stiffen before we get that far, freeze, get so hard and cold it'll have to be crushed with sledgehammers. In the bed at the other end of the room under the window, Arnold, who has been awakened by the sounds, sees the thin moon above Tempreinuten Peak and, half-asleep, hears the faint weeping and the muffled, unintelligible words in a language from a foreign land.

Hadle is no longer there. His bed has been moved to the attic. His clothes no longer lie in the drawers. Hadle has not thrashed him or fought with him or tortured him or grabbed him between his legs from behind or anything like that in many days, but death is something different. Death is the little living room out at Høysand (like most country folk, Selmer uses the name of the farm as his surname, although some use the names of the three sections of the farm—Røyse, Steine, Berge) when Arnold is there with his parents and listens to the sermon on the radio echo through the small rooms in the pensioners' part of the house and Grandmother stands in the doorway, straight-backed and solid and somber, and the living room is cold and everything as motionless as in a photograph, and to move anything in it or move yourself or say even a word are all equally impossible. Black clothes and faded colors. Grandmother speaks. Her mouth is a thin, tight hasp that closes her face; her eyes, the nails that shut it for good. Her gray hair, pulled in a tight knot at the back of her neck, is rubbed shiny with sugar cubes. It is summer, free shift or weekend, morning. Quiet once the radio is turned off. No smells, no sounds, no tastes, no sweet clattering of the cover on Kielland's big candy jar. God is the oldest person in the world. To grow old is to become almost like God, in age, wisdom, goodness, justice. Eighty—ninety—a hundred! Percent? Good? The sun shines on the flowers in the vase, the flowerpots, the porcelain washbasin, the teeth brushed with toilet soap. Arnold in an easy chair, motionless, like a Nordic child buddha. A blue five-kroner bill in a white envelope with wavering slanted handwriting on the outside. The acrid smell of yarn and knitwear. Hadle is dead, but this is the living death. Out on the steps in the dark. We'll stay till tomorrow! Yes, do that. Lights from the city, the factory. It looks like a city, especially over there at the factory it looks like a city! Is that what a city looks like? Night. Next morning. *Christian Missions Magazine.* The wild black girl, Gondane, with swelling dark heathen breasts. Gondane saved, wearing a gleaming white blouse and a necktie tight around her throat in the sunshine at the mission station in the Cameroons. Squares of sunlight on the attic floor. Can Arnold see through them down into the parlor? Yes, Arnold sees through the worn floorboards, through the multitude of phenomena, through everything. He sits without moving and looks, and he sees nothing. Empty space. A chubby little boy who always sits overdressed, stuffed, and motionless, without saying a word, in the chair where he is placed after the unavoidable replies to how old he is and whose boy he is today.

Six-and-a-half this spring! Grandmother's boy! The brief chorus of adult voices above him: And so, so grown up! And so, so big! And so, so good!

IN SUMMER'S SUNNY DAYS

And these are not empty words. Arnold is good. Very good, like Kåre Vangen in the comic books. He sits quietly. He gets enrolled in school, is taken to school the first four days, and sits quietly, still a calm, patient, stuffed boy who slowly and sadly takes out his ABC book and learns the alphabet, his arithmetic book and learns the multiplication tables, his colored pencils and draws the flag in red, white, and blue along with the United Nations flag and Teacher with a black hat and broad shoulders in the shadow of a huge tropical coltsfoot. At the blackboard at the front of the classroom stands a light-haired boy doing a division problem so fast the chalk spurts around him, moving commas and three decimals and remainders, while at the desk next to the back in the second row from the window Arnold's eyes get more and more listless, more and more empty—as if he sees straight through and past the disorderly numbers, where the clever boy now borrows from a five, through which he puts a broad slanting line, in order to be able to subtract 3 from 0 and get 7; as if he sees straight through the value of being able to perform these complicated operations and only see the black, empty, clean board. And Arnold continued to see the emptiness and the darkness, listless and heroic and without blinking an eye. He remembered the light-haired boy doing division at the board and the fall sunshine because from then on he no longer kept up with the class. This is indisputably confirmed by the grade book he brought home each spring, which had a drawing on the cover of a boy climbing over a gate that blocks the road toward the sun shining up in the left-hand corner, while a girl standing behind the gate looks at him admiringly. Two apostles walked on a road, period, is Arnold's brief retelling of the Bible-story lesson. But Arnold, Arnold! What were they going to do in Capernum? You mustn't forget the most important things, what they were

69

going to do in Capernum, and whom they were going to meet there! Two apostles walked on a road, Arnold repeats in a firm voice. For woodworking class, Arnold brings the half-meter-long hull of a boat, a polar vessel, says Selmer, who has hewn it with an axe for him. Arnold is going to make a deck over the empty hull; a board is going to be cut to fit and fastened down, planed smooth and flat and fine, and then given a slight arch toward the middle like a real deck. Is going to. But Arnold adjusts the bench clamps, screws the hull firmly in the vise, and sits down on the workbench after the teacher has come by and given instructions and made marks showing how far he must plane. He sits on the workbench and stares out into space, and once in a while, at rather regular intervals, he lifts his round, sweaty right hand and gives a heavy, flabby slap against the wood of the hull. When the hour is over, he loosens the vise, takes the board and the hull, one under each arm, and locks them up along with the breadboards, the wastepaper baskets, the bookends and the three-legged living-room tables of the master carpenters in the class. After school was out at two o'clock and Arnold had eaten his dinner, he could stand for long periods, whole days when he did not have school, the live-long day, week in and week out, just watching the leveling over by Runnane, the huge Muir Hill trucks that drove up at great speed, turned around, stopped, shifted into reverse, and backed over to the dump, the fill that poured down from the truckbed, the payloader that crawled around on a caterpillar track leveling off the heap. The laborers who took five minutes beside the yellow and red construction machines taught Arnold songs with strange words, The house on the hill is fine and dandy / There you can buy liquor, soft drinks, and brandy / And eat your girl's pussy just like candy, stubbed out their cigarettes, stamped them into the fill, Well, we'd better drive over for another load, climbed up and got into the truck again. Or simpler things, the man who came rumbling along the road in a rig, swung the seat around with himself on it, set the outrigger firmly in the ground, pulled on the four levers with round black handles, and Wonder of all Wonders! The clam shell worked! The clam shell dug! And a box of stones as a counterweight! Or even simpler: municipal laborers with pointed spades, crowbars, jacks, tackles, a tripod with a chain around the biggest stones in the trench being dug for the water pipes to Kleppeker, the jack hammer drilling through the asphalt. Eat your girl's pussy? Arnold did not understand all of this teaching either, but he kept on listening, and looking, and counting every single spadeful. Arnold got to fifth grade and wanted to learn English. He remembered letters from America, a gold watch, a ten-dollar bill, the color photographs in the entry at home, and the daily trickle from his cousin, Steinar Høysand, who was in the same grade at school and who read comic strips, listened to Finn Moe and Birger Kildal's international news and commentary on the radio and Sigurd Evensmo's sermons on film, collected and wrote down license plate numbers, knew the names of popular singers such as Thor Raymond, Elvis Presley, Frankie Vaughan, and Åse Wentzel, who opened the newspaper first to the Brylcreme ads every evening, who had over seventy books (whereas Arnold had two, *Grandfather's Child* and *The Grouse Hunters of Rust Mountain*, carefully read word for word), and who studied English. Arnold sat down near the front of the class, looked at the back of the English teacher in his gray smock, and watched the hand that wrote strange signs on the blackboard, even worse than division: backwards *e*'s and upside down *v*'s, and *d*'s with minus signs above them and long, thin things that looked like something between *s*'s and *f*'s. But then, English had to be difficult. Arnold followed with interest, and wrote things down in his notebook as best he could, until the teacher, who had a small, bright yellow moustache and was a captain in the National Guard, turned to the class, wiped the chalk from his hands, and said they had taken the first step toward pronunciation and now they could start to move forward toward mastering English itself. He was deep into a difficult sentence about how English is a world language, understood throughout the entire free world, when, for the first time in several years, and for absolutely the last time in this connection, Arnold Høysand spoke out in class of his own accord, without so much as raising his hand, and demanded to know what kind of language he

71

had just learned, the one with the strange letters, if it wasn't English. When the teacher restrained a tight-lipped smile and said they first had to learn phonetic spelling, which was an absolutely necessary weapon in conquering the art of how to pronounce English words, Arnold at first appeared not to understand at all, but did not respond, and the teacher quickly went on with his general interpretation of English as a world language. While he was speaking, Arnold Høysand got up deliberately from his desk and leisurely packed together his books and pencil case, put them neatly in his school bag, fastened the two buckles on the bag, and walked quietly and calmly between the rows of students' desks, past the teacher's desk, and over to the door, paying no attention to the amazed expressions of the teacher and the other children. Without turning around, Arnold opened the door to the corridor, went out, held the door for a moment, and then slammed it with all his might. A whoosh went through the classroom, the wall shook, an inkstand tipped over, and the map of Europe behind the teacher's desk fell out of its rack, unfolded nicely, and descended upon the brave English teacher. The time it took for the teacher to escape from the European borders was undoubtedly what saved Arnold, for the teacher flared up like a rocket, fought his way loose from the map, and raced out into the schoolyard. From the window, the rest of the class saw fat little Arnold win a swift sprinting duel with the fat little English teacher (who gave up at the schoolyard gate) and disappear down into the Factory Housing. This was the only outburst of anger, or rebellion, or flight, or *ressentiment* that Arnold showed throughout the seven years he helped wear out the grade-school desks. After that, he went to junior high. Arnold remembers to this day that they had metal shop, and that everyone made metal lamps. And metal lamps and metal lamps and metal lamps. He himself made a wrought-iron lamp that was lacquered black and exhibited at the year-end celebration in the spring. To conclude the festivities, they sang the Swedish song "In Summer's Sunny Days," girls with clear voices and boys whose voices were changing. We walked through woods and gardens / Wandered where we walked, ha-la, ha-la! No, no, no, no! *Singing* where we walked! Singing where we walked, ha-la, ha-la! But when they came to the refrain again, the tall rascals around Arnold gave one another a conspiratorial look and joined in,

> Wandered where we walked, ha-la, ha-la!
> Ha-la, ha-la!
> Ha-la, ha-la!

TAKORADI

Arnold Høysand is fifteen years old. Selmer, his father, is the head tapper on the tap floor of one of the furnaces in the old furnace room. Arnold has finished the required seven years of elementary schooling and the standard one year of junior high school. He is not conscious of being a "laborer's son," or of belonging to a particular class. *Proletarian* is a word he has never heard. He never opens *Factory Worker*, the magazine for members of the Norwegian Chemical Union, which his father receives. The fathers of everyone he knows work at the factory, except for those who are engineers or teachers, but they are so unusual he doesn't count them. He reacts to the fact that in the short stories he occasionally reads in weekly magazines Tony and Philip always go to the office. His father goes to work on rotating shifts, and every third week Arnold has to be quiet in the morning so his father can sleep. That's how it is. Selmer half humorously refers to a shift strike early in the fifties as "the time we went home from work." When Arnold turns sixteen, the factory will be a possibility for him, too, but Arnold does not want to work at the factory. In the fall after he finished junior high school, he informed his parents that he wanted to go to sea and then stay in America for some years in order to get rich. It had all begun about midsummer, when Helge, who lived a little farther up the street, came home after a voyage to Takoradi with the *Vistafjord*. Arnold was sitting down by the river drinking with Helge and the *Vistafjord* fellows. Or rather, Arnold was probably not drinking, but he was with them, and Helge and the *Vistafjord* fellows were drinking. It was about three in the afternoon when Selmer, who had seen them from the factory, rode up on his bicycle. He got off, lowered the kick-stand with his foot, and left the bicycle. Then he came down to the rocks by the river where Arnold and Helge and the *Vistafjord* fellows were sitting next to a puddle and, without a word, took hold of Arnold by his upper arm, lifted him to his feet, and half carried, half pushed him over to the bicycle. Arnold did not say anything, either, nor did his companions. Then they bicycled toward home. The most humiliating part of it was that Arnold had to sit on the baggage carrier with his feet dangling down into the gravel. Back home, a drubbing on his bare bottom, a good old-fashioned thrashing. Two days later, Arnold had a job as a rod man for the road construction on Mo Street. Four days later, he was unemployed again. For the first time in his life, Arnold behaved like that bad boy, Larris, in the comics, and was just impossible at work. But it took two more months before he found a boat and had acted crazy enough for his parents to allow him to go to sea. It was the *Vistafjord*, which was unloading manganese at the factory pier and was to leave again for Takoradi with ballast. Arnold went aboard about four in the afternoon, and the boat was to sail the next morning. Selmer even came out of the furnace building and down past the locomotive shed in order to wave to him. Arnold looked to both sides and waved back. Then the second mate showed him to a cabin midships that had two bunks, a couch with drawers under it, a desk, a washbowl, and a bookshelf with a box of Blenda soap powder behind the fiddles. The upper bunk was taken. Arnold set down his suitcase and sat for a while on the lower bunk. Then he went up into the mess. Most of the crew were ashore. The watchman, a small black or brown man (Arnold did not know whether he was a genuine Negro), shivered, smiled at Høysand, then went down to his cabin and put on a navy-blue pea jacket to protect himself against the September night. Yes, Høysand was the new deck boy. Up in the mess, Arnold sat with an older, gray-haired man who was asleep with his head on the table and his arms hanging loosely on either side of the swivel chair. The table was covered with a light-colored oilcloth with a design of squares and red clusters of grapes, and on the side near the wall was a stand holding oil, vinegar, salt, and pepper. There were four such tables, each with swivel chairs around it. The walls were brown and had teak moldings.

Arnold slept on board that night and was awakened several times, the last time when a big man lay down in the bed beside him. Early the next morning, he came trudging up through Factory Housing with his suitcase. Selmer and Alvhild had just gotten up and sat eating breakfast. They saw him from the kitchen table. The wind sent leaves scuttling to the edge of the sidewalk. Arnold went straight upstairs with his suitcase, and when he came down again he had taken off his suit and tie. Alvhild had put out a plate for him, at his usual place. He did not drink coffee yet. Selmer chewed a piece of bread and said nothing. Arnold sat as though guilt were dripping off him, drank a large glass of milk and got a refill. Alvhild was the only one who said anything before they got up from the table. "The smoke's really bad again . . ." (Silence.) "I almost didn't realize it was you coming up the street, I . . ." (Silence.) "And I just washed the windows before I went into town yesterday . . ." (Silence. Composed by Grieg.) The next week that Selmer worked the morning shift, he talked with the personnel office (they saw him from outside, standing in the middle of the old-fashioned tobacco-brown room as he let his workman's cap glide through his fingers like a rosary in the hands of a priest, and knew what kinds of prayers he mumbled before *his* lord) and with the machine shop foreman, and he got Arnold in as a plumbing apprentice at the factory. The following day Arnold found out about it, too. Apprentice! Yes, now Arnold Høysand would really have to learn to listen. He had already learned. Arnold, you're to be at the Shop on Monday! Yes, Massa Ned, said Blossom, rolling his eyes.

A-1

He's turned into a fine-looking fellow, that Arnold Høysand, now he's outgrown his baby fat, people began saying, while Arnold, without haste or waste, struggled through the last difficult years as a teenager (as those between twelve and twenty now began to be called) and started to look like a fully grown

75

man in his twenties. You know, the son of Alvhild, Alvhild Høysand, they added, for to tell the truth, Arnold had not made much of a mark for himself up until now and there weren't many people, aside from his relatives, neighbors, and the men he worked with, who had a very clear idea about what sort of fellow this Arnold was. You know, the son of the Høysands over in Factory Housing, he had a brother who died, you know. Oh yes, that boy. The one who drowned near the pier. Oh, now I know who you mean. You're right, he's turned out to be a very fine young man.

In the summer of 1962, Arnold Høysand was nineteen years old and had one year left of his apprenticeship. He was broadshouldered and almost exactly average height; in June of that year he was measured as one meter sixty-seven centimeters when he registered for the draft at Sand. At the same time, on the basis of medical examinations and tests for general and technical intelligence, he received the military status of A-1 in his new draft registration book, and his name and number were entered in the army rolls. On the boat coming back from Sand, Arnold gets drunk on beer for the first time (he didn't have to go to work until the next day) without liking it at all, but he drains his glass when the others do and says he thinks bock beer is better, and if you have to drink pilsner, then it's got to be light beer, to show the whole world that Arnold Høysand is no weakling, and to emphasize the brotherhood in arms he has entered. A photograph taken at Infantry Training School at Heistadmoen near Kongsberg about a half a year later shows Arnold Høysand in uniform, trying to look serious, but the picture, taken in three-quarter profile, nevertheless cannot hide something very attractive about the round, regular face with large, clear eyes and a snub nose, the hair in a fine lock on the forehead and clipped very short at the back of the neck, which the times and the situation demanded. He looks young, younger than his twenty years, and his new responsibilities as husband and father do not seem to weigh heavily on him. Judging only from this photograph, most women would think he was a very handsome fellow, whereas many men, probably out of envy or in self-defense, would characterize him as a pansy or a pretty boy or a Caspar Milktoast.

Arnold Høysand was not one who went around noticing that older women talked about him and that the girls his own age gave him long looks. Had he noticed, he would not have understood anyway what there was about him that could be so interesting. Arnold minded his own business; went to work (aside from one winter at vocational school); put in as much overtime as he could get; read his lessons; went to the movies occasionally, especially Norwegian films and love stories and the three C's—crime, cowboys and car chases; stopped in at a café afterward; saw all the Sport Club's games; went now and then, as if by accident, to the People's House and stood in the doorway of the Big Hall watching, as though this were the same kind of entertainment as the Fourth Division soccer games at Sletta Field. Women were the visiting team, but Arnold didn't join the home team. Furthermore, to his parents' mute despair, he never went to the Youth Club, not even to the door. He had no particular criticism, no particular attraction, but he realized immediately, as if by the smell or something, that he was not comfortable with the scraping fiddles and cozy conversations over coffee cups at the Youth Club, that there was clearly too much disparity between this and his everyday life at the factory. So it was on his way up the steps to Café Torgheim, just a couple of weeks after he had registered for the draft at Sand, that Arnold met a girl named Bodil, a junior college student who had the reputation of being quite forward. Arnold did not know Bodil and moved to the side of the stairs. It was summer, and Bodil said, Say, isn't your name Høysand? Say, do you know Ingunn wants to talk with you? Arnold stopped short and stood looking straight ahead. He barely knew who Ingunn was—yes, he knew who Ingunn was. She's been crazy about you for a long time. Awwww, replied Arnold, and continued walking up the stairs. He didn't know anyone at the café, but from about that same day both Selmer and Alvhild began to notice unmistakably that something had happened to Arnold. He did not become lethargic or distant, nor did he get lost in dreams in front of the mirror in the entry. Quite the opposite. He became more open, livelier, often talked eagerly and coherently, both at home at the dinner table and during breaks at the factory. Something or other had become clear for Arnold Høysand, some heretofore unknown possibility had revealed itself in all its power, set him in motion, and turned him into a helpless and most cooperative victim for the first girl who had the opportunity, or the courage, to thrust herself upon him. Maybe I should buy myself a car, said Arnold, both at the dinner table and at work. Get my license, and buy an old car. Or a Folks-wagen, like the guys at work said. Either a car or a Folks-wagen. All the time he was saying this, Arnold was thinking, Ingunn. Yes, he knew who Ingunn was. He tried to close his eyes and think about exactly what she was like when, for example, he was threading, or to see her in his mind when he had rung the bell and stood waiting to have work tools issued at the tool room. Yes, he saw her clearly. She was pretty, no doubt about that, sort of neat and orderly, with a resolute way about her and a short, plump body, and she was a forward on the women's handball team, even though she still could only play on the junior team. And wasn't she always good-natured? Didn't she always have a smile on her face? Anyway, she worked at the telegraph company, lived in a house in an Own Homes tract of land, had taken a course in Bergen (and had it not been for the hasty marriage to Arnold, she would have been transferred the following year when the telegraph office was automated). She met Arnold on Sønna Hill just three days after he had talked with Bodil on the Café Torgheim steps. It was a beautiful day with a mild east wind. She was on her way to work the night shift, and Arnold was heading up to see Knut Åge, who lived in Brekke, and had taken only a slight detour. Knut Åge. Knut Åge, the hero. What has happened to our childhood heroes, those who always won when we fought each other, who dared to go a little farther out on the cliff, who dived from one meter higher, who never got caught when we played hide-and-seek, who were the sheriff when we played cowboys, the chief when we played Indians, who played center on the soccer field, scored the decisive goal, saved the decisive goal when they were the goalie, who had hair on their prick from the age of three and screwed from when they were ten? They're on the other side of the world, aboard a boat sailing with its bottom upwards, on skid row in Hamburg, in a bar in Rotterdam, in the backyard polishing the car, in the corner of the sofa reading the

Stavanger *Evening News*, in an early marriage that resulted in a large family; they're substitutes on the Park Board, grandparents at thirty-four, relief foremen in the shop, powerless, tamed, passive, crushed, out of the picture. The best. Knut Åge, the hero. Why? Where is he now? Ingunn and Arnold met there on Sønna Hill. She has seen him, Arnold sees only her. Farther up Sønna Hill, the Brass Band is out marching and playing "Freedom's Frontier." Perhaps they are practicing for May 1, perhaps they only want to celebrate spring and to blow sorrow and melancholy away on a long march. Ingunn was the first to take courage.

You've talked with Bodil? she said. She was breathing as if she had just made a rush attack, throwing a curve as she leaped into the mouth of the goal. Arnold had stopped, too. He nodded, the smoke from the factory was blowing seaward.

It's going out today, he said.

Oh?

The smoke. It's going out today.

Yes.

The gas, too.

The gas?

The gas is going out, too.

Oh yes, the gas, yes. Don't you work over there?

Yes, yep.

What do you work in, anyway?

In the same shit as other people. That's plumbing, you know, working with the same things others shit in.

GOD AND EVERYONE

This was one of the wittiest remarks Arnold remembered from his job, and he used it as soon as he had the slightest opportunity, if not before, even though in his case it was actually not a very accurate description of the skill he spent his youth learning. Plumbing work at a large smelting plant had little or nothing to do with float balls, high-tank toilets, or low-tank toilets, water traps or cisterns. So although Arnold knew almost everything about these things as well, working with what other people shit

79

in every day was not the aspect of plumbing in which he and his coworkers were experts. Their main job was to oversee and maintain the cooling systems for the fifteen to twenty manganese smelting furnaces lined up in various technical versions divided among three different furnace rooms. The first time Arnold went along to fix a leak in the cooling pipes of one of the furnaces in operation, he was sure he had chosen the wrong work. He was sixteen years old and was sent with two shift repairmen over to one of the closed furnaces in the old furnace room. It was late fall, and the black heaps of raw materials were rimed with frost. The men had brought a hauling wagon and took the elevator at the far end of the shop. Arnold went first, pulling the wagon, while the two repairmen walked behind him talking about salmon fishing in the Vikedal River. Occasionally they plopped their asses down on the wagon and let Arnold pull them along the corridor that went past the laboratory. It was about two, near the end of the morning shift. Down near the Number 1 furnace a fellow sat pounding on the lining of a furnace pot with a chipping hammer. Arnold stopped with the wagon. Are you Kristiansen? one of the repairmen wanted to know. The man stopped hammering and shoved his safety glasses up on his head. No, he said. I'm Fløgstad, Fløgstad with Kj. No, not Fløgstad spelled with Kj, but . . . But are you the furnace operator? No, not me, said the man and pushed his safety glasses down over his eyes again. I sit here banging on a wall of silence and listening for the empty spaces in the language. Arnold gripped the handle of the wagon again. I see! said the repairman, beginning to walk away. So you don't work in the furnace room at all? No, I work for Cooling, said the man and raised his chipping hammer. Arnold took the wagon and sauntered across the operating floor. Behind him, he heard rhythmic hammer blows. The foreman stood in the doorway of the control room for the Number 2 furnace, glaring at the clock on the wall and checking his watch when they came in. He did not say a word, just gave the trio with the wagon an angry look and sprinted up toward the office. One of the repairmen pointed, and Arnold pulled the cart over to the furnace pot. Then they talked with the furnace operator. Kristiansen hung over the handles inside the control room, looked out at the furnace through the window and the green shield, and to the right and the left on his gauges. The second man and third man on the operating floor crew sat on the bench outside earnestly watching the flames lick up around the three electrodes. There was flashing and creaking and clamor. Total uproar. Arnold felt quite dizzy when the two repairmen emerged from the control room again and said, Oddvar got one that weighed thirty kilos in the estuary right across from where Øystein was standing. Then they could tell by the flames and the mix that the furnace operator had lowered the voltage. All three went over to the furnace pot and threw in old dented and torn sheets of corrugated iron on top of the mix. Arnold could not believe his eyes when he saw both repairmen climb up onto the pot and the mix and reach out their hands for wrench and hacksaw. The flames around the corrugated iron were practically licking their legs, and Arnold was supposed to be the assistant! Cooling water dripped down from a pipe, the water lukewarm, body temperature. (After cooling off the furnace, it was used immediately to warm up the swimming pool on the other side of the river. The pool had been built as a volunteer effort early in the fifties. Arnold himself had learned to swim in water that was 33 degrees Celsius.) Now he set his foot on one of the pots' covers and crawled up onto the mix with the big plumber's wrench and a three-inch copper tube. He felt hot and sluggish, and had to push himself, but he managed. It must have been at least 300 degrees, or 5,000, as it said on the temperature gauge inside the control room. And there they stood, right in the midst of the stabbing flames, screwing things like the devil and looking as if they were repairmen in Hell, where the Devil was dissatisfied because he couldn't get it hot and hellish enough for sinners against the Holy Spirit! And, so help me, they were still talking about the one that weighed thirty kilos! Arnold was mute with admiration. No buts and maybes, no dear God, with these guys. Right to it, with no fuss, no drama, while you talk about something else. That's how Arnold wanted to be, too! Fishing and hell! The world was banal and brutal. Thirty kilos! Heedless and full of the devil, they jumped up on the mix, gave hell to God and everyone. Total control, knew how to do everything. Arnold thought he knew how a pork chop felt when it was flipped out of the frying pan and onto a dinner plate when he finally jumped down onto the operating floor and began to play with the sheets of corrugated iron. But here a new and terrible shock awaited Arnold Høysand. After the repair there were large pools of water on the floor around the furnace pot. Arnold took one of the stoking bars lying on the mix and tried to use it to drag the sheets of corrugated iron over toward him. He wasn't wearing gloves, either. Naturally, he touched one of the electrodes with the iron stoking bar and made a fine circuit-ending with his feet in the pool of water and the stoking bar on the electrode. And himself in the middle. The shock made his whole body curl up. Arnold let out a shriek, dropped the stoking bar, and fell full-length in the water. Whew! he said, dazed, and got to his feet. Then the furnace operator turned up the voltage again, and the dazzling white blows leaped around the black electrodes. The other two men on the operating floor put on their safety glasses, each gripped a spout, they pushed the start button and began the circle dance of adding the mix to the furnace and laying it lovingly and evenly around the electrodes. So you got a shock, did you? said the repairmen as Arnold sat on the cart, pale and weak, looking at them with frightened eyes in the elevator on the way back down to the shop. You look sort of wiped out, they added, but it was only a 5–6,000, so you'll be okay!

POWER PULLS THE TRAIN

Arnold did this work for two years, at miserable apprentice wages. He was far from all thumbs and never made any big blunders. The third autumn, he started vocational school, taking the bus back and forth to Saudasjøen each morning and evening. His friends, who had been out and earned money at sea, zoomed past the left side of the bus on their motorcycles, swerved sharply back into the right lane, and pushed the speedometers up close to a hundred on The Strip, as they called it. Arnold watched sadly through the rain-streaked front window as they disappeared around Saunes.

He enjoyed school. Mathematics was still a problem, but he liked technical drawing (his neat, precise constructions were often shown to the class as an example of clear, well-planned working drawings), and he knew about and understood most of the practical work they did during the course. Moreover, for the first time Arnold saw the utter seriousness behind religious convictions—there was a boy in his class who could not wear long trousers and therefore always wore knickers under his overalls, because he believed in God. This scrupulous consistency Arnold admired with aloofness and awe. He was also a second-string back on the class soccer team and played in a total of three games during the spring and fall. Arnold was the classic type of back player who stood solidly at the end of the sixteen-meter line and kicked at everything that moved nearby. But what Arnold remembers best about vocational school was the train of decorated vehicles that the students worked on all spring until it wound through the streets as the Vocational School Parade on the 17th of May, Independence Day itself. The sidewalk was jammed with people as the parade rounded the corner by the BP gas station and began making its way up through town. First came a little boy from Saudasjøen carrying a long stick with a sign on it that read: POWER PULLS THE TRAIN. Behind him walked Power, who later became well-known and admired as a strongman and body-builder and safecracker, hunted by the police and bailiffs of several districts. His bare torso bulged with muscles even then, and around his waist was a double loop of buzzing wire that was fastened behind him to the bumper of a truck. That's how the parade began. The back of the truck was decorated with Norwegian flags and fresh birch branches, and in the midst of all these decorations stood the Shotguns band, with Charles Iversen as soloist on the electric guitar, celebrating life with Shadow music. Behind the truck came a bus that the sheet-metal students had fixed up to look like M/S *Fjordsol*, the boat that made the trip to Stavanger in four and a half hours. In the smoking lounge on the *Fjordsol*'s lower deck sat the Sauda boys, all fired up, with huge clouds of smoke above their heads, as they drank beer and talked at great length about lots and spouts and life on the foredeck and were in tune with the times and the future. The

83

poor fjord idiots who boarded at Marvik, Hebnes, and Jelsa scarcely dared to peek in the door of the smoking lounge before retreating hastily to sit on deck chairs and stools and storage containers for life-preservers out in the rain and cold. People on the sidewalk laughed and clapped.

Then came a boy from the mechanics class who hobbled along on one foot juggling thirty-six ball bearings in the air, and simultaneously swallowed flames, like one of the tilting furnaces in the new furnace room, as practice for fire-eating on the job. Behind him was another bus. This bus represented a vehicle rented from HSD Autos to give a special tour for the members of the Commerce Committee in Parliament. Arnold played the part of a member from the Conservative party and had to clutch the man beside him and peer out the window in stark terror and swoon, because it was seven hundred meters straight down into the fjord, and he had to yell and scream for help and demand that the crazy bus driver pull in to the side of the mountain and stop immediately. But the driver just sat calmly at the wheel, his uniform cap pulled down on his forehead, his eyes straight ahead, a stub pipe between his teeth and big clouds of smoke above his head, totally indifferent to the fact of being millimeters from death for twenty-seven curving kilometers. Behind the bus carrying the Commerce Committee came a fellow from the same class as Arnold. He balanced a nineteen-meter copper tube on his lips. At the top of the copper tube another fellow lit fire to the carbonic oxide streaming out of the tube, which made the gas flare up in a blue flame and turn into carbonic acid. Behind the copper tube came a man wearing a tropical helmet. He also wore a red-checkered flannel shirt and carpenter's pants, carried a woodworker's pencil, and talked out loud to himself in a Bærum dialect. He was following a political Silva compass, which showed The Correct Line, with blue deviation to the right and red to the left. People clapped politely. Then came another truck. On the back of it sat a man reading newspapers on a bench at a trolley stop. Beside him were a pair of cross-country skis and a pair of ski poles. The man was wearing a hiking outfit and a top hat, a blue parka with a hood lined in wolf fur, polar mittens, coarse wool socks, ski boots, and spats. He sat humming with an Oslo tone and reading Oslo newspapers without so much as a smile, without the least hint of laughter. He picked up and opened the *Morning News*, paged through the morning edition of *Evening Post*; *The Nation, Our Land, Way of the World, Daily News, the Evening Post* evening edition—all were read, folded up, and put into the pockets of the man's parka without even the beginnings of a smile. But it was quite the opposite with those who stood watching on the sidewalk along the parade route. They didn't smile, they collapsed with laughter, red-faced, with tears in their eyes, aching diaphragms, and trembling feet. When, for example, the man opened the morning edition of the *Evening Post* to the editorial page with an alert, serious, and socially conscious expression in his eyes, there were many spectators who couldn't stand it. They laughed themselves nearly to death and had to be taken to the hospital by volunteer members of the Red Cross rescue team. After this success came yet another truck. The back of it was set up as a tropical barroom, with wicker chairs and bamboo walls. A couple is dancing a tango to a tune by Carlos Gardel. At the bar stand a big, black Negro in a yellow suit with dark stripes and a girl wearing a white rose behind her ear, a red grass skirt, and a blouse with a low-cut square neckline. Above them, a large fan whirls round and round. They talk together confidentially in low voices. Suddenly, the barroom door is flung open. They turn and look at the man who enters. The girl gives a start, and turns white as a ghost. A shudder runs through her body. What's wrong? asks the big Negro. She has to take a large gulp of bamboo brandy before she is able to answer. Either it's the Devil himself, she finally manages to gasp, or it's Rasmus Høysand from Sauda. This is followed by an interlude. Two fellows from the electric class fasten electrodes to a doll that looks like A. P. Østberg, head of the Employers Association, and send enormous electric shocks through the doll, which trembles and wails. Then comes a new truck. A huge gravel heap has been dumped into the back of it. Two laborers are digging in the gravel with pointed spades, each in his own corner. Around them stand eighteen men in white coats and yellow helmets with stopwatches and questionnaires and tape measures. Then they descend on the two workmen and begin measuring and timing and noting and evaluating the laborers from all sides and ends. It turns into a wild battle, with white coats and blue work shirts and coarse gravel and pointed spades hitting against yellow helmets and ticking stopwatches and extended tape measures and pages of time-studies that flutter behind the truck as it speeds away through town and disappears. At the very end of the parade comes a naked woman, running. Her entire body is covered with tattoos, and she looks as though she came from Takoradi. She doesn't show off at all, simply runs after the truck and the parade as fast as she can. Anyway, this is all Arnold Høysand can remember. Oh, yes, in the evening there was a dance outside on the cobblestones at the Town Hall square, where Arnold waltzed to the music of "Cockcrow" for the first time. Do you remember that?

Yes. Oh, heavenly days! replied Ingunn with a smile.

HEAVENLY DAYS

All these true stories, told with just such honest detail and precision, Ingunn heard as she gradually became better acquainted with the handsome Arnold Høysand, at the Kløver, at the Torgheim, in the cross-fire of envious girl friends' glances, under the publicity posters at the movie theater, on the long way up to the Own Homes tract (Yes, I think I remember the vocational school parade), and on the one trip they made to Tjelmen, where Ingunn Bernhardtsson got pregnant in a wooded grove right next to the huge pipes carrying water to the hydroelectric plant, across from the big water tank and where a TV relay station was later built. At that time she and Arnold had known each other exactly thirty-six days. It was a bright Sunday morning in early summer. Afterward, they sat looking down at the town in its weekend calm. To this day, neither of them can fully understand that children can result from so little. The small glimpse of naked skin and brown hair between the pulled-up crinolines and the pulled-down panties, the big blue head that

86

peeked out of the half-unbuttoned fly of Arnold's trousers. And such a short, short time! But when Ingunn's heretofore absolutely regular menstruation did not occur for over eight weeks, she went to the doctor, and the test was positive. And that corresponded exactly with the date of that Sunday. There was nothing to discuss. They moved in with each other after having been to the church one Saturday afternoon in a white dress and veil and a dark suit with a carnation in the buttonhole, with his large number and her small number of relatives sitting in the front pews of the church. Arnold was impeccable as always, whereas Ingunn appeared to be longing for her jogging outfit as she waded up the aisle in her bridal gown, sparkling and strong, her solid back swaying like a tugboat that now had Arnold in tow, headed for a safe harbor called marriage, where (they had both accepted) all on-going connections would lead into death. The wedding celebration went fine, the gift table was well laden, and nobody had too much to drink. On Monday, an alarm clock rang in an attic apartment with two small rooms in Sønna. They blinked, looked up at the ceiling, a little uncertain of each other and of what they should do, and how. But they learned quickly. They got up, Ingunn put on the coffeepot, Arnold was given cake and cold steak from the wedding dinner in his lunch box, and he headed off to work for the first time in the fifty years remaining until retirement, with three hundred working days in each year—$50 \times 300 = 15,000$ times—and after one time they could do every aspect of it more or less. They had overslept by a half hour, but the foreman just grinned and said something about her probably being hot today before he sent Arnold to work up in Cooling, where he got more or less the same comment from his friends.

Arnold still worked only in the daytime, except for overtime and extra shifts, but late the same fall he passed the apprentice exam with a job in the new crushing and sizing building connected with the Sinterworks, and received his plumber's license at an informal gathering arranged by the Craftsmen's Union in the basement at Festival Hall in Factory Housing. Besides Arnold Høysand there were three others who got their trade certification, two sheet-metal workers who likewise had completed their training at the factory, and one baker. Ingunn, who sat in the hall and listened to the speech by the chairman of the union's Trade Committee and clapped enthusiastically and had a permanent and a new dress, was clearly pregnant. Arnold liked his job at the factory; the furnace room did not frighten him any longer; and he liked the atmosphere among his coworkers, which was marked by strong self-respect and professional pride and well-articulated, ironic self-assertion toward the foremen and shop manager. It took Arnold about three years to pick up the tone and to identify with the attitudes, but by then he was able not only to take all jobs and assignments, but also to join in with his own stories or to speak out to those who needed to know who decided the tempo. Arnold was known as a genial, dependable fellow who was well liked, but who could also be a bit impossible (the peasant heritage for which his coworkers had such deep contempt)—impossible in that, for instance, he might let out a fart as he stood straining to tighten something with a wrench and then say, Heavy loads rear explodes, or, It was so bad it wouldn't hang on the dung fork. Politically, the milieu was anti-Communist and antibourgeois, with about equally heavy emphasis on both. The shift repairmen (along with the shift electricians) were the best-paid laborers at the plant, receiving shift bonuses as well as a skilled-worker bonus. Most of them were married and were undeniable male chauvinists; many had previously been active in competitive sports, had been to sea a few times, knew Rotterdam (and the Katendrecht red-light district) better than Oslo, owned automobiles and, in some cases, a house, were hard-working, intelligent, skilled laborers. They saw themselves—in relation to people such as the Chinese, Italians, Arabs, and Russians—as stewards of civilization and of Western culture, Goethe's chromatics, the Sistine Chapel, the alphabet, modern electronics; saw clearly the perspectives that television opened up for people interested in soccer, read the *Rogaland News*, were basically cynical about political issues, embodied most social-democratic virtues, even though their essentially anti-authoritarian attitudes were also directed toward the leaders of the Norwegian Labor party and the national Labor Union with demands (during lunch breaks and on the way home) for specific terms of office for Labor Union leaders and tougher representatives in Parliament. There was never any talk of happiness or freedom. What was on the agenda were the fifty years until retirement (and the unknown number of years after that) that had to be managed in the best possible way in order to survive, without too much wear and tear, without too much subjugation, without being too demeaned; with warm clothes on one's whole body, familiar people around at all times, children who carried on life, stone laid upon stone, sofa, living room, apartment, row house, summer cabin, automobile, auto trip, vacation in the South, single-family house. When the whole construction was completed, with living room and dining room and kitchen and a basement under the entire house and bathroom and individual bedrooms for the kids and a guest room and a garden, perhaps that was what was called—Happiness and Freedom? In any case, when Arnold Høysand waved goodbye to Ingunn, who was now between five and six months along, from the aft deck of the hydrofoil to Stavanger one afternoon early in January the year he was twenty, he felt fortunate and happy, like a man who has found his right niche in life. And he waved goodbye with perhaps just as much sincerity and feeling to the large brown factory that loomed impressively and spewed smoke in the background.

AT ATTENTION

After four months at the Heistadmoen military training camp, among recruits who had to move at a run the entire day, even in chow line, and after having learned discipline, learned to pull a Laplander sled, and learned to drink royal highballs (1 part export beer and 1 part Brandy Special), Arnold Høysand was a sufficiently good soldier to be sent north to Setermoen in Indre Troms, where the main battle against Ivan was to take place. Pointing out that his wife was now nine months pregnant, Arnold asked to be transferred to the navy and Harald Hårfagre on Madla, but his request was denied, and on the fifth of May he found himself sitting in an airplane flying north from a leave in warm, spring-green Rogaland up to the darkness, snow, and ice in Gokk, and barracks fever in Brig N. How many days? bellowed the veterans in the mess hall, and beat their forks and spoons against the tin plates, when the new recruits from the South stuck their closely cropped heads through the door. Arnold had twelve months left, that was 12 times 3 is 36, and then add a zero, 360 days, that's one year, twelve months, damn it! Arnold stretched out on his bunk in the barracks with his hands under his head and felt three seconds pass, 4–5–6–7–8–9–10–11–12 seconds pass, slowly, slowly, 12 times 3, then add a zero, but that was days. Was it 60 times 60 seconds in a day? No, 60 times 60 times 24! And then multiply that by the other arithmetic problem. Arnold rolled over and looked inside the door of the green locker: twelve months, one year, 365 days! In this room, on this iron bed, together with nine others placed two by two next to each other, with all this bunk making and boot polishing, with your private life in an olive-green locker, with clothes folded just so, with evening inspection, with lights out at 2215, with the Garand in the rifle rack, with preparedness, with NATO alarms, with repolishing, with reveille at 0600, with maneuvers, big Swedish tents with wood-burning stoves, combat rations, corned beef in cans, field uniforms, thick long underwear, woolen watch caps, primus stoves, Kapok sleeping bags, web belts, anklets, chow lines, afternoons at the canteen. Arnold—37–Høysand—rolled over again and stared straight at the olive-green door of another locker. Then he looked at his watch. Forty-eight seconds had passed. He closed his eyes. Twelve months! Twelve long ages. Arnold Høysand managed to make about six of them pass before any officer or noncommissioned officer was in a position to realize that there was a private in the communications section with the number and name 36537/63–Høysand. He never said anything an officer could overhear, never asked anything, never criticized, never made irritating mistakes, never was the very last man in any activity, be it military sports or shoe polishing or bunk making or coming out of the barracks onto the parade ground after lunch when it was 37 degrees below zero. However, 37–Høysand very often came *next to* the last (and left next to the first from duty), stood in some inconspicuous place in the middle of the olive-green flock and was air, nonexistent, when the last man arrived and got thoroughly chewed out. This everyone understood and admired, but very few were sufficiently relaxed and deliberate to be able to copy it. After twelve months (including recruit training), some officer or other checked off the troop lists and, to his great amazement, discovered the existence of a certain 37–Høysand in the platoon whom no one could recall ever having noticed, but who, on the other hand (or precisely therefore), had never been reprimanded or sentenced to the guard house. They called 37–Høysand in to company headquarters where he, along with four others in the platoon, received a single stripe on each arm of his uniform jacket as well as an armband for his field uniform, and was given the rank of vice-corporal—insulted private—with a raise in pay of fifty øre per day, and then sent back to the barracks to the scorn and disdain of the others in the platoon. Even this misfortune Arnold managed to take with stoic calm and impassively continued to trudge next-to-the-last in the company with the heavy field-radio equipment on his stomach. He was still accepted, although not exceptionally popular. A dependable guy, that was Høysand. Never any nonsense about Høysand, they all agreed, all the nine others with whom he shared a room in the barracks. He watched enthusiastically when his buddies, for example, loosened two mattress springs on the bed of status-seeker or stargazer 12–Risnes, so that in the evening 12–Risnes fell on the floor instead of falling asleep. But Arnold never took part himself. On the other hand, it often happened that he came out with humorous comments, such as, This is just as damn hard as putting toothpaste back into the tube! (when they changed the batteries in the ANPRC 10 in the basement under the classroom barracks), or, This place looks like a bombed-out bordello (when he entered a Swedish tent that the platoon staff used on maneuvers). Or he sat at the formica-covered table (with its lead selvage fastened with copper screws) in the barracks reading aloud as he replied to one of the 483 letters Ingunn sent during his first tour of duty (or to the few half pages Alvhild wrote for herself and Selmer), distant and inaccessible to his roommates because of his marriage and family responsibilities, which implied experience they lacked but the seriousness of which they somewhat understood and accepted.

It looks funny, Arnold might say.

What does?

I wrote, "I ain't got no complaints," but it looks funny to write I ain't got no. But that's what I say, ain't it?

Ain't it supposed to be *am not*?

Am not, how?

Ain't is *am not* in right grammar.

"I am not got no complaints?" I guess I'll just leave it: "I ain't got no complaints. The food here is better than at Heistadmoen, and on Friday the whole company except the company staff is going on 'maneuvers' on skis. We're in for a lot of trekking, trekking yourself bow-legged, like the ass't platoon leader says. So you can tell there's still snow up here, at least when you get a little ways into the mountains."

A man from Jaeren sitting at the other end of the table putting the finishing touches on Correspondence Course Number 144—the one about the transition from farming to plow factories and machinery stores—glanced up angrily from Book 19, and his look alone stopped Arnold from reading everything aloud as he wrote it. This Jæren man later had his picture in *Troop News* and *We Men*, after setting the Norwegian record for correspondence courses completed during the first tour of military duty. The picture, which was used in both publications, showed a long, dark, serious face, sad eyes that only aimed at and hit the bull's-eye on the rifle range, and a thin mouth that had resuscitated dead domestic animals long before mouth-to-mouth resuscitation became common among people. Arnold didn't say another word and continued writing, but now and then he glanced up furtively and would not have been more amazed had it been a five-legged ibex sitting there doing one correspondence course after another, so far was this man from his own dreams and ambitions. Arnold got along fine with the others in the room and never had a real blow-up with anyone. Easterners were impossible, he knew that, brazen and boastful, like the folks from Odda, and without being what they bragged:

At home everyone calls me Sexy. It was the same with the men from Trøndelag, and there was no one from Bergen in the room. But the northerners were fine, and so were the men from Stavanger, even if they talked the way people from Stavanger have to talk, letting the last letter in all the sentences go over into long laughter: It was funny-y-y-y-y-y!

REPORT MY SIGNALS

The march in the mountains that Arnold wrote home about took place four days later in the Sikka-Paras-Rieppevarre-Treriksrøysa area and proved to be very tough going with springtime ground conditions there. "You boys are here to fight for freedom," the army commander, Lieutenant General Bjørn Christophersen, had shouted to the brigade as it stood in formation. He made a dramatic pause, the echo of his words died away among the barracks as he looked out at the rows of expressionless twenty-year-old faces between the collars of their field jackets and the brims of their field caps. The general found no further words. He was cold. Battalion Commanders, take charge! he ordered. He saluted. The men in front of him returned the salute and then began running and shouting, and the order was transmitted through the ranks. Ten long ages later, the evening of that same day, Arnold moved into battle formation southwest of Govddavatnet as communications officer for the leader of Pi (code for Pioneer) Platoon, a lieutenant who in civilian life had been a blasting foreman on the construction of the Ulrik Tunnel between Indre Arna and Bergen. Now, under his uncertain leadership, it was Pi Platoon's job to detect mines and to build a road for the battalion's heavy-baggage train, which was to advance toward Paras where a regiment of experienced vets from Infantry 4 had taken up a position as the Fiend, code-named Fi. During the evening a thin crust formed on the wet snow, making the terrain slippery and dangerous. The platoon leader ordered his men to bivouac for the night, and they put up tents and established a command site. Arnold set up the radio and calibrated it to 6120, with a reserve frequency of 3770 for platoon communication. Then he began to call:

Ninety-nine, Arnold said into the microphone on the hand-set. Ninety-nine, this is Nine. This is Nine. Report my signals. Ninety-nine, this is Nine. Over.

Loud and clear. Nine, this is Ninety-nine. Over.

Ninety-one, this is Nine. Press the microphone button on the handset before you start sending. Ninety-two, Ninety-two, this is Nine. Report my signals. Over.

Nine, this is Ninety-two. You're weak but readable. Over.

Ninety-three, this is Nine. Report my signals. Over.

Nine, this is Ninety-three. Oooha! Things are really swinging here, man, swinging. Have you heard the one about the guy who dreamed he was hanging wallpaper, and then he woke up with paste on his stomach and the brush in his hand? Over.

Ninety-three, Ninety-three, remember transmission regulations. Ninety-four, Ninety-four, report my signals. Over.

Nine, this is Ninety-four. Can you tell us where they eat steel and shit chains? Over.

Ninety-four, this is Nine. On Jørpeland, Kiruna, Mo-i-Rana. Ninety-five, this is Nine. Report my signals. Over.

Nine, this is Ninety-five. When Johnny comes marching home again, hurrah! hurrah!

Ninety-six, this is Nine. Report my signals. Over.

Nine, this is Ninety-six. The devil is in heaven compared to us. Over.

Ninety-six, this is Nine. That figures, you could hardly manage cooking classes in school. Ninety-seven, this is Nine. Report my signals. Over.

Nine, this is Ninety-seven. We want to talk with a general or something with -ral in it, like a vice-corporal, for instance. Over.

Ninety-seven, this is Nine. You want Odin straightaway? Over.

Nine, this is Ninety-seven. No, Smirnoff straight up. Over.

Ninety-nine, Ninety-nine, this is Nine. Transmission completed.

Lieutenant, radio contact established, said Arnold Høysand and crept into his sleeping bag with the handset on his collar.

94

The next day was sunny, with no wind. They marched in a long column south toward Paras, two men to a sled, without meeting Fi. The company marched as a unit, with Pi Platoon about in the middle. It was nearing the end of the first stretch when the helicopter carrying the battle judges flew into a chasm toward the northwest and set down on a patch of ground to the right of the company. An orderly hung onto his cap and ran over to talk with the executive officer. Everyone figured it took five minutes. The xo stood listening. He nodded. The orderly put his hand to his field cap in a salute and ran back to the helicopter. The xo waved the company on the march again. It was heavy going, wet and slippery. The straps on the backpacks cut into the men's shoulders, thirty kilos, backs ached, the runners on the sled paralyzed hips and thighs, seventy kilos, feet got blistered, eyes ran, mouths were dry. The orderly's words began to travel back through the column:

Høysand has a daughter, Høysand has a daughter, Høysand has a daughter, pass it on, pass it on, Høysand's got a daughter, Høysand's got a daughter, Høysand's got a daughter, Høysand's got a daughter, Høysand got a girl, Høysand got a girl, Høysand got a girl, Høysand got a girl, pass it on.

No, that's me, said Arnold Høysand and stopped short, as though an extra weight had been added to the sled.

REIULF

Politically, Arnold Høysand was never in any doubt. Politics meant that every fourth year he got checked off on the roster of eligible voters and dropped the list of candidates supported by the local Labor party into the ballot box behind the curtain at the Town Hall, and two years later repeated the same lonely and liberating action with the Rogaland County Labor party list, which was headed by J. M. Remseth the first time Arnold voted. Remseth, who for a long time was Number 2 on the list—just below the old Mot Dagist candidate, Trond Hegna—had worked at the slag dump before becoming a member of Parliament, although Arnold cold not remember so far back himself,

95

he could only remember Remseth as a splendid old man with silver-white hair and a ruddy face who stood in town having discussions, probably about politics, when Parliament was not in session. Later, Arnold helped vote into Parliament Peder Naesheim, editor of the *Rogaland News* (an amalgamation of the *Haugarland Labor News* and *May 1*), a female candidate Sunniva Hakestad Møller, and Edvard Edvardsen, a shoemaker from Egersund. Arnold saw a meaningful connection between his own daily work, his actions at the ballot box, and the work these candidates carried out as his political representatives among the bigwigs in Oslo. You couldn't expect everything, and they certainly did as much as anyone had a right to expect. Arnold also remembered the shift strike in 1961. At that time, the furnace room workers paraded from the factory up past the homes of the factory director and the head of personnel, and then down through town. They filled the street, shoulder to shoulder. It was a dark evening in late fall. The Brass Band stood playing the "International" on the back of Tjelveit's truck as the vehicle followed the furnace room workers, who marched up Skule Street and disappeared into a meeting in the People's House. The thirties all over again. Arnold felt he had taken a look backward in time, far back in time; he interpreted what happened as the final outbreak of something the rest of the country was finished with, but which they were still fooling around with here because they hadn't kept up with progress (including progress in wage levels), and perhaps also because the plant management here was unusually stiff-necked. But the following year when, after several months of open conflict, the big strike over seniority and the number of laborers needed for different jobs culminated on May 1 in a demonstration parade in which over a thousand marchers took part, Arnold had not the slightest doubt that he too should join the march, all spiffy and shined, while Ingunn waited at home with dinner and the kids. But that had nothing to do with what went on in Oslo, with what was politics and was passed or voted down by the bourgeois members of Parliament. What the people here were involved in was a struggle for decent treatment and decent wages at work, whereas Parliament debated the Nordstøldal or Slettedal high-

ways and tax percentages and concessions for boat routes on the
Bokna Fjord and support for Christian Junior College and Sand
High School and the length of required military service, and the
Township Board argued about water and sewers and tried to
maintain some restraints in the face of all the demands from the
teachers, who were so bad they wouldn't hang on a dung fork,
when you considered how little they worked. Now and then,
the two worlds touched each other. Around 1960, Arnold went
to a few meetings of the local Young Labor party, including one
where the head of the national Young Labor party, Reiulf Steen,
was the speaker. The place (Little Hall) was packed, and the air
was damp from the wet rain gear hanging in the corridor. Are
there any questions? Reiulf wanted to know, when the chairman
thanked him for his talk. Questions for Steen? The chairman
repeated the question. Yes, Birkeland jumped up. He was an
energetic middleweight-type laborer. What's the Labor party's
position on the atomic question? ("The Labor party believes the
atom can be split.") Reiulf, in his enthusiastic way, discussed the
national convention's clear vote against atomic weapons on
Norwegian soil and emphasized that the Labor party and the
Labor government would never consider changing current Norwegian policies regarding foreign military bases, before the
dancing was let loose and he trudged across the bridge to sleep
on a sofa at the home of his relatives. Is Birkeland satisfied with
the answer? Birkeland, sitting with his legs crossed and his lips
pressed tightly together, nods. Are there further questions? The
room is silent, everyone avoids the searching look of the chairman. Arnold is silent, too. He wouldn't say anything, not on his
life. But at the same time, he somehow feels this has nothing to
do with him, this isn't politics, this isn't a question of power,
aside from the fact that it gives him and the others an opportunity to see Reiulf and decide whether they have confidence in
him or not. Arnold decides he does, or rather, he decides he has
more confidence in Reiulf and the Labor party than in any of the
others. But he doesn't go to any more meetings. He feels, cor-
rectly, that it's useless, that Birkeland's question is just a ritual,
that there has to be a question from the boldest, most impetuous
person in the local party so the gathering can be called a meet-

ing, so the illusion that communication goes in two directions can be maintained. Reiulf returns to Oslo and his party head-quarters after the young laborers have questioned him about the politics of the party that bears their name and have criticized him on central issues, and after he has learned important things from them. This is the conception that the meeting is supposed to try to keep alive, that Birkeland's question is supposed to affirm, that Reiulf's answer must maintain beyond all doubt. He says, Birkeland, you've asked a good question. Birkeland and Steen are equals, comrades, Steen is Birkeland's chosen representa-tive, they meet and discuss fundamental political questions. That is the conception that the meeting in Little Hall is supposed to confirm. Arnold does not believe this conception is true. It does not have to be true, is his conclusion. Reiulf and the others are my people anyway, even if he leaves here by boat tomorrow morning and dances the cha-cha-cha with upper-class girls in Oslo on Saturday night. Arnold walks home through the same streets as Reiulf, and never goes to a meeting again. Perhaps that's just as well, too. He doesn't go to meetings either a year later when a pale, thin young student named Berge Furre, who has thick, horn-rimmed glasses and who they say is from Sjer-nar Island farther out in the fjord, stands up in the Big Hall and, in a voice that comes out surprisingly strong and resonant from the spindly body, holds forth about the new Socialist People's party and No to Atomic Power and The Third Position—not capitalism, not communism, but a neutral alternative. There is dance-hall lighting, people are sitting in the first three rows of folding chairs, and these listeners, who feared the worst, are pleasantly surprised, perhaps not so much about what is said as about the voice, which carries well, past them and far back across the empty rows of seats into the darkness under the bal-cony. While Furre is speaking, Arnold Høysand, who has now reached one of his greatest goals in life and is a permanent shift repairman, pads around in stocking feet in the small apartment in Sønna getting ready to go on the night shift. It is quiet, the child has gone to sleep, Ingunn will soon be home from handball practice, the radio is on, as always, softly. Arnold empties the water out of a large bottle and sets it next to the warming plate on the kitchen stove. He makes coffee himself, tests the bottle with his hand. Yes, it's warm enough, it should do. He pours in the coffee. Six hours later, he thinks back on it while drinking from the bottle and looking at the darkness under the timber rafters in the silent, empty machine shop. He thinks about it as a happy memory—the quiet house, the sleeping child, Ingunn out at practice, the brown liquid trickling down through the neck of the bottle as he aims the spout of the coffeepot exactly above it. Arnold sets down the bottle, finishes eating his packed lunch, drinks more coffee, puts the still half-full bottle into the warming oven, claps the helmet with the round Protection Officer mark on his head, and ambles back up to his job again. He has been issued his tools, there are only a couple of hours left, he'll be finished at five o'clock, he can manage that. Outside, the rain turns into snow. He whistles under his breath going up the stairs from the shop floor. The bosses and the engineers are sleeping like babies in their homes, and Arnold opens the door to the furnace room and feels a blast of heat hit him. No, Arnold Høysand has no doubt about where he belongs.

FALL IN, DRESS AT TWO PACES

But it took time for Arnold to become completely adapted to civilian life again. The first days were the best. His friends at work listened patiently and with a certain degree of interest to his stories about the sergeant who was so stupid he had failed business school seven times; and the lieutenant who had been demoted to second lieutenant for having given an order to fire in position while a squad was on its way out to the trenches below the targets on the firing range; and the captain who assigned the entire company extra duty to make the men learn to answer loudly enough, Good morning, Captain! when he said, Good morning, soldiers! at morning review; and the trumpet player in the Royal Guard (a well-known soccer player) who played the mess call as if it were a fanfare for the King's arrival at the palace

with the entire guard standing to arms; and the guy at Mauk-
stadmoen who asked the colonel on the field radio if he had
heard about the fellow who dreamed he was hanging wallpaper
and then woke up. Then there was the story about the non-
combatant at Heistadmoen who never got discharged because at
every discharge bash he beat up one of the officers and got
twenty days in the guard house and at the next discharge bash he
beat up another officer and got twenty days again, etc. etc. And
then there was the one about the guy who was supposed to
polish the table in the officers' mess at Skjold and was issued a
cleaning rag along with a whole bottle of Golden Cock gin—
and guess what he did with the gin. And the one about the guy
from the same club as the cross-country skier Pål Tyldum, who
pulled two sleds during the entire mountain march to help those
who couldn't pull their own. And there was that guy, Borsaas,
who had been the Junior Division regional champion in five-
hundred-meter speed skating in North Trøndelag and had a
45.2 average, and haven't you heard about him? He's pretty well
known and beat Heikke Hedlund in pair skating in the Junior
Division. For once in his life, Arnold Høysand was almost a
fluent talker. His friends at the factory listened willingly for
some days and made comments. For example: In basic training,
I was in the same platoon as Frank Sending, the soccer player
from Vestfossen; he's the guy who played center-half on the
national youth team in the early fifties. And: So they're still
using the old German schmeisser; well, well, that's an easy
weapon to clean, but its shooting capabilities . . . But when
Arnold began standing at attention when the foreman gave him
a new job, or shouted: Fall in, dress at two paces, close ranks left
face! to the other workers (at the same time, it's true, glancing to
both sides and winking broadly with each eye), most of them
thought, now he's going too far. After a while, Arnold realized
this as well and, feeling mortally wounded, abruptly withdrew
into himself again. About this time the rumor spread at the
factory that Arnold Høysand had been given the job of holding
up the lamp pole down at the far end of the shop, because Arnold
stood pressed against it, staring blankly out into space for long
periods during the morning shift. He spent nearly one year in

this position before he understood that the special camaraderie from the dreary barracks in Indre Troms was useless as a social lever in other situations, was useless for everything, at least in a sober state, was as useless as the knowledge of calibrating and reserve frequencies was worthless in establishing any contact other than with Ninety-nine and Odin on the field radio. Arnold was more gloomy than usual, and Ingunn, who had gazed into space with large pupils and a distant expression when he began telling about the machine-gun guy from Ørsta who had become practically a millionaire by selling aluminum flagpoles to the farmers on Jæren, with a fancy house on Varhaug and a fancy wife and a fancy car and everything, began focusing her attention once more and gave Arnold a worried look when he lay his knife to the side and began eating dinner without a word. She was pregnant again and had not told Arnold. That fall, their name came up on the list for an apartment in Factory Housing, and in December, well before Christmas, they moved into two small rooms and a kitchen on Håkon Street. A couple of months earlier, Arnold had been elected as the Protection Officer for his department, and his mood had begun to improve. He could be seen holding endless technical, as well as polite, discussions with foremen and engineers, and with representatives from the local Labor Commission when they made their periodic visits. Arnold took his new responsibility seriously, and conscientiously he began to gather information and form an objective view of the relevant problems by studying, among other things, the Worker Protection Law, the Factory Work Hours Law, and the Labor Commission Law, all passed on December 7, 1956. Arnold believed that the law regarding bargaining between labor and management should be respected, and he became silently stern and angry when anyone began calling it a law to protect employers. But he thought that he saw progress, that the managers listened to him when he presented the issues in a knowledgeable, nonfanatic way. He and Ingunn celebrated their first merry Christmas on Håkon Street together with Asta, who was now big enough to stand by herself without anyone holding on to her, and with Ingunn's belly very visibly giving renewed hope for Arnold's desire to have a son.

THE PLAIN OF JARS

This is in 1965. It's the time when in every Norwegian city and town one found an open space or field called the Plain of Jars (at the factory it was the warehouse lot) and some sort of representative for international capitalistic interests named Tsjombe or Kasavubu (at the factory it was someone from intermediate technology in Gothenburg). In May, the son was finally born, two weeks late, and although Arnold did not give much outward show of emotion, he was a very proud father, and one wintry day in early June when there were snowbanks all the way down to the fjord, Ingunn's mother carries the baby to the baptismal font and, in front of the sparse congregation in a white church built to the honor of God and Johnsonian pietism, the pastor announces to the entire world that the baby's name will be Svein. In 1973 Svein is a study eight-year-old with a long "bowl haircut," as the old people called it, a boy who greatly annoys his grandparents, blue T-shirt with SVEIN written in large letters across the front of it, blue windbreaker, red American corduroy trousers with bell-bottoms, sticks of chewing gum in his mouth, and Adidas tennis shoes, who runs with a whole group of boys over to the soccer players warming up for a game at Ullevål Stadium in Oslo and gets Bob McNab, an Arsenal back, to sign a shiny blue plastic autograph book with a picture of Dopey on the cover. This is before the kickoff in a sensational game that Frigg would win 1–0, a fact that did not help in the least later the same fall when Frigg fell unmercifully, and most deservedly, into the Second Division, where they have been ever since. Arnold and Ingunn are in Oslo on an auto trip with the whole family, which now consists of two boys and two girls. They are all sitting in the bleachers and Ingunn is ashamed of her eldest son, who has climbed over the fence and onto the field, and comes back to the rest of the family before the game starts, awed and solemn because of the treasure in his autograph book, and Arnold is allowed to open the book and immediately sees the name Bob McNab, and Svein thinks Bob McNab is the best player on the field and is on the point of tears when Arsenal does not manage to make a goal after the Frigg score. They take down their tent at Bogstad the next morning and start toward home along the Sørland highway and up through Setesdalen in the Anglia with its funny back window that slants inward. No, says Arnold afterward, when their vacation is over and they are back in the everyday routine and sit at home under the great and genuine pathos of the gypsy woman in the wall-hanging above the sofa in the living room. No, Arnold repeats with all the surrealism of ordinary speech, we didn't stop at Roligheden and them places down South. Easterners got there before us, and you know how it is, once the car's headed home again, it ain't easy to stop it. And: Sit down, if you've got some time to kill. And: We sure were lucky with this weather! We always take good weather along with us in the trunk of the car when we go on a trip. And: We saw Lars Roar Langslet come out of Parliament. What did he look like? A politician! He was white, he was black, in front he was behind. And: How did I know I'd draw a trump card? I did like this: Arnold's hand makes the sign of the cross in the air above the deck of cards. And then I drew the trump ace. It's easy, if you just know the trick. Making a mystery of the connection between cause and effect is necessary in order for weakness to endure. Ingunn deals. Yes, says Arnold, Frigg deserved to win. If I hadn't seen it myself, I'd never have believed it, but they deserved to win, and Jan A. Hovdan played like a first-rate back. It's the best game I've seen since I saw England beat Germany in the final game of the World Cup in 1966. That tournament, and especially that particular game, has a very special, sentimental place in Arnold's memory. It was the first World Championship soccer tournament he watched on TV; in fact, that was one of the first years you could even see proper TV, after the transformer at Flatskår was built and the cables were buried and the picture on the screen didn't change according to the weather and the road conditions. It was the same year, 1966, that the cross-country skier, Gjermund, was in such tip-top condition and won three gold medals in the winter, and Wirkola did the same in ski jumping. And then in the summer the world soccer championships, which ended with that German, Weber, managing to stick out that long leg of his in the last second to tie things up 2–2. Arnold could almost have cried, and it really wasn't the same with the extra inning and the disputed English goal and the Russian linesman and the TV replay that was shown again and again: the ball at the crossbar and down on the goal line and out, the ball at the crossbar and down on the goal line and out, the ball at the crossbar and down on the goal line and out, the ball at the crossbar and down on the goal line and out. Had it been inside? The Russian linesman signals a goal. Yes, those were great days, Nobby Stiles and Eusebio and Portugal coming from behind to win against North Korea. Arnold was working shifts and got to see most of the series, but not that particular game, although it was described to him so many times that he saw it in his mind anyway. Eusebio putting the ball inside the North Korean goal, the tall center, Torres, and the fiery North Koreans. Ingunn and Arnold still live on Håkon Street, but Ingunn is expecting a third child and the apartment is beginning to feel crowded, even though they have built a loft space for Asta and Svein. Arnold buys a piece of property in an Own Homes tract and builds during 1968–69. The work on the land and cellar and foundation shows that the old custom of building–bees has not been completely destroyed along with the old peasant society; Arnold does most of the labor himself with the help of his many relatives living nearby as well as his friends from work. Some of them have already built their own homes, some are experts at welding or plastering or concrete construction; all of them help to screen sand and shovel cement from Portland Valley into the hopper of the cement mixer, and those with strong arms push the wheelbarrows filled with mixed concrete along the narrow plank walks and empty them into the concrete forms. The young boys clean up the forms afterward, and the wives bring coffee and food. Arnold does not have much to do with building the framework, walls, and roof of the house; it is a prefabricated home that satisfies the Home Loan Bank requirements and is erected in just a few days by carpenters from the prefab company. The plumbing is not exactly a problem for Arnold, plus he knows an electrician who is building on the same tract and the two men agree to help each other, which keeps labor costs down. The family moves in early in the fall, and Ingunn, who now has more than enough to do just being at home and no time, interest, energy, or desire to keep up her handball practice, gives birth to her fourth child in January the following year. Arnold sits in his own house and watches the 1970 World Cup soccer games, but it is something of an anticlimax; the only things he remembers are the two goals in the final quarter of the game between England and Germany, when old Uwe Seeler faked out Peter Bonetti twice. Arnold gets an extra long vacation that summer because of the furnace room strike, and in the years that follow he experiences sudden and welcome rises in his earnings, until he is making over 70,000 kroner on a four-shift plan—with all his extra bonuses, about 75,000. Arnold is satisfied. He ought to be satisfied, he tells himself. He has managed things well. He is a skilled worker; his job is secure—skilled workers are not fired. If Arnold goes, everything goes, the whole factory, the community around him (and then the Labor government and the state would surely step in to help?). If I fall, thought Arnold, many people will fall with me. It was a good thing to know, now that Arnold is thirty-four years old and his youth is behind him. Arnold is still a handsome man, but he has begun to put on weight again, drives a car to and from work, likes to work shifts, often sleeps until three or four on the night-shift weeks, has about ended his sexual life with Ingunn. He begins to notice he isn't the young man he used to be in other ways, too. He no longer gets the same pleasure from feeling able to do the work at the factory well, has drained the content of most of the jobs and situations there, and knows exactly how he stands in relation to the other laborers, the foremen, and the management. The work, when he thinks about it, he experiences as a ruthless, unseen force that saps his strength. In 1972, Arnold finally votes "no" in the national referendum on joining the Common Market, after countless, and sometimes agitated, discussions with Ingunn and his parents (who, in his opinion, represent a fanatic "no" point of view) in which he has maintained that factually and objectively there are probably both good and bad things on both sides of the issue, and that surely there must be some wisdom in the joint recommendation of both the Labor government and the majority in Parliament, and that it's not absolutely certain that hordes of small, dark-skinned Italians will come and pick all the cloudberries on Skitt-kleiv before they are ripe if Norway joins the Common Market. But Arnold's name is not among those on the list of "The Cream" in the local newspaper (where the names of many of his friends in the Labor party appear) who urge total affiliation with the Common Market. On the big day, he drops a "no" slip down into the ballot box and helps to make history, still in doubt and of two minds. Arnold feels the times are off the mark. People are no longer content with what they have—it's just buy, buy, big houses and big cars. And getting pleasure out of your work, for example, is now a thing of the past. This becomes a favorite topic with Arnold, and he often gets quite worked up about it. He still has fun with the men at the factory during the lunch breaks and on the job, and this is the main thing that keeps him going, yet he is often more interested in finding an unseen corner where he can relax and sleep, at least on the afternoon and night shifts. Sometimes, as he stands under the shower at the end of the shift looking down at his own body and at the bodies of those showering or just washing their hands around him, he may have the passing thought that he is alone, that aside from Ingunn he has no friends with whom he quarrels. He finishes up with a cold shower, shivers, and clatters out into the locker room on wooden-soled sandals. Standing in line at the time clock after having dressed and combed his hair and tucked his lunch box under his arm, he tries to lighten the mood by saying something funny or making a joke—for example, The card misuse / And the joker will lose, when the first man in line misses the slot in the time clock as the whistle blows—but he doesn't get much of a reaction. The others are quicker with their time cards, get them stamped 1500 and placed under the correct letter on the OUT side, and hurry straight for the door. On the way home for dinner, Arnold usually stops at a fruit store and buys cherries for the kids and candy for Ingunn and him to eat when the kids are outside or have gone to bed.

THE PROGRAM FOR TOMORROW

It is a warm, pleasant summer evening near the end of August. The kids have gulped down the cherries and rushed outdoors, and Ingunn is in the kitchen washing the dinner dishes. Arnold goes out into the garden and feels the plums, tastes the red currants. From the smokestacks at the factory, which he does not see, the smoke rises straight up; not as much smoke as before, but enough so that one can tell the factory is operating. He would much rather have the smoke than have those crazy environmental protection people able to shut down the whole factory because they sense the smell of working life and get manganese dust in their elegant noses. No, Arnold is against extremism of all kinds. It's already been shown what *that* leads to. He walks around the house and hears Ingunn clattering with something in the kitchen. People who haven't been married and had kids, people who have only themselves to think about, don't know what it means to live. But he knows. Now he sees everything around him improving, the lawn is getting greener and thicker, the loan is getting smaller, economic worries about the house decrease in opposite proportion to inflation. He has his solitary joys—the warming thought that now Bjørn Nilsen must surely have gone too far at last (didn't you see the *Rogaland News* yesterday?); his youngest boy's strange comment: My best days are over now, as he said when he started nursery school (which has just opened); the wonderful singing on TV by the Scottish baritone Kenneth McKellan, who sang himself into everyone's heart; the Labor party's upward trend in the Gallup polls. Arnold, who has been a registered member of the Labor party for many years, has now become active in politics—not in the local Young Labor party, which is in a bad state, but in the local Labor party itself, where he has been both a board member and the treasurer and is also high on its 1975 list of nominees for Town Council as a representative of young people.

Arnold goes inside again. Ingunn has finished washing the dishes, and she is sewing. They open the box of Sphinx chocolates while they watch the evening news, and Ingunn notices with some irritation that Arnold is on a first-name basis with the people who appear or don't appear on the screen: Per Øivind, Kjell Arnljot, Trægde, Herbjørn, Harald Tusberg. She does not say anything. Arnold has strictly forbidden anyone to listen to the radio all evening. There will be a report from the Norway–Soviet Union game on TV at nine-thirty, and during the three hours between when the game starts in Oslo and when the television report is broadcast, Arnold isolates himself entirely, his home an unassailable fortress against all news of the game's progress and against the final score. Things go fine until nine-thirty; the kids are sent to bed, Ingunn shuts the door and sits down in the kitchen and will probably go up to bed before the game is over. And then, first, a Russian movie that lasts far past the scheduled time—typical television, to bore people with such things when they *have* to watch! But finally the game begins, we switch to our reporter, Rolf Hovden, at Ullevål Stadium. Arnold's stomach churns at the thought: the suspense will be over in seven minutes. There's a goal! And another goal! Two to nothing in seven minutes! Arnold sits nervously looking at a gray screen on which twenty-two men in short pants run after a ball under floodlights in Oslo. And Arne Dokken, who was supposed to be such a good scorer! Well, you saw what kind of scorer he was when he let his team end up with 0 in the first half. Arnold follows dully all the way to the end of the second half, sits as if paralyzed, watching and seeing nothing. He is never so lonely as when the national team has lost another game, the players have slunk off the field, and Rolf Hovden has rolled his eyes and said that with 3–1 in favor of the Soviets we say goodbye for now from those of us here at Ullevål. The single bright spot Arnold can see is that he has already figured out what he will say about the game at work tomorrow. The only hope for a stronger Norwegian showing? he will say and look around calmly, Who can tell me what that is? Nobody knows? It's for Brann and Hardy to join one club under the name of Brandy.

Nobody has heard that one before, smiles Arnold. As he gets up to turn off the television set, a female announcer takes over after the late news and says, Now we will take a look at the programs on television tomorrow and on the radio for the rest of this evening.

Yes, let's do that, replies Arnold, and keeps standing in front of the screen. Ingunn has probably already gone to bed.

THE PROGRAM FOR TOMORROW: 17.55 Afternoon News. 18.00 Children's TV. Ole's Ski Trip (Color). 18.45 Sports (Color). 19.30 Evening News—Weather. 20.00 Election News (Color).

20.15 Perspective. Report from Abroad. 21.05 Detective Hour. Law and Justice (Color) (Subtitles). British series starring Margaret Lockwood as Attorney Harriet Peterson. 21.55 Our Primitive Ancestors (Color). Part 4. Our Human Aspects. 22.30 Late News.

The announcer goes on to list the radio programs for the rest of the evening, while Arnold stands with his finger on the switch, waiting to see her say Good night, good night.

She finishes reading, smiles, looks straight at Arnold, and winks at him.

And with that, we wish all our viewers a very pleasant good night! Good night, Arnold Høysand, good night, good night!

Arnold presses the switch that sends the picture out into the darkness.

Good night yourself, he replies. When we wake up after tonight, it'll be Saturday tomorrow.

El Dorado

THE WAY BACK

Rasmus Høysand set his foot on the lowest step and felt the gangway lurch. Above him, the superstructure and the white bridge of the Wilhelmsen boat rose proudly like the spires and towers of a fairy-tale castle. Below him lay the dark coal wharf in Genoa. The way forward was far to go. And the way back was just as far. And out and in were just as narrow. The way in and back Rasmus Høysand knew. It saw him stop at the edge of the wharf, turn himself inside out, travel north in the world, backward in time—go across the crane tracks on the pier, in among the jumble of storage sheds and warehouses, up along the street of small shops and sailors' bars, out of the city, into the fertile Lombardy countryside, through the jagged Dolomites and snow-clad Alps; continue on through Switzerland and blue Bavaria as quickly as possible; disappear into the beech forests of Baden and Pfaltz; cross the hilly country along the Neckar; enter the wheat fields in Hesse; come out again into the smoke from the ironworks and steelworks and chemical industries of the Ruhr; put behind him meter after meter of Lower Saxony's rich fertile soil; awaken the cows and bulls (which get up, stop chewing their cuds, and bellow bitterly) in Schleswig-Holstein; penetrate the entire length of gentle Jutland in just a few hours; wait for the ferry in windy Hirtshals along with the lighthouse and the shrimp trawlers in the fishing harbor; be stowed bumper to bumper on the auto-deck; fumble around the center of Kristiansand looking for the right road to get onto the Sørland highway;

follow the curves through the barren landscape of Dalane with its heaths, lakes, mountain peaks, and slopes; pollute the carrot beds and fields of fodder-cabbage moldering on the lowlands of Jæren; round the corners of Christian meeting houses in Stavanger en route to the ferry at Jorenholm pier; pass Munkholm (which is the local name for Finn Island) and see the red glow of tomatoes behind the greenhouse glass; chug up the Smea Sound; drive down the ferry ramp at Haugesund and onto the Heilar highway, the E76, toward the northeast, through Haugarland, past Vats, farther inland, where the mountains' base of gneiss and gabbro sticks farther and farther out of the sandy topsoil and gravel, through the smell of the swineries in Etne and Skånevik; speed past one more crossroads with a yellow sign, and then another, away from the Heilar highway, through the narrow canyon in the Halland Valley, and then the final stretch on unpaved county roads, at a lower speed, on the narrow curving infrastructure at the edge of the legal expansion of capital.

Yes, Rasmus Høysand knew the way back. But the way forward? He took another step. The gangway lurched beneath him. And then another. It held. He chose the trim bridge, the shining superstructure, the Soria Moria dream palace, the fairy-tale ship, the carnival boat, El Dorado, the *Fjordsol* from the vocational school parade. He went aboard. Many things could have been different. The boat cast off. Dreams billowed westward in the trade winds, out into the unknown. Høysand heard the sound of sleeping people around him and felt the rocking rhythm of the sea within himself. He kept a tight grip on Åge Holte's arm. It was still too dark to see anything.

HIGHWAY BANDIT FROM BADAJOZ

After three months, the ship was laid up in dry-dock, Rasmus Høysand continued. We got kicked off in Baltimore, with wages paid in dollars. After two weeks, I found a new ship. It was a Panama-registered tanker that was loading oil in Maracaibo. I was to go aboard the next day. I sail as a bo'sun now. The flight from Baltimore to Miami was like all flights. Noth-

111

ing happens. In Miami, I changed to a plane that flew nonstop to Maracaibo. It was one of the ten exclusive days in the year without sunshine in Miami. A strong southeaster, and heavy gray clouds. Standing in the transit lounge with my ticket in my hand, I wondered if the difference between a seaport and an airport is the difference between the nineteenth and the twentieth century. And I wished I could go back to a hundred years ago. When I was traveling. I sat on a leather couch in the tax-free area and tried hard to seduce an elegant Spanish woman sitting beside me named Teresa de Cuellár Ourique y Ledesma Mazagón, according to her ticket (how they found space for all that, I don't know), who smelled coolly and discreetly of perfume, but even more coolly and discreetly of money—old, aristocratic money. But when I suggested an exclusive lay in the toilet at 30,000 feet she stood up suddenly and walked away. She wasn't only highborn, but highfalutin', too. It had been many annuities since a bearded highway bandit from Badajoz had acquired the original fortune by striking down and robbing a skipper of the caravel *Santísima Trinidad* in Moguer, Huelva. The skipper (his full name was Blas de Diego) in turn had first acquired the money (in the form of Indian gold and jewels) as a fifteen-year-old soldier on the successful expedition that Pizarro's deputy officer, Sebastián de Balalcázar, led to the interior of Venezuela and Colombia in 1539. From then until 1544, Blas de Diego lived in revelry and riot in Cartagena de Indias, a godless, sinful life that ended in sudden terror when the pirate Robert Baal raided the city that year. Blas de Diego, along with hundreds of the inhabitants who weren't already killed, was taken prisoner and bullied and beaten for years; but then he had a rapid career at sea, and when French pirates under Martin Cote plundered Cartagena anew in 1549, Blas de Diego was among the most bloodthirsty participants. He survived many wild years as a pirate, though he lost one eye and one arm, and ended a notable career as the captain of one of Sir Francis Drake's vessels in the successful raid of the West Indies in 1589. After that, Blas de Diego went ashore with chests full of silver and gold, and a few years later he returned to Spain under a false name, but with genuine syphilis, and with brazen tales (the truth of which readers can judge for themselves) about endogamy, poisoned daggers, and subsequent inheritances in the palace of a fabulously rich Transylvanian prince. The skipper was then a vigorous fellow in his late sixties, with a ruddy face and a strong barrel-shaped body, and he was clearly very drunk when he was first seen by Agustín, which was the Christian name of the highway bandit from Badajoz. Agustín, who had a thin, fanatical monklike face and had not slept in a bed, but on the ground wrapped in his cape, for a full ten months, drank only water (which he begged at the bar) as he made a close survey of the smoke-filled sailors' saloon. He noticed immediately that before the red-faced skipper fell asleep with his head on his arms he was spilling gold and silver coins on the table as freely as wine. Agustín drank the water, set the cup down on the bar, thanked the bartender with a humble smile, and quietly left the tavern. Outside it was a green and cool sunny day in April which suddenly, about eight o'clock, turned into a cold, black night. Agustín pressed up against the wall of the building, wrapped his cape around himself, and waited. The whites of his eyes gleamed each time the tavern door opened and one or more drunken persons were thrown out or staggered out on their own into the weak light of the lamp above the door. The skipper must have been awakened by the owner before closing time. He came through the door alone, stopped, swayed dangerously back and forth a few times, and fell flat onto the cobblestones in the narrow street. Agustín looked around in every direction, toward heaven and hell, crossed himself quickly, then followed the dark shadow of the wall and went over and helped the dead-drunk skipper to his feet again. The skipper thankfully lay his one remaining arm around Agustín's neck, made a futile effort to open the eye he had lost, and as they walked he sang English sea chanties he had first heard as a prisoner and later had sung as the captain of English sea pirates on Henry Morgan's island, San Andrés:

> And this is what I've seen with my own eyes,
> Sing falleri, sing fallera,
> A day lies bleeding just before it dies,
> Sing falleri, tra-la!

113

The song (which had only this one verse in Blas de Diego's version) came to an abrupt end after a few hundred meters and exactly seventy-five minutes, when Agustín made sure to place his deft thrust of a cheap Moorish dagger on the left side between the skipper's shoulder blades (more than anything else, to end the wretched song, it might seem) and transferred the coin purse, which was still heavy, from the skipper's belt to the folds of his own cape. Agustín then walked the long distance to Seville in one day and two nights, and slept the next afternoon near Bollullos before continuing on his journey, whereas Skipper Blas de Diego bled profusely during the night and was found early the next morning, with the dagger still in his back, by three women who were on their way to the river with their washing and who heard him whisper his last words, which were, Sing falleri, sing fallera! They looked at each other in bewilderment and then back down at Blas de Diego, who breathed his last. The next day, newly shaven and scarlet clothed, Agustín sat in the office of the Casa de Contratación in Seville and spent about half of the silver coins for bribes to get himself a royal monopoly on cocoa imports to the Basque provinces and the Kingdom of Navarra. He left on the long trip north early in the morning three days later, with a golden carriage drawn by four horses and fourteen livery-clad servants besides the coachman and the page, and after eleven days en route he reached Bilbao on the 28th of April, 1596.

Then the DC-9 began boarding passengers. I didn't see the elegant Spanish woman again, but I'd gotten the inside track on her and put her in her proper place. Gotten the rat, if not the pussy. The plane taxied out to the runway and headed straight south with a layer of clouds between it and the Caribbean. I fidgeted in the middle section of seats and exchanged a few words with the stewardess, at the standard rate of exchange, and with the passengers next to me. The man to my left put his index finger on the document in front of him and said, no, he worked in the U.S. Weather Bureau, before moving his finger and reading further. The man in the seat to my right worked for an English printing company, Thomas de la Rue. He pulled out his airline ticket and showed me the full name of the company printed in small letters in the margin. But currency bills is what we make money on. We print them. Inflation is good for business. He smiled and stuck the ticket back in his pocket.

Nothing happened. Nothing happens. The clouds beneath us thinned. I caught a glimpse of the sea and watched as we followed the Río Catatumbo in to Maracaibo Lake before passing over the city itself and heading in for a landing. The plane lost altitude and circled the airport. We straightened our seatbacks and fastened our seat belts and extinguished our cigarettes. Two circles, three, four, five, six. Ten circles. Then a voice came over the loudspeaker in English: a landing-gear signal indicates that one wheel cannot be located. Before an attempt was made to land, the plane would stay in the air and circle over La Chinita Airport until the fuel tanks were empty. That would take about two hours. In the meantime, the airline would be serving free drinks.

I had no chance to think about my own sinful life. The two briefcase carriers on either side of me threw themselves upon me in tears and started confessing their sins. The meteorologist from the United States asked for forgiveness because he had spent his youth in research and renunciation, because he hadn't wanted to acknowledge that he came from a family of Mexican braceros who ran a hamburger joint called El Olor de Jalisco in Seattle, because his knowledge of women was no more intimate than what he had gotten through Walt Disney's portrayal of Daisy Duck, and because he had taken part in a research project aimed at affecting the path of tropical hurricanes by "seeding" the storm clouds with a quicksilver solution in industrial magnitudes, as he put it, and thereby steering the dangerous quadrant of the hurricanes away from rich industrialized areas of the United States and in over the poor countries around the Caribbean Sea.

At this point he was drowned out by the printing company representative, who, with tears still in his eyes, admitted he had worked to increase inflation in the countries that were his company's customers, even though he had been fully aware of the catastrophic effects of inflation on the economies of those countries and their inhabitants.

THE COUP

He had stood beside the currency presses and watched them spew out miserable, worthless bills with pictures of romantic liberation heroes, saw them spew out thousands, millions of bolívares, cruzeiros, sucres, guaraníes, soles, escudos, gourdes, quetzales, colones, lempiras, pesos, córdobas, balboas, and realized that soon the head teller in the Banco de la República in Medellín, Colombia, will sit in his bulletproof cage and pay out this money in crisp new pesos to two employees of the Buc Medellín rum distillery who have been assigned to bring the payroll money safely back to the factory. Under the stern gaze of four armed guards, two with machine guns and two with just carbines, the money is placed in a brown cowhide briefcase, which is then handcuffed to the wrist of one of the two Buc Medellín employees. They walk stiffly out of the bank building, looking carefully to the right and to the left, and hurry into an armored car parked at the back door. So far, everything is going fine. At the intersection of Avenida John Foster Dulles and Calle de la Independencia, just by accident it appears at first, the armored car is involved in a chain collision, and then it is forced open by eight or ten masked bandits who send a chatter of machine-gun salvos into the car before seizing the money and speeding away. By then the man with the briefcase handcuffed to his wrist has had his lower arm chopped off, but he lives long enough so that one hour later, in great agony, before bleeding to death, he is able to describe what happened to the police inspector, whom he can barely make out through the strange mist surrounding his bed in an isolated room at Nuestra Señora de Luján Hospital. The next day, the same police inspector receives a not-insignificant number of the still-crisp new bills in exchange for a promise to let the innocent burn, but by far the largest part of the money accompanies two men and a woman that same evening as they drive a new Ford compact south on the rough roads leading to Pasto, at the Ecuador border. Two days later, the same trio is staying at the Tequendama Hotel in Bogotá, where a good deal of the money remains at the reception desk, in the bar, the beauty shop, the restaurant, and the

116

boutique when they fly north along the Magdalena River in a private single-engine Cessna heading for the seacoast town of Barranquilla. In a forest along the main highway between this city and the neighboring city of Santa Marta, somebody finds, six weeks later, the battered corpse of one of the two men from the Cessna. The body is identified and a photograph of it reproduced in four colors in the popular press as proof that crime does not pay. Meanwhile, the remaining members of the trio, a man and a woman, dance the merengue in La Fuente nightclub at the Jaraguá Hotel in Santo Domingo, where the song "Moon Over Jaraguá" originated, and change crisp new (and actually nonconvertible) Colombian pesos at a ridiculously low rate of exchange without it occurring to the cashier (who himself has a bundle of crisp new pesos in his inside pocket) to check the serial numbers. One such evening in March, as the trade winds blow in from the Caribbean with gale force and scatter all the refuse from the day's business into the deserted streets, where no one ventures unless absolutely necessary, a stocky, middle-aged truck driver at the Union Carbide Corporation plant on the west side of the new Urdaneta Bridge walks through the slum streets in the oil town of Maracaibo. On one such evening at the end of the afternoon shift, he heads home to his ranchito in the Corazón de Jesús section of town where his wife and children are waiting for him and his money in the darkness behind the flimsy, locked wooden door. He walks quickly, looking straight ahead, with a large stone in each fist and two knives and a pistol in his belt and a week's wages in a yellow envelope in his pocket, 587 inflated pesos, which are no longer crisp and new, but limp and disintegrating with use, the portrait of liberation hero Simón Bolívar invisible after having gone from hand to hand, from fist to fist, from thieves to prostitutes, to clerks at the La Concha Sagrada pharmacy, to the Royal Bank of Canada, to a cheap café that serves cool fruit drinks, to a grocery wholesaler, to an air-conditioned bar in the Cacique Mara section of the city, to the Tropical Telegraph Company, to a French tourist, to a Guajira Indian in a wide-brimmed black hat, sandals, and white cotton clothes who sells ruanas, a type of poncho, in the blazing sun opposite the Joyería Moderna goldsmith shop, to a grocer who pays interest on a loan from the Bank of London and South America, to the wage office at Union Carbide Corporation, to a truck driver scared out of his wits who makes his way home amid the darkness and the movie-star photographs—William Holden (paying for a lay), Ernest Borgnine (whittling a small piece of wood), Holden (coming out into the bright light), Borgnine (exchanging a look with Holden), Holden and Borgnine (walking together toward death), and Pierre Clementí (watching, wearing a leather coat and a schizophrenic expression)—and the Coca Cola ads and the angst in the slum, with a yellow wage envelope in his pocket containing a white wage slip and 587 almost disintegrated pesos.

RESTLESS HEARTS

Two hours had gone by. The money merchant still hung over me, begging forgiveness for his evil deeds. The loudspeaker informed us that the fuel tanks were empty and that the plane would go in for a landing at La Chinita International Airport in Maracaibo. We began to lose altitude. We fell and fell. I sat with my body hunched over and my muscles tensed, as at the start of a hundred-meter dash. The starting gun did not fire. Air resistance howled against the wings and body of the plane. Then it came. A crash. Farewell happiness and riches. A new motion, the plane crested forward with its tail in the air, and I made a swift dive from ten thousand meters without being able to straighten out properly. I felt the wild pain as the seat belt cut into my stomach.

I don't remember anything from the next three months. I lay in a respirator at Espiritu Santo hospital in Maracaibo, while a coal-black girl on monitor duty in the next room occasionally lifted her eyes from the Spanish edition of Gray's large anatomy textbook, or from the photo-novel *Restless Hearts,* and glanced at the EKG screen to make certain that my heartbeat was following a normal curve. Exactly three months after the accident, I opened my eyes and looked up at the ceiling. Then, from my bed, I looked around my room. On the night table stood a vase with a fresh red rose in it. Next to the vase, on top of a large pile of documents, lay a brand-new Norwegian passport with its crest of the crown and the lion and the axe and the word *Norge* on the cover. I carefully took it in my hand, kissed it, and shed a couple of warm tears before I opened it. Surname Høysand, given name Rasmus, citizenship Norwegian. I turned to the next page. A photograph of me in the most beautiful bloom of my youth. I pressed the passport to my breast, cried just a drop out of happiness, and carefully lay it beside me on the bed. Under the passport was some money. I dried my tears. Two bundles of crisp, newly minted bolívares. I held them a moment in each hand before putting them on top of the passport on the bed. Hard currency. Under the money lay credit cards. Six altogether, all in my name. Might as well take them, I thought, and put them on top of the money. Under the credit cards lay a guidebook of Maracaibo, barely visible through the exhaust fumes, but useful anyway. I had gotten down to the clothes. They lay under the guidebook, a light summer suit, elegant and airy cotton underwear, a raw silk shirt, hand-sewn moccasins. I put them aside, on top of the guidebook. At the very bottom of the pile I found the newspapers.

I was a famous man. I'd been a famous man for three months without knowing it. Well known and unknowing! "Plane Crashes at La Chinita Airport. 163 Dead. One Survivor." That must be me! I was the only one to survive the plane crash at La Chinita Airport in Maracaibo! There was one page after another, with text and photos, almost life-size. Høysand taken from the burning wreckage. Høysand in the ambulance, Høysand at the hospital, Høysand hovering between life and death, Høysand in a respirator. The last article, which was from the previous day and lay at the very bottom, showed Høysand on the road to recovery. The motor road to recovery, judging from all the equipment around the bed. On the front page! Along with a huge headline that shouted:

HALF OF ALL HUMANS
BORN ON EARTH
ALIVE TODAY!

Another headline, farther down the page, read:

DO I EXIST? IS THERE A GOD?
DOES LIFE HAVE A MEANING?
NORWAY'S PRIME MINISTER
RAISES THE QUESTION

I didn't get through that whole long article. However, I did read a shorter one even farther down the page which had the simple headline:

PRESIDENT CRASHES

LA PAZ, 18 May (Prensa Latina—Eduardo Galeano) A transport helicopter hit telegraph wires near Canadón del Argue in Bolivia yesterday and crashed to the ground. On board was Bolivia's President René Barrientos, along with two suitcases filled with currency (pesos bolivianos). The helicopter was a personal gift to President Barrientos from Gulf Oil Co., the telegraph lines were government-owned. The President intended to distribute the money himself, bill by bill, among the farmers of the district. But that was not to be. As the currency caught fire and began to burn lustily, the increasing heat also caused the machine guns of the soldiers in the President's bodyguard to go off, sending a shower of bullets out of the sea of flames. This prevented rescue teams from going in to save the life of the dictator. He was burned alive in the wreckage of the helicopter.

The article ended at the bottom of the next-to-the-last page. I folded the newspaper, laid it aside neatly, and got out of bed. The suit fit perfectly, hand-tailored. I put the passport and money in the inside pocket and the rose in my lapel before I left the room and walked out of the hospital and my heartbeat was no longer visible on the EKG screen.

MR. BURKE

In bourgeois European towns the center has traditionally functioned as an urban reconciliation or as a neutral area for the different classes in society: the extortioner inside the stock exchange, the beggar outside; demonstrations for peace and so-

120

cialism around the bank palace, money exchange within; red banners, and neon advertisements for ITT. But this expression of social reconciliation has collapsed in the large North and South American cities. In the United States, Big Business owns the city by day, the Mafia owns it by night. Elsewhere, in places like Los Angeles, Bogotá, Caracas, Maracaibo, there is no center at all. I took a taxi into town from the hospital and soon discovered that the beautiful colonial architecture in the center of Maracaibo was simply a large, deserted ruin, with no social or economic function. I could not arrange anything; each class had its own commercial center, which was geographically isolated from those of the other classes, but which had everything that was right and necessary—bank, store, boutique, pawnbroker, restaurant, fortune teller, café, movie house, and an open-air market supplemented by a supermarket. I couldn't find my way. Which class did I belong to? All my efforts came to nothing. I drove back to the hotel and lay down on the bed. I lay on the bed in the green room with the green lampshade, thinking. Do I exist? Is life a dream? And dreams dreaming? Is there life after death? Does the dialectic apply to the laws of nature? I think? Therefore I am?

Then the telephone rang. Telephone? For me? Therefore I am? The sound went through the room like a fifty-inch circular saw. I reached out my hand, put the receiver to my ear, and opened my mouth to a YES?

At first I heard only a jumble of different noises that all together sounded much like a street fight. Then there was silence. Then a woman's voice asked if she could speak with Mr. Burke.

Sorry, I said, you've got the wrong number. There's no Mr. Burke here.

But isn't this Room 811?

I looked at the key, and she was right. It's 811, but there's no Mr. Burke here anyway. The telephone operator must have given you the wrong number. I hung up.

I sat on the edge of the bed with my left hand on the telephone and my right hand in my crotch. I drew the left one slowly toward me. Then I sat on the bed with my elbows on my knees and my head in my hands. A bent back against the sunset outside the window.

The telephone rang again.

Mr. Burke?

This time the voice was clear and easy to understand from the beginning. It was a dark, pleasant voice, almost beautiful as it came through the ITT network of wires.

Wrong again, I said, and lay back on the bed holding the receiver with my shoulder and chin.

But isn't this 811?

Yes. It's just that there's no Mr. Burke here. However, let's suppose—

But both the operator and the person at the reception desk say that Mr. Burke is in Room 811.

Let's just suppose that I was Mr. Burke. What could I do for you?

There was silence at the other end of the line. I could almost feel her breath against my face.

You *are* Mr. Burke? she finally said.

Well, since I have Mr. Burke's room—

Are you, or aren't you, Mr. Burke?

I'm not, but I could be a sort of stand-in for Mr. Burke this evening, since he doesn't seem to be here in 811 himself.

Are you trying to make fun of me?

No, quite the opposite. I mean— What is it you want from Mr. Burke? Maybe it's something I could help with as well.

Oh, now I finally understand! That's very kind of you. You're a friend of Mr. Burke—

No, no, no, no, no! I'm just staying in Mr. Burke's room.

But then where's Mr. Burke?

I don't know! I don't know any Mr. Burke!

And still you admit you're staying in Mr. Burke's room. So what do you have to do with Mr. Burke then?

What does 69 have to do with 31?

You aren't even an American?

American? My God, no! No, definitely not. Norwegian. From Norway!

I'm from here. My name is Melody.

My name is— Well, it's a little hard to pronounce. I'll spell it. It's R— R, yes, Rrrrrrr, a-s-m—

I'm tall and slender and have long black hair and green eyes.

I'm tall and blond and—

I'm nineteen. How old are you?

I am twenty-five. Twenty-four.

And you're sure Mr. Burke isn't there?

Absolutely sure.

Then please excuse me, and have sweet dreams about me. Good night!

Uhhhhhh . . . wait a minute!

Yes?

Are you far away? From the hotel?

Much too far away, unfortunately.

But tomorrow? We could have lunch. I mean, it's surely possible to find a good restaurant?

Yes, it's possible to find a good restaurant. But no. Well, let me think . . . Tomorrow? Tomorrow would be all right.

Where? When?

The Arepa Restaurant. One o'clock.

I pointed the pistol toward the telephone receiver. One false word and you're dead!

I sat with the receiver in my hand and her laughter in my ear. Then came the dial tone, and I put the receiver back on the hook.

ASH WEDNESDAY

The next day was Wednesday. The clock in the hotel lobby showed 12:30, local time, when I dropped the key through the slot into a bulletproof box under the counter and walked out of the hotel. I squinted against the heat and the blazing sun. On the street corner just opposite me, two young Indians with black broad-brimmed hats and wide white pants stood selling colorful ruanas and shoulder bags with pearl embroidery. Next to them squatted two girls with a board in front of them displaying leather belts, hair clips, and plastic watchbands. And then next to them was a bank where white letters painted on the windowpanes announced that the employees were on strike. Outside the entrance, strikers were pacing back and forth shaking the coins in their collection boxes. On the two other street corners were marimba bands, each playing its own tune. Bits of confetti still floated down slowly from the sky, and faded garlands swung in the noontime breeze. I put out my hand for a taxi. An overcrowded bus with red-checkered curtains and amulets of saints cluttering the front window and a red roof and blue sides went by. Then came a Range Rover, and after that a taxi stopped. It was an old American car with glowing-hot plastic seats. The driver looked at me in the mirror and nodded when I said the name of the restaurant. I sat in the back seat, diagonally behind him, as the taxi navigated through a sea of cars and the confusing streets of an unknown town. The taxi meter ticked its commercial seconds, the driver talked about soccer and inflation. (Over his shoulder: Atletico Maracaibo up to Second Division, food prices up sky-high, but when God is dead everything is possible after all, maybe the food prices rose to heaven?) While he wondered about this he drove one block and then turned left past stops with their iron curtains pulled down for the lunchtime closing. Four—five blocks farther, and then uphill, still to the left. My name is Melody, I thought. I'm tall and slender and have long black hair and green eyes. Nineteen years old! The car turned left again, onto a broad avenue with a strip of yellowed grass down the middle and rows of palm trees arching overhead. And traffic lights. The driver braked slowly and stopped to wait for the green light. I leaned forward and asked whether we still had far to go. The driver sat with his arms crossed on the steering wheel in front of him; he was no longer asking about things himself, his stream of words had stopped. He did not answer. He stared at a refined-looking, well-dressed man walking in the pedestrian crossing in front of the car. Do we have far to go? I repeated, and looked at my watch. The driver still did not answer. Instead, the well-dressed man turned toward the taxi, came rapidly to the right side of the vehicle, and opened the front door. Just as he got into the front seat, the yellow light flashed, and then the light turned green, and the driver stepped on the gas and screeched across the intersection. The elegant gentleman sitting in the front seat calmly turned around to me, smiled, lay his left arm on the back of the seat and on top of it his right hand, which held a pistol.

124

The smile and the pistol were equally steady, but I remember the smile best. It was white and hearty, in broad contrast to the pitiful little moustache that hung down on either side of it, the long nose with wide nostrils above it, and the sad brown puppy-eyes stiffly fixed on a point a couple of centimeters above my heart, which was wildly pounding between my fifth and sixth ribs. I shifted my glance back and forth between this face and the small black mouth of the pistol, which was turned toward me equally full of expression. It was a terrible weapon, black and heavy and deadly. A Bernadelli 69. The nonreflective stripes on the road streamed toward me. If it had been warm before, now it was at least forty degrees hotter. Nothing was said, but there wasn't time to say much either. We weren't going far. I didn't dare to mop my sweating face. After a couple of blocks the driver left the avenue and drove down into narrow cobblestone streets, past a playground with slides and a swing made out of tires and a primitive merry-go-round, but no children; across an open square where there was a dry fountain, an old-fashioned printing shop that printed wedding songs and a populist weekly, a man leaving a barbershop, two women dressed all in black standing in a doorway, a dark-skinned man in a blue smock raising the iron curtain of a tobacco shop using a pole with a hook at one end; on down a wide, dusty, completely deserted street lined with one-story houses in worn-out colors and thin trees that barely cast a shadow. The taxi took a sudden turn to the right between two of the thin trunks, continued on between two low houses made of dried clay, past a vegetable garden, an outhouse, a chicken coop. Then through a clump of tall, stout trees. Still the unmoving smile and the mouth of the pistol. Then we came to the river, brown and swift. It was the end of the road. The car lurched twice, came to a complete stop, rocked a couple of times on the riverbank, and the driver turned off the motor.

The smiling face nodded toward the door and, just to make sure, pointed the mouth of the pistol a moment in the same direction. I opened the door and got out. The man with the pistol followed me. The driver opened his door and got out on the other side. The doors were left gaping wide open. The taxi meter was still running. It was twenty or thirty meters from the car down to the river's edge. We stood in a small clearing. Everywhere else, on both sides of the river, a thick tropical forest stretched all the way down to the water. Over in the underbrush was a heap of junked cars, Renaults produced under a special manufacturing license, Volkswagens from Brazil and Mexico. I felt the barrel of the pistol prodding my ribs. I looked at the smiling face. It made a sign for me to turn around. I caught a glimpse of my wristwatch. The time was 13:12. Wednesday, March 3. Carnival Sunday, Monday, Tuesday. Ash Wednesday. I turned around slowly, shut the rear door, and lay my body against the automobile. There was nothing to see, just thick green underbrush and a couple of tall palm trees thrusting up into the haze of heat. When I turned my head a bit to the left I could see the river flowing past, thick and brown. Red herons and purple parrots with ruffled tail feathers and orange breasts glided downwards with the stream. Dense jungle vegetation covered the opposite riverbank. I heard movements directly behind me. They still hadn't touched my money or credit cards. I lowered my neck and waited for the blow. The taxi driver had come up behind me, too. I caught a couple of words he exchanged with the man holding the pistol, then he leaned the upper part of his body into the front seat and turned on the radio, and immediately a seductive voice began to sob from the dashboard. The driver emerged from the car again. One of the men gripped my left arm. A large bird fluttered up among the tree trunks, others followed. The birds screeched, and I heard a whirr as if the forest itself were taking flight. Then I felt a distinct prick in my left arm, and almost instantly I felt my legs weaken and turn to rubber beneath me, and I pressed my face against the roof of the car and my upper lip turned inside out and my teeth scraped against the paint and my eyeballs rolled down the auto body, and my own body slid slowly down the door. Somebody turned up the volume on the car radio, and I could clearly hear the singer's words as I slid downwards. I fear the bird that lands to judge my life, dadada. I fear the nights that choke me with memories, dadadada dadada. But the wanderer who flees, late and early he must leeeeeave, dadadada dadada,

126

even when the white veil of forgetting has fallen and covers aaaaall, dadadadada dadada. Then I felt myself falling. I fell backwards with arms outspread, and I got a quick glimpse of the sun, which had torn loose from the sky and was falling, too. The light failed and poured ooooover me, dadadada dadadada dadada.

THE ROAD THROUGH THE JUNGLE

The man was a truck driver at the new UCC plant for industrial gases. He found me in a wrecked car in the underbrush down by Río Catatumbo while looking for spare parts for his '47 Pontiac. He couldn't get me to come to down there, but with some effort he managed to put me over his shoulders and carry me up the four hundred meters to the house where he lived. When I opened my eyes later that night, I saw he was a strong, middle-aged fellow with hair as short as a military recruit's and a mouth that looked like a horseshoe magnet when it curved into a smile and pulled countless small iron filings of wrinkles up around the poles in both cheeks. Small, brown teddy-bear eyes shone in the weak light as he looked down at me. Then I fell asleep again. The next morning I managed to eat—fried green bananas, manioc, fried eggs, and a glass of ice-cold thin oatmeal. Then the truck driver exchanged a few soft-spoken words with his wife and went off to work for the day. A black T-shirt on a broad back. The two children were asleep. I lay on a bed with uneven springs and felt around on my body. They had taken everything, the money, the credit cards, the passport, the watch—that fine quartz watch—everything. I was on my feet when the truck driver returned. He smiled and asked how I was feeling, while his wife set out a soup made with bananas and manioc. She was wearing a black dress that followed the lines of a beautiful, buxom body, and had long hair pulled back smoothly into a bun and a warm smile, which she tried in vain to control because of two missing upper front teeth. The children stared at me, wide-eyed. I broke corn bread and dipped it in the soup and looked around the room, wide-eyed, as I ate. I was sitting at a white-scrubbed wooden table with two chairs beside it, and the truck driver was on the other chair. His wife and children sat on a crate-board bench fastened to one wall. The room also contained a bed that had two springs sticking up through the mattress; a gas stove with two burners; a large iron pot; various wooden spoons and tin ladles; one picture of Jesus on the Cross and one of the local saint, San Roque; a transistor radio in a black plastic case the size of a large box of matches; and photographs of movie stars on all the walls. The woman held the transistor radio in her lap clasped between both hands, with the sound turned on and a listening child on each side. I broke a new piece of corn bread, put it in my mouth, and scooped up a large piece of manioc on my spoon. It was beginning to get dark when I said goodbye to them. The wife smiled without trying to stop herself. The truck driver gave me his hand. I ruffled the children's hair and left.

The truck driver had told me what I could do. I could go to one of the main streets, stand at an intersection where there was a stoplight, and, when drivers had to stop for the red light, I could ask them for money or a job. I stood on the divider on one of the large avenues. It was a black tropical night. Car after car came by, all types of models, all types of drivers. Some rolled up their side windows the moment I approached them, others drummed their fingers on the steering wheel and listened to me with a disinterested look until the light turned green and then spewed exhaust at me in farewell. Eight hours! Lost everything, señor. Just what I'm wearing. Need a job, mister, anything at all. Eight hours at least, for it must have been past midnight when the driver of a pickup truck looked up from the wheel and out through the open side window at me. It was a face that had been young and handsome not too long ago, but now looked merely puffy and red under a curly blond head of hair. The eyes that examined me were blue, and cold as those of a marksman lining up his sight on the bull's-eye three hundred meters away, taking aim. I stood waiting for him to put out his hand to open my mouth and bare my teeth, or to lift up my trouser leg and tell me to give him my hoof. Ahead of us the traffic light changed to yellow and was reflected on the hood of the truck. Nationality? he said quickly. The light turned green. Swedish, I replied. He thought, while openly appraising me. A driver behind him leaned on his horn. Get in, said the man in the pickup, pointing to the back of the truck.

He drove all night, rested and ate in the morning, and then drove the whole next day. I lay in the back bouncing on a couple of empty burlap bags, slept occasionally, and was shaken awake to a lofty night full of stars, and the shadows of dark forests against the earth, and the outline of foliage against the sky— araguanay, apamate, bucare, acacia, samán, jacaranda; or to some slumbering town with whitewashed walls, a sleeping marketplace, a dog slinking in the shadows, crossbars on the windows, and dull streetlights made of wrought iron; and, above me in the cab, the puffy face of the driver like a large, lonely red light in an amusement park. He asked me to wait for him the next morning and didn't give me any food when we drove on. I figured we were driving west, but didn't notice that we crossed the Colombian border. Through the bars on the back window of the cab I saw that now and then he studied his direction on a well-used Esso Colombiana road map and later switched to a hand-drawn sketch. Sometimes the route was no more than two faint wheel tracks that would disappear in the next rainy season. But we were still driving on a narrow road through thick jungle when the sun rose and streamed down toward us from above snow-covered mountains, which I figured must be the Sierra Nevada in the northwest. The driver stopped the truck for a moment, not to study the map, and even for me—who was used to the view north toward Folgefonn Glacier from Nordeskår- nuten or Kvanneskårnuten peaks and the Suldal Mountains seen from Napen and toward the southwest, or the Selsnip Ridge in the late summer—this was an impressive sight.

About lunchtime he stopped and gave me some bread and a little water from a canteen. The road had led upward, and the luxuriant jungle slowly had given way to dry savannah. I let the tepid, life-giving liquid trickle through my dry body and looked at the desolate grasslands stretching toward the south like a huge nature-colored bedsheet wrinkled by energetic love- making. The sun was at its zenith. We stood in the shade of a jacaranda tree, sweating. Far to the southwest a jagged range of

129

mountains turned blue in the distance. Not a person, not a farm, not an animal, not a town to be seen. Just dry bushes, sand, and occasional tufts of grass. A sad corner of the world.

It might have been about six in the evening when we arrived there. The first thing I saw were the woods, a long green avenue of tall ahuehue trees. When we got closer, I saw the ditches and irrigation canals. The truck drove fast, but the road was better here, and I was used to being shaken up. I sat hanging on to the sides of the truck, with my back against the cab. Behind me, the savannah was spread out in the sunset like the glowing remains of a huge prairie fire. When I glanced again in the direction we were headed, I saw the buildings, and then, at the very last, I saw the armed guards. They were dressed like ordinary peasants, with leather sandals, loose white cotton clothing, and cheap straw hats. But they had rifles and carbines in their hands and cartridge belts slung over their shoulders. Motionless, with weapons at the ready, they watched the pickup drive, slowly now, along the avenue of trees and come to a stop in front of the largest building.

I got up. My teeth were gritty with sand, and a cloud of fine brown dust rose from my clothing when I jumped down from the truck. It was dusk. Around me, five or six buildings were spread out asymmetrically in an open yard. The main structure was a long whitewashed building with two stories, a porch along the entire front, and a pretentious false façade, in the middle of it, which had some sort of coat-of-arms and AD 1823 carved into it. Beneath the façade, a wide stone stairway led up to the porch and on into the building. Besides this main building, I also noticed another large structure, which was perhaps a barn or a storehouse, and two long, low concrete-block buildings with small windows that had bars on them. The driver was already out of the truck and on his way up the broad stairs of the main building. One of the guards met him halfway, and I heard them exchange a few short words. Then it was only a matter of seconds before two new guards came along the porch from the left and down the steps toward me. One of them was wearing North American jeans and a denim shirt, and boots instead of sandals. He also had a big pistol stuck into his belt. The three guards came down the steps and stopped in front of me. The driver disappeared through the door of the main building. At the same moment, one of the guards stuck the muzzle of his carbine into my chest. Then he slammed the butt into my ribs, and I crumpled up nicely and fell silently at his feet. Before I had even reached the ground they grabbed me, one by each arm, and dragged me over toward one of the low cement-block buildings. It was practically dark; the last drops of sunlight dripped from the trees along the avenue before darkness hardened into total night. The long cement building lay dim and gloomy. I was flung to the ground in front of a solid wooden door. One of the guards fumbled with the lock and slid back a heavy iron bolt. The door squeaked on rusty hinges and opened into a square of thick blackness. I was thrown in full length and lay there with my face against a damp earth floor as I heard the door slam shut behind me.

At first, I didn't see anything, didn't hear anything. Then I saw the pale squares with the dusk outside, and the iron grates. And then I heard that I was not alone. I heard heavy, uneven breathing, as though many people lay sleeping all around me. I braced my arms against the earth floor and stretched out my neck. Still I saw only the small squares of the duller dark outside and heard the multivoiced sleeping sounds. I got to my knees and then stood up. Somewhere in the darkness someone turned over, and someone let out a brief snore. I took a cautious step forward and immediately stepped on a sleeping body. He did not wake up, and I quickly pulled back my foot. I tried in another direction, and went two steps before I trod a new body with half of my weight. He swore softly and strangely as I stood motionless on one foot, and then I heard him turn over, and all was silence again. Silence, silence from many sleeping people. I thought I could begin to see them vaguely, too, those closest to me, like dark bundles rolled up across the floor. I also thought I saw a vacant space and started to step carefully over the bundles in that direction. But the first thing I did was to tramp on a body lying curled up right at my feet. As if I had stepped on a trip

131

pedal, he swung his body into a vertical position, grabbed onto my leg, and said in a ringing Austfold or Vestfold dialect: Ævvv! Helvete! Faen! It's the amulet again! But they can be damn sure!

Yes, said Åge Holte, after a long and bitter pause. It's me. And I've got good reason to be careful and expect the worst.

In the Act

THE BENDS

You said Ålvik? Åge Holte began. That's where you're from? Well, it was over in that part of the country everything started for me, too. On the West Coast, not far from Ålvik, at a place called Sauda. It all started in Sauda in April, 1950. April 11, 1950, to be exact. Then and there was the beginning of the road that led me here. I can even give you the exact time. I remember everything as if it happened today. We'd made a successful bid on the new steamship pier, tearing down the old wooden pier and building a new one out of concrete. We'd finished the demolition and the dredging and laying the foundation for the new pier, and I was lying down on a four-meter doing some welding, nice and cozy, and thinking we're way ahead of schedule, and besides, you need some pliers and a cigarette. Especially a cigarette! *That's* what you really need right now, to get this job rolling, I thought. So I signaled and surfaced through the green, brackish water. That was, of course, long before they had diver phones in the divers' suits.

Topside it was a bright, beautiful day. I slowly climbed up the ladder to the pier in the bow of the dive boat, and I can still see in my mind the clear spring morning that came to view when I dried the drops off the port of my helmet. The temperature had been sniffing down around freezing that morning, and mist lay far out across the quiet fjord, where the ice was beginning to break up in big pieces. Across the river, the smoke from the Electric Furnace plant gushed from the furnace building smoke-

133

stacks and rose straight up among the snowy mountains until it got lost against the blue sky. The snow had started to melt, both rivers were high and packed together the ice floes there where the two rivers flow into each other in the estuary between the factory and the steamship pier.

My helmet had been unbolted from the breastplate, and I was standing there like that, just breathing in fresh air, when I saw Feigum, who was sitting on a bench in the shelter by the shipping agent's office with his shoulders hunched and his knees together and his hands in his pockets and a tense smile on his face, looking very cold. He was surrounded by the bunch of boys that was always on the pier watching whatever they could see of the work, when they weren't out on the river jumping on the ice floes or doing other equally crazy things. That's Holte for you! was the first thing Feigum said, Works for five minutes and then takes five for fifty-five! And that's typical Feigum, even though he didn't have any more of a say in the business than I did, for example, or Bryde-Olsen. But he always had to play the little chief like that. Of course, he needed a way to show off, too—a guy like him, who was too weak to take the professional diving course. But anyway, we all agreed when we started that each man would put in an equal share, and each man would have an equal say, and be equally responsible. Personally responsible, that is, because we didn't register ourselves as a corporation, meaning that if we went bust, they could take both the car and the one-family house in Tennvik. And the wife, too, as Feigum used to say. That was the hell of it. But whatever we might have planned, it had turned out that Feigum was a sort of overseer who did the office work and made calculations and cost estimates and contracts and traveled up and down the country and kept an overview, as he put it, when we had jobs at different places, like right then. And that was probably because his brother always sided with him and supported him a hundred percent, and then it wasn't so easy for the rest of us to say anything one way or the other, and not too pleasant either. Because we were five altogether in the company, me and then Feigum, and his brother, and then Bryde-Olsen and one other guy, who was on a job in Mo-i-Rana at that time, and we'd all known each other for a long time and put a lot of importance on having a good feeling amongst us. Anyway, Feigum sat there now on the pier in Sauda, shivering and shaking with cold, and he wondered if I had a cup of black coffee to offer him. So I tromped across the pier in my lead boots and breastplate and lead weights and all, with Feigum and the bunch of kids trailing after me, and into the shanty where we'd painted UNDER-WATER INSTALLATION on the wall in big black letters. Feigum closed the door after himself, shutting out the white, curious faces of the boys. Cold! he said, and moved some tools and sank down onto a bunk fastened to the wall, and I got out my thermos and wondered what he had on his mind now. Then I started to roll a cigarette. Cold! Feigum said again with a shiver, as I moistened the glue with the tip of my tongue, shoved the loose tobacco back in the package, and lit up. How long before you're finished down there? Feigum asked, helping himself to coffee. Two weeks, I said, and saw Feigum grimace as he tried to warm his hands on the coffee cup. We'll be done in two weeks, easy. At first we had trouble finding our way down in all the muck, but once we got that cleaned up, everything's gone just fine. It was probably discharge of process water from Electric Furnace that caused most of it. Hell! said Feigum. First I burn my fingers, and now I burn my lips, too! What kind of stuff is this anyway? I didn't answer, and opened the cover of my lunchbox. Then I asked what brought him to these parts, and after making a couple of unsuccessful tries at lighting his pipe and taking a slurp of coffee, he had to come out with it. A big one! he said. A big contract! he added, and puffed smoke at last. Really big, he continued, finally looking relaxed and happy. You remember that mate I talked about? And if I hadn't heard about any mate before, I sure got to hear all the details now. Feigum had met him by chance in the restaurant at the Wassilioff Hotel in Stavern ("Was there to negotiate a contract that never came to anything, hm, hmmmmm,"), they started talking and had a couple of extra cognacs after dinner, and then followed that up with a bottle of whiskey in Feigum's room. The next morning, Feigum knew all about how Underwater Installations was going to haul in big money. *Haul in* were the right words.

We were going to go to the Caribbean and hoist the wreckage of an ever-so-small Mexican cargo boat that had sunk in the entrance to the harbor of a city called Barranquilla in Colombia. That was the main thing in what Feigum told me, sitting on the tool shack on the steamboat pier in Sauda that morning. He also knew exactly what the cargo of machine parts from the USA was worth. About ten million kroner! said Feigum expansively, gazing down into his mug, which he slowly twisted back and forth in good Protestant church-social style, before taking the last sip. Ten million! And that's just the declared cargo. Think of it! I preferred not to. I preferred not to think about it; I put the cork back in the thermos and preferred to go down again, to dive into the cold green water, but running away was no use now, no, there was nothing to do but think about it right away, and Feigum was already in full swing, making deals with Alfred Næss or Chargeurs Réunis or Lampart and Holt or Koninklitke Hollandesche or La Véloce or whoever it might be about chartering a salvage vessel and sailing it down to the Caribbean in November or December, then throwing a couple of lifting straps around the hull of that dago boat, hoisting her up, and bringing the cargo ashore. The mate had already looked into a Mexican salvage company, and then one in Colombia, and he'd never laughed so damn hard and didn't believe it could possibly be any problem for Norwegian technicians to haul up that tub of a cargo boat, which was lying in just seventeen or eighteen fathoms and not far from land besides. I was still worried, but, Hell, man, are you out to pasture already, do you plan to sit up here in Vestfold in your little one-family house listening to the ivy grow up the Pearly Gates and the cellar walls till you hear the angels' song instead, or what? In short, when Feigum took the coastal ferry to Stavanger early the next morning, I wasn't filled only with his whiskey (we stayed up all night, and then he went straight onto the ferry), I was also filled with a pious belief that the expedition to the mouth of the Magdalena River to salvage the motor ship *Tlatelolco* of Vera Cruz was an intelligent business venture that offered the prospect of enormous profits for the Underwater Installations salvage company and a life of

136

revelry and riot for the five equal partners in the company and their families.

Bryde-Olsen was the only one who had doubts, but even he was almost convinced when he saw the *Lolita* for the first time, at the Loenga pier in Oslo. We stood on the pier looking up at the superstructure and the cranes for a long time, totally overwhelmed, before we went up the gangway. She looks good, said Bryde-Olsen. How much can the Clyde crane in the bow lift? Good! exploded Feigum, stopping in his tracks. They were standing right under one of the traveling gantry cranes on deck. Good! She's got a lifting capacity of 1,600 tons! Guaranteed by Transports Maritimes. You call that just "good"? Bryde-Olsen made no reply and calmly started up the ladder to the operator's cab. Feigum threw out his arms, rolled his eyes, and looked at the rest of us one by one before going after that crazy Bryde-Olsen. Sixteen hundred tons! he shouted. She swings free with 1,400 tons! Plus you've got the traveling gantry cranes, with a combined lifting capacity of 1,200 tons! American-made? asked Bryde-Olsen from inside the cab, his back still turned. Yes, but mounted by Clyde! shouted Feigum. And there are sponson tanks mounted on both sides of the ship to give proper stability while hoisting. We compensate for the list by pumping in water as ballast in the tanks. A clever system! Bryde-Olsen jiggled the handles inside the operator's cab. Without a word he swung the whole crane, with us in it, around 360 degrees. A real panorama show. Then he turned abruptly, walked past us, and began climbing up the boom. We climbed after him and hung on at the top of the ladder, out of breath, looking down at the cranes and warehouses of Loenga and Sørenga below us. It was a clear, late-summer day in Oslo. The smell of phosphorus from a Polish bulk carrier just beyond the *Lolita* stung our noses. Do you see that deck? shouted Feigum, when he had caught his breath again. Two thousand square meters, and each can take a load of 8 tons. Try hitting it! The whole thing is a solid gold mine! A generation before its time. And when we're finished with this salvaging job we can stop in the Gulf on the way back to take the bearings of jackets and lift modules onto the oil platforms. So

137

there'll be a Christmas bonus this year, too. For widows and fatherless children! What do you say to that, Bryde-Olsen? Good boat, said Bryde-Olsen, and began backing down the ladder. But we need to take her out in the open sea to check the anchors and winches.

The second week in October, Feigum flew Oslo–London–Miami–Barranquilla, and returned Barranquilla–Caracas–Madrid–London–Oslo eleven days later. Vigorous and tanned and far too lightly dressed, he walked through the rain toward the terminal building at Fornebu and waved to us with his passport, smiling and worldly wise, as he waited for the baggage to arrive in the customs hall. Afterward, we drank coffee with him in the airport cafeteria, Bryde-Olsen and me. Eso es, said Feigum. We've got the contract. At least we've landed the contract, he-he; now we just have to do the same with the cargo boat. Eso es, Feigum repeated, slapping his jacket pocket. Did you go down and look at her? asked Bryde-Olsen. I was out and looked at her, Feigum corrected. The place is ideal. Absolutely perfect. All we've got to do is put a winch into the ocean and haul up ten million, at the very least. But how are things here? Have you checked the anchors and winches? Bryde-Olsen nodded. Eso es, said Feigum, and clapped us on the shoulders as we headed out to the parking lot.

Six weeks later we were ready, and we sailed from Tønsberg the first Sunday in Advent, delayed an extra two weeks. The problem was that Feigum's mate didn't have a skipper's license and couldn't take the boat over himself, and besides, the third mate signed on with a Jahre boat and sailed to the Far East early in November. But then Feigum found a Danish skipper with his papers in order at the Seamen's Hotel in Oslo, and the first Sunday in Advent the whole family and I took a taxi in from Vestskog. The snowfall earlier in the day had veered more to the south and turned into sleet and dismal rain by the time we drove over the bridge and into Tønsberg. Hildegunn cried through the whole trip, and was embarrassed, and tried to hide it from the driver as best she could. I held her hand (over the seatback, because I was sitting in the front next to the driver) and talked with the children, who were four and seven at the time, about

Indians and American chewing gum. As I paid the taxi driver at Market Square and Hildegunn dried her tears and got the children out of the back seat, the Christmas-tree-lighting ceremony was going on in the square. They had lit the tree and said a prayer, and now the school band was playing "O Christmas Tree." We joined in when everyone sang "Silent Night," and something in my chest felt so funny when we came to, All is ca-a-alm, all is bri-i-ight, and I noticed that my voice was getting thick and didn't dare to look down at Hildegunn because I was afraid I'd start crying, too. Sleep in heavenly peace. Then we walked slowly through the Christmas streets, looking at the decorated store windows. The children ran ahead of us, and we couldn't drag them away from a window with mechanized figures of a shoemaker and his apprentice who sat repairing shoes. Each time the apprentice's head nodded and his needle went more and more slowly as he began to fall asleep, the shoemaker gave him a kick and he woke up with a start, shook his head, and went back to half-soling a shoe for dear life. It wasn't easy to say anything to Hildegunn down at the pier, but I picked up each of the kids in turn, and tossed them in the air a few times. Mo-o-other and chi-i-ild, I heard in my mind. Then I went aboard and helped to cast off.

We were lucky with December weather in the North Sea, went through the Channel, and headed out across the Atlantic north of the Azores. Everything went fine, the weather stayed good, the Dane on the bridge was in full control, Feigum sat in the mess holding forth about the girls in Barranquilla. The same color as Freia milk chocolate, and just as sweet. After fifteen days at sea we went through the Anegada Passage. Three days later, we anchored outside Barranquilla.

The wreck existed and lay where Feigum had said it would lie, but I'll never forget Feigum's face the morning he was the first to go down and actually see the *Tlatelolco* and we got him back up on deck and took off his helmet. It's swarming with sharks down there! was all he said when he'd caught his breath enough to talk. Then he staggered heavily into the mess and started drinking rum straight from the bottle. Bryde-Olsen was the next man to go down. He just shook his helmet when he came up on deck again. The sharks are one thing, he said, but besides that, there are stronger currents down there, because the river flows much narrower and faster. It's just about impossible to stand upright and work down there. Plus, it seems as though all the sludge from half of South America flows into the sea right here. Sometimes I couldn't see even as far as one foot in front of me.

That evening, after everyone had been down for a look, we decided to go ahead anyway. There just might be a chance, everyone except Bryde-Olsen thought, after I don't know how many bottles of rum. The boat *did* lie in very shallow water, and we could at least hope the current would ease up and the river flow with less force. Furthermore, Underwater Installations was in debt far deeper than the Plimsoll mark, and besides, little brother Feigum was crying.

The rest of the project, aside from the fact it was a wonder none of us were eaten by sharks, can be described in three words: fiasco, fights, break-up. Bryde-Olsen was the first to leave. He borrowed money for his ticket at the Consulate and flew home in anger early in February. A week later, the rest of us gave up, too. There was no cash left, and we hadn't been able to secure a single lifting strap on the boat. I was the last one to dive down to her deck, which was listing more and more during the last weeks, and now heeled over so much it was impossible to stand on it. It was just a question of time before the current would take the entire wreck and Feigum's ten million far out to sea. If only we had stayed at home building concrete piers in Vestland! I was in such despair that there no longer seemed any reason to come up again alive. But no dangers were in sight; I didn't see a single shark, hardly saw farther than my nose, felt only the current sending the thick brown sludge past me and out to sea. Then I surfaced into the sunshine with the others. The next day we went ashore from a gig in Bocas de Ceniza. Our dreams lay shattered. Transports Maritimes flew over a crew to take the salvage vessel home again. Wangen and little brother Feigum stayed on the ship until the new crew arrived. Back home, the bank sharpened its claws and poised to leap at us. The night after the others left, Feigum and I were shown into a thirty-five-cent hotel room that had twelve beds with filthy sheets and a view of Caño de las Compañias, the marketplace in Barranquilla. We were the first ones. Gradually, the other beds filled up, too. Feigum fell asleep immediately. I lay on my back with my hands under my head staring up at what was left of the green color on the ceiling and thinking about Hildegunn and the kids and about how this fall it would be two years since we moved into the house in Tennvik and about what it would be like when the bank came and took the house. Suddenly, I felt there was somebody by the bed touching my suitcase, trying to open it, so I rolled over. But no, it was only Feigum, my eternal sidekick, who had turned in his sleep. He lay on the coarse jute-straw mattress, his face toward me, his mouth open, fast asleep. I lay awake the whole night, afraid of being robbed as I kept thinking about how long it would take before we could save enough to go back and settle our affairs. The next day, as we sat on a bench in the shade inside the bus station at the hottest part of the day, this guy, who looked honest and European, came over to us and said he was looking for two men who didn't scare easy and were willing to take a chance. Feigum looked at me, I looked at Feigum. Well? said the guy. Okay, said Feigum, and looked at me. When one of us dies, I'll go to Norway with the money.

THE LAND OF GOLD

The honest European was a German. He drove us south from Barranquilla in a prewar Dodge truck. All three of us sat crammed together in the cab. The German drove with his left hand. With his right hand he waved an old parchment in the air and then quickly stuck it back into his shirt pocket again.

You know the story of El Dorado? he asked, putting both hands on the steering wheel to straighten out the truck. El Dorado is the legendary land of gold in the heart of South America. But with this map—he patted his shirt pocket—El Dorado is no longer a legendary treasure. It's drawn by an old, old medicine man in Tamahuate and shows the exact location of the land of gold. The drawing fully corresponds with classical sources, which haven't been precise enough, but this map leaves no doubt as to where the place is. In the past, El Dorado has been connected with the idea that the Garden of Eden was on the American continent. A map of South America in León Pinelo's book, *Paradise in the New World,* published in Madrid in 1656, shows a Garden of Eden in the heart of the continent, surrounded by the Amazon, the Río de la Plata, and the Orinoco and Magdalena rivers. The banana was the Garden's forbidden fruit, and Pinelo's map indicates the exact place from which Noah's ark set out after the Great Flood. El Dorado lies in the same area; all the sources agree on that. The most likely location is somewhere in the Colombian highlands, because we know definitely that before the European conquest great quantities of gold and emeralds were to be found in that area. When the high priest of the Chibcha Indians, who was also the tribe's chief, took over his ritualistic duties his whole body was first smeared with resin and then covered with a thin layer of gold dust. Then he walked out into a holy lake called Guatavita and washed himself clean. This is probably the origin of the name "The Gilded One," which is what El Dorado means. Another thing that shows there was plenty of gold and jewels among the Chibcha Indians was their custom of throwing idols made of gold and emeralds into their holy lakes during their religious celebrations.

When the Europeans came here to this beautiful part of the world, it didn't take long before they heard these stories, and they immediately began to look for El Dorado in the strangest places. In 1528 Carlos V pawned all of Venezuela, which at that time also included what is now Colombia, to the Welser banking firm in Germany, which then spent the next generation in a futile search for gold mines, mountains of diamonds, and cities built of silver. But the race did not begin in earnest until Pedro de Limpias traveled all the way to Bogotá on Federmann's expedition and returned to Coro on the Caribbean coast in 1540 with the first rumors of a land of gold, the fabulous El Dorado. Already in 1541 Gonzalo sailed off with Francisco de Orrelano and a huge army. They searched everywhere in Canela, but all they found was a godforsaken place where they soon died of tetanus and gold fever. Filip Hutten and Fernán Pérez de Quesada, who explored the Colombian part of the Andes in 1545, were equally lucky. In 1556 the Welser firm gave up, and the Spanish king took back Venezuela. A year later, he equipped a large expedition led by Pedro de Ursúa, which looked for El Dorado in the highlands in the interior of Venezuela. The only lasting results of this expedition are the large finds of splintered marrowbone that archeologists of today have dug up in what are now the provinces of Meta and Casnare. These marrowbones are the remains of the orgiastic meals that the anthropophagous Indians made of the Europeans who were unfortunate enough to fall behind and who were rapidly transformed into dishes in which the light, sweet-tasting meat disproved, once and for all, the Indians' long-held theory that horse and rider are one and the same. You could taste the difference between horse and Spanjol!

But the Europeans didn't let themselves be discouraged by such things. Martin de Proveda and Nuflo de Chaves poked around in 1560, and in 1579 Gonzalo Jiménez de Quesada— who earlier had discovered the Chibcha Indians, conquered them, and founded the town of Santa Fé de Bogotá in 1538— made a grand attempt but didn't bring any fabulous treasure to light. A few later expeditions, Sir Walter Raleigh in 1617, Aimée Reichenbach in 1874, and Arthur Lodge Shawcross in 1911, found most of the gold now spread around in anthropological museums in Europe and the United States. Treasures, but not The Treasure, not even the reflection of El Dorado itself!

The truck took a sharp curve, and the headlights strewed gold out on the river that followed the road south toward its distant sources. Feigum and I exchanged dubious glances. I hope you can handle weapons, said the German. And money. And women. We're going to be the richest men on earth.

THE EMERALD MINES NEAR MUZO

Maybe the German became the world's richest man, Holte continued. I never saw him again. He drove Feigum and me to a camp for slave-workers in the emerald mines in Muzo, and turned us over to the guards there. I'm sure he got his money for that, which started him on his first million at least. Feigum and I were put in a camp like the one we're in now. Conditions here aren't much worse than in most of the haciendas here in the interior. The landowners rule over life and death, just as the mine owners do. The mines are controlled by a mafia from a section of Bogotá called Santa Isabel, although officially they're run by the Colombian government. Feigum and I were in the first camp for four days before being sent on to the mines. It was pure slave labor; people dropped their pickaxes, crossed themselves, and collapsed all around us. We talked constantly about escape and listened to stories about what had happened to people who had tried. Told with a quick, expressive gesture: a slash across the throat with the edge of the hand; and people said no more. Most of the prisoners were natives, just a few beach-combers like us, Americans and Frenchmen. One Lebanese and one Finn. Two years went by. Feigum and I worked side by side, our hands gripping a primitive tool as we kept one eye on the brutal guards and any possibility for escape while the other concentrated on the hard work. Emeralds are the softest of all jewels, just a little harder than quartz, and we had to be very careful in digging them out. We found the stones in isolated crystals, often as six-sided prisms with smooth sides and a dull green shine. The special color comes from the very small amounts of chromic oxide the stones contain, which is also what determined their quality when they finally were evaluated and cut in Bogotá. But we didn't have anything to do with that, we just dug them out, from sunrise to sunset, in sun and rain, year in and year out. Four years had passed when Feigum escaped together with a Bolivian, who was found dead two days later. Since then, I've heard only rumors about Feigum. But in any case, he never came back to the mines. Nor to Norway, with the money or without it. He was last seen in Leticia, a jungle town near the Amazon, where the borders of Colombia, Perú, and Brazil come together. There he stayed one night at the Ticuna Inn and told the innkeeper, Mike Tsalikis, that he was searching for a lost city in the jungle. Feigum was even news-paper copy at that time; the last article about him in the Bogotá press said he had disappeared without a trace in the jungle, probably eaten up by an army of giant red ants. Mike Tsalikis also personally told the same thing to a friend of mine in a sidewalk café near the Lido in Santa Marta as darkness was falling and a North American was beaten and robbed two blocks away.

As for me, I stayed in the mines. I advanced to a sort of overseer position. I became a slave driver myself. I learned that emeralds are dichroic, a type of beryl, and that Klaproth and Levy believe they are a double silicate of aluminum and glucinum, with the formula $Gl_2O_3(Si.O_2) + 2Al_2O_3(Si.O_2)_3$. And that in many places emeralds have traditionally been associated with wisdom, and have been attributed other remarkable qualities as well. It was my team that found the big emerald, the one that weighed 570 grams. It was dull green-blue and eternal as a sea under the dichroscope. Three years later, I escaped with a stone weighing just over 65 grams. I had planned my escape carefully, step by step, but I wasn't able to sell the stone. This forced me to be careless. After six weeks, I was caught in a dilapidated tropical hotel inside the old fortress walls in Cartagena while waiting for the photographer who was going to get me a new Brazilian passport. I made it halfway from the bed over to the wrought-iron balcony when I saw who was standing in the doorway. Before I fell forward on the cool tile floor, I caught a glimpse of the last jeweler I'd contacted, a North American who roared through the midday stillness of the streets on a powerful motorcycle, and I heard loudspeakers from a political meeting nearby demand, Power for the Coast! I swore revenge. Then I heard the shot. You can still see the scar. After that, I was shipped to the mines in Somondoco. There they ground stones with the same famous green color as in Muzo. Now we're en route to Coscuez, which is another mine. That is to say, the others are en route.

FLIGHT

During the whole last part of the story Rasmus Høysand had heard voices outside, and doors slamming, and feet running down steps and walking back and forth in the yard with a heavy tread—all of which made Åge Holte tell his story more and more briefly and hurriedly. Now he heard a powerful auto engine start up, then stop, then start again.

Høysand gripped Holte's arm tighter.

Listen! he whispered.

Holte nodded.

Yes, we're going to leave. They'll come and get us. We're going to Coscuez tonight. Tomorrow morning we'll be standing with our pickaxes. But not me. I know a place where I'm going to try to escape. What about you?

Høysand thought for a moment.

The others? he asked, making an invisible gesture toward the sleeping bodies around him in the dark. He felt Holte shake his head, and then he answered with his mouth as well:

Most of them are too wiped out with yopo. We don't have to think about them.

Yopo?

It's a hallucinatory drug that's extracted from the seed of a plant known in this part of the world as ñopo or yopo, but its Latin name is *Anadanthera peregrina*. The drug is made this way: you remove the outer husks and dry the seeds, first in the sun and later over a fire. Then they're crushed into a paste and wrapped in large leaves. When you're going to use the yopo, you have to mix it with ashes from the bark of some tree, and knead it and dry it until it's hard. Then it's dissolved in a pot over a fire and dried again, and then immediately crushed or ground with a stone into a fine powder that can be inhaled. You take the drug through a thin tube that can be up to a meter long and is about fifteen millimeters in diameter. One end of the tube is stuck into the nose of the person who's going to take yopo. Someone else places the amount of powder to be inhaled into the other end of the tube and then puts that end into his mouth and blows.

Høysand did not answer. In addition to the sounds from outside, strong floodlights had now been turned on out in the yard, perhaps the headlights of a truck. Light came in through the small windows and drew bright yellow squares on the opposite wall. Otherwise the room still lay in pitch darkness, filled with deep sleep.

Yes, said Høysand. I'm with you. What's the plan?

Åge Holte had about finished explaining when suddenly he stopped talking. Høysand heard, too, that someone was opening the door. The key in the lock, the bolts being dragged to the side and falling heavily to the ground outside, the creaking hinges.

After that we try to get to Facativatá, each man on his own and as best we can, said Holte quickly. That's the junction for the railroad through Cundinamarca and the railroad up from Girardot. When we get that far, we should be relatively safe. Then we'll meet again in Buenaventura.

Light from a strong lantern appeared in the doorway and wandered hastily over the floor and walls of the room. Behind the light Høysand saw bodies moving in the darkness and the glint of long rifle barrels. He tried to catch a glimpse of Åge Holte beside him, but the light was already gone. Then he heard a harsh voice command everyone to line up in two rows and come out the door two by two.

The room awoke suddenly and chaotically. Høysand stayed beside Holte, far back in the crowd. They were among the last who put their hands behind their heads and followed the undertow out through the door. It was still too dark to see anything, outdoors as well. They shuffled at the heels of two others toward the outline of a large truck. High above them, the night sky was filled with stars. A couple of guards hurried the line with blows from their rifle butts, and then went back into the house with swinging lanterns. Behind him, Høysand heard swearing and the thud of several rifle blows. Then he climbed up after Holte onto the back of the truck. It was already overcrowded, but there wasn't a sound, not even low conversation. Shouts and quick steps outside. A heavy tarpaulin stretched over four large hoops covered the back of the truck, and there were benches along each side and against the cab. People were sitting everywhere. Høysand kept a tight grip on Åge Holte, and they squeezed themselves into a space on the floor with their backs against the rear panel, which had been swung up and fastened from the outside by the guards. They sat in the truck waiting, about fifteen or twenty minutes, Høysand judged, before anything further happened. It must have still been early in the night, because the small patch of sky visible between the tarpaulin and the sides of the truck did not yet show any sign of morning. Out in the darkness, Høysand kept hearing shouts and commands coming from different directions. Then two guards suddenly climbed over the rear end of the truck and positioned themselves there, one on each side, with their rifles pointing in threateningly. The next moment the engine started and the truck jolted on its way, perhaps down the long avenue of ahuehue trees along which Høysand had ridden just a few hours earlier. The beams of the headlights of the vehicle behind them swept in under the tarpaulin now and then. Otherwise, the road was completely dark.

A couple of hours' drive, Holte had said. Then they'll stop for the bridge on the dam across the Río Negro. The guards will get out there. That's when it happens. He was right. The truck stopped suddenly, and the two guards swung off the back of the truck down onto the road. The next vehicle behind them approached, dimmed its lights, and turned them off completely. The vehicle stopped. It was a Willys jeep with a machine gun mounted on it, Holte had said. That's the one you've got to watch out for. But it, too, has to drive slowly over the bridge. We've got to get around to the front of the truck for shelter right away. The guy next to the driver in the cab only has a semiautomatic rifle. And he doesn't see well in the dark. Høysand was abruptly torn out of his thoughts as he felt Holte's hand grip his shoulder hard and Holte's mouth against his ear. Wait! he whispered, pressing Høysand down against the floorboards. Not yet. When the truck starts up again! They have to drive single file over the bridge, one by one. The bridge can't take more weight than that. But we've got the jeep behind us. We each take one of the guards behind the truck, just knock them to the ground, we don't need more than a second. Then ahead of the truck, and over to the other side of the bridge. The drop from the middle is too high. And then over the guard rail. You know the rest.

The motor started up. Holte still held Høysand down. Not yet, not yet! he whispered. They sat motionless, their hearts pounding. The wheels began to roll. Somebody farther in under the tarpaulin said something in a low voice. Otherwise, all Høysand heard was the hollow, slightly singing sound of the large wheels against the deck of the temporary bridge.

Now! Holte whispered breathlessly. He gripped Høysand's arm hard, and let go.

The jeep was fifteen or twenty meters behind, low beams. Høysand got up quickly and said nothing. Just one guard on either side of the truck, rifles at the ready. They jumped down, both at the same time. Høysand saw the white-clad figure following the wooden walkway a couple of meters behind. Only that. He leaped. A long leap, the chilly night air, the water below on both sides of the bridge making the darkness deeper. Høysand sensed this before he felt the rifle against his body, then the blow against the other body, soft and heavy. A shout from somewhere else, the light from the jeep farther back. They toppled onto the walkway, the guard cried out, amazed, close, and unintelligible. Høysand was above him, on his feet, and tried to kick away the rifle now lying on the walkway The guard reached Høysand's foot first. He fell. More sounds now, shouts and screams, warm breath, a body. Høysand pulled himself free, threw aside an arm that reached out for him, got up, the red tail-lights of the truck thirty or forty meters farther ahead, too far, he began to run. Another shadow moving to the right of Høysand, nearer the truck; he set out after Åge Holte. Then he heard the machine gun start firing, just heard it, did not feel any bullets, ran, only heard them like whiplashes against the water somewhere under the bridge. The bridge's deck was just a thin boardwalk on either side of a narrow-gauge railway track. Through the sleepers Høysand could dimly see the water, far under the bridge. He had caught up to Holte, could hear him breathing. He leaped across the tracks onto the other boardwalk. A couple of machine-gun bullets sang against the rails. The iron-mesh guard rail was lower here, easy to climb. Høysand reached it first and began swinging himself up the netting by his hands. Holte was right behind him. The machine gun chattered, a couple of single rifle shots. Then Holte screamed. A short scream that ended abruptly and told everything. When Høysand turned around, Holte's silhouette was hanging in the air, dark against the faint dawn light. Then he fell, flat onto his stomach, as if he had been struck down from behind by a huge sledgehammer. Høysand let go of the iron netting and bent over Åge Holte. He had chewed the blood pill. A thin dark stripe was already oozing out of his mouth. It was still too dark to see his face clearly. His hands were clenched and stretched out in front of him on the walkway. Holte turned his head and tried to say something. The words would not come. With his last strength he lifted his arm and laid something cool and heavy in Høysand's hand. A large, shining, golden figure gleamed in Rasmus Høysand's palm, an Indian god with a large emerald embedded like a fertile womb in its belly. Høysand closed his fingers tightly. Bullets whistled through the air. Holte threw out his arms and flopped over on his back. For a moment, everything was silent. A monument of silence on a grave of oblivion. Two rifle shots threw yellow roses on the grave. Åge Holte lay dead on the wooden walkway. A bullet scratched Høysand's cheek. He got up, without noticing the bullet. The guards ground their teeth in fury, and the words they used were so gross and godless that it's impossible to repeat them in print. Their wickedness, their demonic plans, made them powerless, vile, and helpless. Høysand was beautiful and as invincible as his good actions. He smiled toward his pursuers, heard the machine gun crackle nearby, felt a new bullet burn against his thigh, and swung himself with playful ease up the guard rail. There he took aim, and dived, like a large white bird, out into the darkness.

FAR-OUT ODE

Stars like the eyes of beasts in the tropical night
Gazed down on me as I drifted along the stream:
From Atahualpa's hoard I'd stolen the moon's rare light
Until the morning sunlight ripped apart the dream.

In the rushing water cold death held me fast,
Cayman and anaconda lurked there by the score.
In water red with blood that poured from my open chest
I summoned up my strength and staggered toward the shore.

Who was she who pulled me to solid ground,
Who kissed me, washed my wounds, and dried my tears?
We met for just a moment then but found
We'd been together for at least a thousand years.

Life is a stream: I follow it afar:
Me quedan grandes esperos
Es tan difícil olvidar
Aquellos tiempos pasajeros.

Hear the limousine approaching, Angelina!
Hear the killers' knuckles pound incessantly!
It's deathly quiet now in the cantina:
Your lovely eyes now seem to question me.

Oh, Angelina, they have killed my friend!
And from a thousand perils I must flee;
I've lost them now but they will come again
And in my mind this is the scene I see:

A shot, a scream, a riddled body falls
And at a throat the blades of bandoleros!
Uprooted constantly like bouncing balls,
We flee again those cruel caballeros.

We sense the terror, smell the stench of rum,
Pay off the barman to provide our cover,
Give him the stars—a five grand minimum—
The final seconds now like vultures hover.

Life provides you with an answer:
Te quedan grandes esperos
Es tan difícil olvidar
Aquellos tiempos pasajeros.

We dodge the bullets and pursue our flight,
We commandeer a jeep, chase down the sun,
With one hand on a loaded gun at night,
Make passionate love in the dark with our boots on.

Your gentle breath now soothes me to the bone,
Your dark skin under my hand, Angelina,
Your mind in mine like yopo powder blown,
Like *Anadanthera peregrina.*

We gallop beside the ocean, then dismount,
Bring time to a halt as merry as can be
above a bar more whores than you can count
Give us the time of our life at Barranquilla.

Prisoners yesterday, tomorrow free,
We stare at Death as at someone we know,
We beg for time and swear we'll faithful be
And sleep to pounding surf while trade winds blow.

151

Now hear the distant sound of a guitar:
Nos quedan grandes esperos
Es tan difícil olvidar
Aquellos tiempos pasajeros.

I waken to strange noise. Who's there? I cry,
Get out of bed and go to have a look.
A shot rings out—behind the fire I spy
None other than José, the dirty crook.

Another shot, then pain. The end of me?
The Chibcha god that hangs down on my chest
Is smiling still, and looking down, I see
He's stopped the bullet like a safety-vest.

Oh, Angelina, answer me! I fear
The story's ending somehow you heard tell.
Sweet Angelina, what has happened here?
A shot was fired, and it was you who fell?

José is gone, as the black stillness shows.
I light a match and lean down over you.
Your empty gaze is like a pale, moist rose;
Your lips emit a tender last adieu.

All that's left now is an ugly scar:
Le quedan ningunos esperos
Es tan difícil olvidar
Aquellos tiempos pasajeros.

Sleepless are the nights, no rest by day;
An awful odor now where the agave grows:
And there I take revenge upon José
Where Río Soledad to the Pacific flows.

Dozing, he awakens with a start
Beneath a saint on his white-sheeted bed.
My machete quivers in his deceitful heart;
The sheets pour red with blood: José is dead.

The streets are empty; I have kept my vow.
Santísima María, the darkened doorways say.
A ship that's heading north weighs anchor now
And as it sails the dogs begin to bay.

The engines rumble and we cross the bar:
No quedan grandes esperos
Es tan difícil olvidar
Aquellos tiempos pasajeros.

THE DANGEROUS QUADRANT

The curve with which the bus approached the station became a full geometric circle before the vehicle stopped, as if the driver wanted the wheels in the gravel to demonstrate graphically that this stopping place was the end of the world. The bus station in Chomala was a long low café made of adobe and corrugated iron, with two tables outside in the shade. At one of them, a girl wearing no bra sat peeling sunburned skin off her arms. The chairs around the other table were empty. Inside the café, a dark-skinned man stood motionless behind a massive bar. Ten meters away he saw most of the merchandise in a primitive country store. The storekeeper, who was wearing sunglasses and had greasy hair and looked like a nervous mafioso, dozed in the burning sun next to a handwritten advertisement for ice blocks by the kilo. On the opposite side of the road, two narrow piers jutted straight out into the sea. The road continued past a row of colorful one-story adobe houses with thatch or corrugated-iron roofs, and then stopped by an oil tank about two hundred meters farther along the bay. Rasmus Høysand paused on the bottom step of the bus, took in most of the scene in one quick glance, and left the bus as the last passenger. He hesitated a moment, then sat down in a chair on the other side of the table at which the girl with no bra continued peeling off dry skin in large flakes, after looking up at him briefly and without interest.

It was quiet and suffocatingly hot. Høysand had ridden past the Mayan ruins in Copán at the border of Guatemala, and after a whole new day on the bus he was still wondering why these ruins were viewed with utterly amoral and apolitical enthusiasm (even by those who evaluated the empires of our day on the most uncompromising political and moral grounds) merely because they showed an advanced level of civilization and were examples of monumental religious architecture. Who speaks today about the humanistic leftist-intellectual criticism of the bloody sacrificial rituals under the late Aztec empire? Who praises the peasant uprising of the tenth century that crushed the Mayan empire in Central America and chased the culture-bearing priests to the Yucatán, where they created a new monumental civilization? Among those who will see the ruins of the Empire State Building in a thousand years, when capitalistic civilization is finally crushed, who will think at the same time of the anti-imperialistic work in Scandinavia in the 1970s?

But that was still a thousand years away. Now sudden gusts of wind came in from the sea every once in a while. Afterward, the air was just as still and suffocatingly hot. Høysand wiped his perspiring forehead with the arm of his shirt and squinted up at the sun, which hung palely uncertain, spreading itself out over the entire sky through a high, thin layer of clouds. Then he bought two bottles of beer, which the café owner went and got out of the freezer. Høysand carried the bottles back to the table, each with a glass on top of it. The girl was still not finished sloughing her skin. She had taken hold of the outermost layer on the outside of her upper arm and was peeling it slowly upward from her elbow toward her shoulder when Høysand opened his mouth and said:

Do you mind if I sit here?

She looked up slightly bewildered and smiled without answering.

Have a beer, Høysand offered.

When she raised her eyes this time, she just looked bewildered.

Beer, repeated the man behind the bar in a deep voice.

Now she smiled and said, Thank you, rolled the thin layer of skin together with the tips of her fingers, and threw it onto the ground.

Is there a bus going on to San Pedro Sula later this evening? asked Høysand, and took a long swallow of beer.

As he put the glass down, without having gotten an answer, he saw that a large black bank of clouds had come up in the northeast and now hung motionless above the rough, oily-looking sea. Like a heap of chromium, thought Høysand. Like a heap of chromium on the shiny speed-skating rink in Davos. He let his glance go further, from the sea and in across the land, but without noticing the inquiring eyes of the girl on the other side of the table. However, he did clearly notice her two voluptuous breasts, and the nipples that her breathing pressed against her blue T-shirt.

154

San Pedro Sula, said the soft bass voice from behind the bar.

The girl's glance met Høysand's gray-blue eyes, and she suddenly appeared to understand. Høysand did not understand anything, and he had long ago forgotten what he had asked.

No, she said. We're going to take the bus down to Limón and try to get a boat over to San Andrés.

For the first time now, Høysand could hear the distant noise of breakers crashing against the reef far out in the bay. When he listened, he could also hear the wind waving the tops of the palm trees overhead and the rustling of leaves in the tropical underbrush behind the café.

Why San Andrés? he asked.

As he completed the sentence, the first wave crashed in over the pier down below the café, sending a brief shower of fine spray onto the land. Then the wind stopped momentarily, and everything got deathly quiet. The air was oppressive, and it was hard to breathe. Out at sea, the water still heaved in great swells.

It's the last island, said the girl. It's the last island with endless blue sea on all sides, white coral reefs, bloody history, quiet lagunas, an unbroken circle of white sand, sensuous people, green and impenetrable jungle. It's the last island.

Was, said Høysand, and intended to go on to say that she was ten years too late, when a new gust of wind threw two coconuts in quick succession onto the roof above them. They sat and listened to the coconuts roll down over the corrugated iron and finally fall onto the sand outside the café. From a short distance away came the sound of frenzied hammering. Two women ran past on the road. The man with the bass voice opened a hinged leaf in the bar, walked outside, and stood motionless, looking out to sea. The sun crept slowly toward the horizon, turning the high clouds brown and crumpled, like fire on thin paper. Low rain clouds swiftly followed the sun toward the west, and in the north Høysand could see the black heap of chromium growing. Far down the road a man tried to run against the wind, toward the café, without making any headway.

The storekeeper next door had taken down the placard advertising ice blocks and now came out of his store. Høysand watched him as he struggled across the road over to the café owner, who was still standing motionless looking out to sea. The man running on the road approached with invisible forward steps, like the minute hand of a clock approaching midnight. Straight ahead, Høysand saw the café owner turn and try to shout something to the man with sunglasses and greasy hair. They put their arms around each other, put their heads close together, but nevertheless had to shout in order to hear one another. It was still possible to distinguish individual sounds: the heavy surf far out in the bay, the waves crashing onto the shore, the coconuts that thundered incessantly against the roof, rolled downward, and thudded onto the sand beside the café. Høysand thought he also felt the first drops of rain as he watched the lone man running on the road struggle forward the last meters and finally arrive under the lean-to roof in front of the café.

He was a tall, athletic-looking boy who could hardly have been more than twenty years old. His face was wet with surf or rain or sweat. The girl on the other side of the table had risen and now stood looking questioningly at the boy, who was doubled over trying to catch his breath.

No, he finally managed to get out. There's no bus going to Limón tonight. Everything is cancelled. And the hotel is closed. All boarded up, not a soul. Everyone who can, has gone up the river. It's supposed to be safer up there.

San Pedro Sula? asked Høysand.

The boy shook his head, still breathing hard. Darkness fell as in a movie theater, lightning raced across the sky, thunder rumbled under the horizon. Høysand just waited for the curtain to go up for the rain.

Everything is cancelled, said the boy, more calmly now. It's impossible to leave. We've got to find a safe place down here until the storm is over.

It was so dark that Høysand could only vaguely make out the boy's face as he said this. The sun had fallen heavily beneath the horizon after having burned the white paper sky black. On a patch of clear sky in the southwest a lonely cluster of moist stars trembled close to Earth. Ten meters away the storekeeper began to pull down the iron curtain in front of his shop. The café owner came calmly into the café again.

Hurricane, he said, but he had to shout in order to be heard: Hurricane, hurricane! We lie in the dangerous quadrant, in front of and to the right of its path. Tropical cyclone, hurricane! Understand?

He went behind the bar and opened a cupboard. At the same moment the rain roared in over them like a supersonic plane. It drilled a million holes in the ground around the building. The café owner came out with two hammers and gave one to Høysand. All sounds wound themselves together tightly and inextricably. Somewhere far in the distance the surf was still crashing wildly. Høysand held a board and a nail with one hand and tried desperately to nail the board to the window with the other. He hit his fingers, the nail bent, the board fell to the ground. The rain was a thick impenetrable wall. Loose pieces of wood from the pier slammed into the walls around him. Dead birds were flung onto the ground.

Then the wind took the lean-to roof, several sheets of corrugated iron, and sent them tumbling end over end into the jungle. The rain pounded onto Høysand, he was knocked to the ground and could no longer see anything. Out in the darkness, he heard trees crack and fall over. The board got wrenched out of his hands again. He was crouched on all fours without the slightest idea where the door was, when he felt a strong hand grip his arm and pull him inside.

It was almost as wet inside. Wet and chilly, noise everywhere, a salt taste in his mouth. Høysand lay on the floor and felt the building coming apart at the seams. No light, pitch-dark everywhere. He tried to shout, the words were snatched from his mouth, his eyes were bulging so far out of his head that it hurt.

Then Høysand heard the explosion. Somewhere in the darkness someone screamed. Høysand also screamed, weakly against the storm's wild breath. Explosion! Høysand lay flat on the floor with his hands over his head. He had never believed in the end of the world, but now pieces of hail as big as a fist rained down over him. Høysand screamed again, screamed, howled, kicked his feet against the floor. The hail had stopped. He felt the pieces of hail around him on the floor and saw another body near his, and next to his ear someone shouted in a deep voice at the top of his lungs that he should take it easy. Take it easy! Easy, man, easy, that's it, relax. It was only the freezer that exploded. Too much pressure inside, because of the low air pressure.

The freezer! Høysand felt his heart drop down from his throat and start pumping blood again. The freezer had exploded. He was still alive. A kind of warmth spread through his body. He began to move, opened his eyes, took his hands away from his head and used them to brace himself as he got to his knees. It was as dark as ever, he did not see anyone, no longer heard anyone, the storm was just as fierce, the building swayed like a bus careening at full speed through rugged terrain. Høysand was crouched on his knees, fumbling around for something to hang onto, when he heard a new sound.

It was a sharp cutting sound, like two strong men ripping a thick piece of cloth in two with a swift, decisive movement. Høysand screamed again and threw himself flat on the floor once more. Then he felt the rain. It drilled through his body. When he looked up, the roof was gone.

It was now light enough for Høysand just barely to make out that the bar was close by, and that there were people next to it. Through a window he could see that the shop next door had been blown away, its iron curtain ripped open like a beer can and the merchandise scattered into the jungle. Høysand tried to get to his knees. All the bolts on the door were gone, the door was gone, Høysand could not straighten out the upper part of his body. He lay on the floor and wriggled himself toward the bar. Then the storm took the east wall.

Høysand lay motionless, feeling the boards and the tin cans hit his body. They were harder than the rain. Something struck him in the head. He woke up and figured he had been unconscious for a few seconds. In the meantime, the storm had taken the remaining walls. Only the big bar was still standing; Høysand thought he saw people over there. Around him lay battered tin cans, smashed tropical fruits, broken bottles, broken chairs and tables. There was a strong smell of alcohol. Høysand wriggled himself closer to the bar.

He had not yet reached it when he heard the boom of another explosion. This was completely different from everything he had heard up to this point, as if the wind had turned itself inside out, sawed loose everything around it, and dived over Høysand again, but not as air, as another element, as liquid, a glistening greasy squall that stuck to his body, blinded his eyes, made his mouth dumb, his ears deaf.

The oil tank! shouted a deep bass voice close by. The oil tank exploded! The oil tank! Rasmus Høysand managed to think. Over two thousand liters of diesel oil! The oil tank! The oil tank! he tried to shout, too, but could not get out a word, could not hear, could not see. Oil was thick in his mouth, black before his eyes, plugging his ears. Everywhere. Now for a match! A spark! Now for the Apocalypse!

WAR SAILORS SYNDROME

From 27,000 feet, where a jumbo jet belonging to Braniff Airlines in Texas (with exterior design by artist Alexander "Sandy" Calder) was about to start landing procedures prior to its arrival in Guatemala City, the Mexican Gulf looked the proper azure blue, changeless and unmoving as a blue mountain, and completely harmless; indeed, for the passenger in the window seat in First Class, who occasionally glanced out between mouthfuls of steak, the Gulf looked definitely inviting and made him eagerly look forward to a morning dip in the swimming pool at the Guatemala Biltmore. The young sun-tanned navigator on board, who had been in constant contact with the U.S. Weather Bureau in Miami and also was able to verify with his own eyes that the barometer reading was no longer threatening, could confirm this superficial impression. But neither he nor the passenger saw, or were in any position to see, even by a fortunate accident or with the magic telescope of Pastor Meyer in Vangje, the small 3.5 x 3.5-meter log raft that was drifting ever farther out across the open blue sea in the wake of tropical hurricane Gala. The meteorologists of the North American weather services had long ago taken note that, after an inexplicable and unexpected swerve in over the Central American mainland inside the borders of the Republic of Honduras, Gala had suddenly turned northeast again and moved out into the Gulf leaving massive, though still unassessed, damage behind. Before being

159

smashed to firewood by the hurricane, a wind gauge on Roatán (the largest of the so-called Bay Islands on the Atlantic coast of Honduras) had measured a wind velocity of 296 kilometers per hour (a number that later would make experts at the National Hurricane Center open their eyes wide and would create waves in academic circles and at scientific conventions that were almost as large as the waves Gala herself had caused in the Caribbean), but by now the velocity had diminished so much that the meteorologists no longer hesitated to allow normal air traffic in the area, and at the same time they were able to give categorical assurances that Gala would be completely harmless by the time she reached the coast of Texas or Louisiana.

The world breathed easier, and for that matter, so did Rasmus Høysand when he sat up with a jolt and, to his great joy, found he could see again. He still had oil stains over his entire bare body, but he could open his eyes, and see, see, see! The light streamed, clean and fresh, into his retina and created beautiful shining pictures back in his brain. I can see! cried Rasmus Høysand, wild with happiness. But nobody responded, and his jubilation immediately became more restrained when he looked around and discovered what he really saw. He was on a tiny little raft (alone, there would not be space for two) in the middle of a huge blue circle of ocean, which stretched endlessly in every direction. Not only that, Høysand felt lukewarm water splash up over his feet and nervously shifted farther in toward the center of the raft. There was a good breeze (from the south-southwest, though Høysand could not know that for sure, simply make a guess, which he did immediately like the old sailor and workingman he was), the waves still rose about five or six meters, the sun shone brightly, and high stratus clouds sailed across a blue sky. On the raft beside Høysand were five fish the sea had thrown up (robalo, rape, abalone); the eyes of all but one had been forced out by the low atmospheric pressure, and all of them were dead, lying motionless side by side with their white undersides in the air. Høysand shuddered and was about to throw them overboard immediately, but he stopped himself, tore the head off one, and greedily began to eat it raw. No land, no ship in sight. The day turned into night, the stars came out, high and unreachable, Rasmus Høysand lay on his back rocked by the immense ocean, Rasmus Høysand slept.

He was awakened by the sun and a heavy sea washing in over the raft. The day was exactly like the one before, the sea was the same, the sky was the same, the raft was the same, not a bird to be seen. Høysand tore the head off the second fish and chewed sadly on the white meat. Finally he threw the half-eaten fish into the sea and lay down on the raft. He lay there on his stomach and cried, as the sun climbed slowly but surely toward its zenith and there, Rasmus Høysand thought, it hung itself up or something, and stayed. He cried and cried, but considering that within the space of a short time he had survived the most incredible dangers (if we trust his own melodramatic and overly romantic description—in rhyme!—of his flight from the emerald thieves in Santa Isabel), he had absolutely no reason to carry on like that, even if the blazing sun bothered him. It could have been much worse. Only a few days ago, if we still trust his rhymed story (which otherwise shows—in a manner his loyal friends find revealing and frankly painful—so many examples of concrete thinking that Høysand would have gotten a high rating on both the Concentration Camp Syndrome and the War Sailors Syndrome, which are characterized by *e.g.*, various bodily pains, lack of energy and initiative, self-isolation, weeping without outward cause, impotence and inability to have an erection, constant nightmares, dyspepsia, poor memory, inability to form mental impressions, lack of ideas: syndromes of which Høysand himself is happily unaware, which is perhaps best, and also, when it comes right down to it, the real strength in his story), he supposedly boarded a ship in the city "where Río Soledad into the Pacific flows" (Bahía de Solano??), a ship (name unknown) that lay at anchor "with course set northward," and then sailed with this ship to a harbor in Central America, which probably cannot have been very far from, for example, San Lorenzo, because just a few days later we find Høysand at a table outside the bus station in Choloma, and everything that happened from that moment on through the next few dramatic

161

hours can be described exactly (thanks to the French couple he met there) using the most precise language and methods of measurement taken from advanced sciences such as psychology, geography, and geophysics. From this point on, Rasmus Høysand is one of the light spoils of Gala's gigantic strength and trails helplessly in the rough wake of the hurricane, in a movement that follows unequivocally the strict laws of time and space and the epic. It should be added parenthetically, and in the name of fairness, that Høysand's desire for adventure and exoticism, which is mainly what has gotten him into all these difficult and impossible situations, is not just an individual peculiarity of his own humble person, but a far broader and more social phenomenon that is particularly characteristic of the ideals and dreams of freedom of young people who have grown up near the factory entrances of Stavanger Electro Steelworks, Electric Furnace Products Company Limited, Norwegian Zinc Company, Tyssedal DNN Aluminum, Odda Smelting Plant, A/S Bjølvefossen, Årdal and Sunndal Works, Bremanger Smelting Plant, Norsk Hydro, and who have become pale and toughened by the smoke from those same industries—something which, for example, the so-called "Årdals Investigation," carried out by the highly esteemed and respected University of Oslo, can fully confirm. The conclusions of this study lead one to exclaim, as does Professor Jens Arup Seip in the Foreword to his extensive *Overview of Norway's History:* "Social realities often provide an explanatory link between economic and political realities."

In any case, it is dusk, Høysand lies on his back hallucinating, dreaming, like the Indians in Copán, that the world rests on the backs of two alligators who start fighting with each other; he sees the stars come out far up above and plop down from the sky, does not notice that a ship glides by in the distance (far away as it is, one can still hear the Latin rhythms of the band on board, the promises of eternal love whispered by those dancing la cumbia on deck, the clink of jewels and champagne glasses: the Norwegian cruise ship *Black Prince* is sailing ahead). It is dark, night has fallen completely, perhaps only Rasmus Høysand is hallucinating, the ship has disappeared, the sea is calm, Høysand has fallen completely to pieces and collapsed on the raft.

MEETING IN THE HURRICANE

It was a young and somewhat romantic mate on the Hauge-sund boat *Amanda Bakke* transporting bauxite between Port Es-quivel on Jamaica and Årdal in Sogn who discovered (and thereby probably saved the life of) Rasmus Høysand. William Oanes from Tasta, who was second mate on board and newly married ashore (or number two in both places, as the chief said), had stood the twelve-to-four watch, eaten a good dinner in the mess, and then gone back on the poop to watch the sun go down into the Caribbean and dream of his wife at home in a one-family house on Dusavig Road. He had already been sit-ting there for twenty minutes and had gradually begun to think this sun was taking a good long time for just a simple sunset, when one of the last rays from the red ball that the sea had already half-swallowed fell in such a way across the broad, calm crests of the waves that Second Mate Oanes could not help seeing that there was a raft just thirty to forty fathoms astern to port and, moreover, that there was a person on the raft, a naked man, jumping around and up and down and wav-ing his arms and legs like a madman. Second Mate Oanes was a clever young sailor and knew what the situation demanded, and less than ten minutes after he first saw this strange sight, a bearded, brown-baked, mentally unbalanced Rasmus Høysand was taken aboard the *Amanda Bakke* (which had quickly made a full stop and back at the gentle *r*-trilled Stavangeresque cry of, Man overbooooooard!). The officer who ended his watch three hours later noted the find carefully in the logbook and observed that the raft and the shipwrecked sailor were found at exactly the same northern latitude as the Tropic of Cancer.

Høysand continued to hallucinate for three entire days after being rescued, until the *Amanda Bakke* had gone through the Straits of Florida and had sailed up between West Palm Beach and Grand Bahama Island. All that Høysand remembers from these days is being lifted from the lifeboat up onto the deck, and having a black man stick his head between him and the sun and ask William Oanes with amazement in pidgin English:

O-dat?

163

The second mate doesn't know. He says nothing. Rasmus Høysand from Norway, whispers the dry throat of the naked man who lies stretched out on the aft deck. That is the last he remembers. A blanket is thrown over him. The only other thing on Høysand's body (aside from the oil stains) is a gold amulet of a thickset Chibcha god with a large emerald in its belly. And he can be glad for that, "For," as Rabelais says, referring in turn to well-known classical authors such as Orpheus, in his book *De Lapidibus,* and Plinius in *Libro Ultimo,* "emeralds possess a strengthening and resurrecting power for the male organ." Høysand lay flat on his back in sick bay holding his hands in front of his face most of the time out of fear that his eyes would roll out of his head and down onto the deck and be washed overboard. The fourth day he was well enough to stand up and swing his arms twenty-five times. The fifth day he could walk alone to the mess and have three hot meals a day, and ten o'clock coffee and three o'clock coffee, and pound cake and coffee after dinner and fried eggs from the galley along with the men who ended their watch at eight o'clock. And it was then that Høysand saw the engine-room crew for the first time. One of the seamen at the Deck table was the first to say it. Where's the engine crew? he asked, turning around on his swivel chair. Where the hell is the engine crew? Høysand, who had just gotten a haircut (a crew-cut, from the cook) and was freshly shaven, did not look too bad at all, except for a strange expression on his face once in a while. Engine crew? he asked. Was the whole engine crew on this watch? And the entire mess laughed, and the man sitting across from Høysand (who was called Miss Johansen or Sande-fjord, Høysand later found out) said, Yes, the whole engine crew was on this watch, ha-ha. For the next ten minutes the talk was about sailors' dives in Tampico, and Høysand did not open his mouth. Then a new man strode across the threshold into the mess. Høysand was sitting in a position to be one of the first to notice the new man. He glanced up at him briefly at first, and turned warm and red, and then gave him a long stiff look, and turned cold and pale, and sweat broke out on his suntanned forehead. The man calmly found a white ceramic mug, poured in some coffee from the pot, and plopped his ass down at the

Engine table. He was a fellow of medium height who looked to be in his late fifties. Deep wrinkles criss-crossed his pale gray face, and his long thick gray hair was combed back on his head in the style of the thirties and forties. His dark blue overalls were covered with even darker oil stains.

Here comes the engine crew! said the seaman at the Deck table, giving Høysand a nudge.

You see, the engine crew here on board is just one man— him, Sandefjord added. All the rest are officers or "reorganized" away. That's a good one, eh, a one-man engine crew!

Høysand did not say a word. The tan from his days on the raft had faded from his face in less than half a minute. He was as white as snow.

Well, I see we've got a new man on board, said Engine Crew in a ringing East Coast dialect. Is he the new bo'sun? The new bo'sun who's drifted in out of the blue?

Høysand made no reply.

Take it easy, Engine Crew! said the seaman next to Høysand. Just take it easy, will you? Can't you see the man is white as a sheet? He's been floating around on a raft without food or water for eleven days, after all.

Okay, okay, okay, okay! said Engine Crew good-naturedly and took a swallow of coffee.

Then Rasmus Høysand got up his courage.

It's been a long time, Johan Jørgensen! he said in a trembling voice. He wanted to say more, but his voice failed him.

Johan Jørgensen looked up.

Gee! That's what I thought, I thought there was something familiar about you. You were the deck boy on the *Eva* in, let me see, it was after they converted from coal to oil, so it must've been in '59, am I right? Mo-i-Rana, Rotterdam, Cardiff, Narvik—?

No, said Høysand, and swallowed hard.

Bremerhaven, Newcastle, Odda—?

No, I'm not from the *Eva*. I'm from Ålvik. Hello from Ålvik, Johan Jørgensen!

You're from Ålvik? You're not—?

Durdei Steine's son.

It was impossible to see whether Johan Jørgensen had turned paler. He set his cup down carefully on the table, opened his mouth, and blew a stream of air out of his lungs. Then he got up, took his cup, and threw the coffee out in the sink.

Well, well. So you're Durdei Steine's son, he said half to himself, and walked out of the mess. His unopened pack of Senior Service and his lighter still lay on the table.

About three or four minutes went by before he returned. Meanwhile, nobody said anything, and one by one the men walked out of the mess. Høysand was left sitting alone. Chilly sea air entered through the open doors leading out to the deck and to the corridor. When Johan Jørgensen came back into the mess, he was carrying a case of export beer, which he heaved with a clatter onto the table in front of Høysand. Then he sat down on the other side.

You weren't a very big fellow then, were you? he said as he lit a cigarette.

Eight years old, said Høysand.

But you remember me?

Of course.

Everyone does. I know how things have gone with Durdei, so we don't have to talk about that. *Skaal!*

Johan Jørgensen took a few swigs of beer. Høysand did the same and said nothing. Johan Jørgensen emptied his bottle. There was a long silence. Johan Jørgensen opened a new bottle. Through the open doors they could hear the wind and the waves outside.

You know, I once thought about going back to see them, said Johan Jørgensen. Johan Jørgensen, go back to see them? Go back to seaman! But that's a long time ago, in '52 it was, for the Winter Olympics in Oslo. I wanted to go home and watch that speed-skater Hjallis beat Sugawara by a lap in the 10,000. I planned to go ashore and make a trip to Ålvik afterward. The Bergen train and the whole bit. I'd saved up a lot of money by the time I signed off in Baltimore, because I got that far, there was over four thousand bucks between the rubbers in my wallet, I want you to know, and that was a lot of dough in those days. I took the train from Baltimore up to New York, and I wasn't wearing nothing from either the church or the Salvation Army that time, I want you to know. I stayed at a good hotel, Hotel Bryant, in the heart of Broadway, believe it or not, and I walked around New York in a tailor-made suit with a rose in my mouth and four thousand bucks in my inside pocket. It was fall, but nice warm weather anyway, and I took off my jacket on Wall Street and my vest on Canal Street and wandered up through Chinatown and over to Little Italy and drank a martini before dinner and a cappuccino after dinner, wearing white gloves and a Borsalino hat, and it was no mean dude, let me tell you, who walked on up Broadway into Greenwich Village, tossing hundred-dollar bills to the Bowery bums on the way, and strolled around Washington Square so many times in my new suit that the ladies all got cricks in their necks from watching me the whole time, and when they couldn't see me no more they had to go get treated by high-class doctors and nerve doctors and German psychiatrists on Sixth Avenue, and the German psychiatrists scratched their beards and pulled their hair and moustaches and thought long and hard before they put on a thick Vienna accent and said the stiff neck was probably part of the general muscular armoring caused by repressed sexuality in childhood and by long summers at Martha's Vineyard and by stealing looks at Blossom, the son of the Negro woman, Flossie, who did the washing and fixed the meals with a view out over Central Park in the winter, and not from stealing looks at Johan Jørgensen before noon on Washington Square!

Those were the days, all right. But then I made a bad mistake. It started to rain, you see, the sun disappeared in a flash, and then it rained, poured cats and dogs. You're from Vestland, so you know how it can rain in America! It wasn't long before all the rainpipes started gurgling, I tell you. And that's when I made the big mistake. Damn well couldn't get my suit rained on, you know, but if I'd had a few brains in my noggin I'd have stood calm and cool right where I was, there on the corner of Waverly Place, till an empty taxi come by or till it stopped raining or till I decided to go into a bar, but no, I had to take the subway, stupid ass that I am. I absolutely had to get up to Carnegie Hall, as if the match for the heavyweight title was going on up there or something. Ran like a damn fool over to Christopher Street and took the orange line Uptown toward Times Square.

And now you'd better listen hard, my boy, because this is something you young folks can learn from and watch out for. It's just after five in the afternoon, see, heavy rush-hour. The subway car I'm standing in is packed, jam-packed, believe me, jam-packed. Meaning, in order to breathe you've got to inhale at the same time as everybody around you. Well, anyway, I'm standing there hanging onto an overhead strap in my blue suit and nylon shirt and breathing in time with everybody around me, and the train leaves the station and disappears into the tunnel, and I'm standing right by the door, squashed between two women, elegant ladies, one in front and one behind. These are real elegant ladies, let me tell you, the way women used to be elegant, with feathered hats and gold hatpins and veils on their faces and stiff masks of powder and red, I mean really bright red, lips and a beauty mark on the cheek, and red-fox and sable furs and live minks that kept licking them in the ear wrapped layer after layer around their necks. I couldn't see no farther down, could only feel, but the woman standing in front of me in that tête-à-tête, as they call it, was wearing such high heels she seemed like she was about ten centimeters taller than me.

She looks down at me and smiles, and I can't help smiling back, you see. So we stand there, smiling, the both of us, and everything's fine and dandy, and I think I just barely feel something moving between my legs, something I ain't got nothing to do with, something that moves up between my thighs and turns into a small, expert hand that feels around in my crotch, finds what it's looking for, and settles around my balls, loose and gentle, like a bird's wing around two fresh-laid seagull eggs. I feel my legs getting weak and start sweating in my armpits and at the back of my knees, and I've got to swallow a few times. When I look at the elegant lady again, she's still smiling the same smile, and I try to smile back, but I feel like I look strange anyway. Because the little hand is still curved, just as gentle, around my balls, and it juggles them, real careful, in its fingers now and then. But the elegant lady's smile is just as charming as ever, and I can tell I'm not sweating as much and I smile back at her in a natural way and my legs still feel just as weak, and I notice I'm starting to think about where we should go when we get off. The Waldorf Astoria? The Hilton? The White House in Washington, D.C.? The Empire State Building, to get enough space? Then I notice a new wave of perfume from the woman behind me, and I feel a slender hand stretch out, real slow, under my right arm, with a steady course for my left jacket pocket and the wallet with the four thousand bucks in it, and not only the money, but pictures of my mom, who danced a waltz across the Frier Fjord, and my dad, who won the Menstad Battle between the workers and the police. No, you don't turn out to be a Conservative from that kind of stuff, but this hand, this hand don't care about that, it just keeps going toward the four thousand bucks and the pictures in the fat wallet in my inside left pocket, and as if that ain't enough, about the same time I feel the small hand holding my balls start to tighten, slow and careful, but noticeable, I tell you, noticeable, otherwise Johan Jørgensen wouldn't never have stood for nothing like that. The hand from behind reaches my jacket pocket, and the hand in my crotch squeezes so hard it starts to hurt. I look at the elegant lady with the diva smile that's just ten centimeters from my own clenched lips, and I'm just about to scream, to object to the entire car, to shout, Stop! I'm being robbed! Help! when the hand in my crotch squeezes so hard that all I get out is a gasp, and I'd have fell flat on the floor if the train wasn't so crowded. And at the same time I see these two fingers, an index finger and a middle finger with long, bright red nails, steal my precious wallet from the inside pocket of my blue suit, pull it, quick and graceful, across my smooth nylon chest, and make it disappear behind me under my right arm. I give the elegant lady with the smile a real entreating look, but she just smiles as beautiful as Eisenhower and Adlai Stevenson, who was asking for votes in posters on the wall behind her, and then she goes right on tightening the vise around my balls. I try to shout again, to get my hands free, to turn around and stop the thief, but I can't do none of those things. I don't move, I don't make a sound, and I let it happen.

The train stops at Times Square. The doors open, and that leaves a little bit more space in front of me and behind me and on both sides. I'm still standing by the door, and the elegant lady with the smile is still holding me just as tight. Passengers get off, and new passengers get on and push past us. But now there's more space around me. The doors start to close, and I figure I'll see that beautiful smile till the next station, when all of a sudden I feel this god-awful pain in my crotch. She squeezes hard and twists, like when you try to pick a plum that's not ripe off the tree. Instead of a tree falling, I fall. The doors close, and the train starts to move. The last thing I see is two elegant ladies, with big hats and veils and ermine around their necks, swaying real graceful along the platform on high heels. Then the train goes into the tunnel, I'm laying on the floor, ready for a coffin, and everything goes black.

I drag myself off at Columbus Circle. A kind man helps me get to my feet as we pass 50th Street, asks if it's my heart, and then takes the rest of my money, the loose change in my pants pocket. I crawl up the subway stairs, doubled over with pain, come out at Central Park, and sleep on a bench that night. It was what I deserved. I'd scattered riches and sowed poverty, like they say. Yep, that's for sure. The next day I went over to the Salvation Army and got some food, and three days later I signed on a ship. Headed for the Pacific. And that's why I didn't come home in '52.

FOR A SONG

There were quite a few empty bottles on the table between them. Høysand sat looking straight ahead, deep in thought. Johan Jørgensen stubbed out a cigarette after three drags. They were still alone in the mess. Outside the ventilators, the night was black. The ship rode northward well in a southwester.

And later? asked Høysand.

Coastal boats for the most part. I built up Lorentzen's fleet with gas tankers in Brazil. Then I sailed with passengers on the Caribbean and with automobiles in the Great Lakes. Souvenir shop in Nicaragua for two years. After that, foreman of a road gang on the Lima–Cerro de Pasco railroad. Nothing but scrub and jungle, and as long and twisting as the Sogne Fjord from Sygnefest to Årdal. Then there was nothing else to do. So I went to sea again. Rough sea. Ships that went down for a song.

Sometimes we got rescued, sometimes not. I was shipwrecked two hundred sea miles straight east of Cabo São Roque in Brazil with a big load of passengers. So there we sat in a lifeboat. Now we're done for, says the skipper. We'll all die of thirst. This is the end, uhu! But then Johan Jørgensen showed everybody he'd been in tough spots before. No, I tell them. We'll make it. How? By drinking from the ocean. But we'll die for sure from that! says the skipper. He didn't know the Amazon sends fresh water about three hundred kilometers out into the Atlantic. So I leaned over the edge of the lifeboat and took a drink. Then everybody else took a drink. And that's how I saved the lives of over three hundred people (we had to stand up in the lifeboat to have enough room). Finally we drifted ashore in Recife. There, more people came to an end than in the Atlantic. In Jensen, Utah, I had my picture taken arm in arm and cheek-to-cheek with Donna Michelle, Playboy's Playmate of the Year in 1964. It was supposed to cost twenty bucks just for arm-in-arm, but them big doe eyes of hers looked at me so deep it went right to the bottom of my soul, and she says, Oh no, for Johan Jørgensen this is gratis. Two years later, I'm standing at the entrance to the Union Carbide nerve center in New York, and I say to the guard, I'm Johan Jørgensen from Norway and I worked in your factory in Norway. Come right in, says the guard, the CEO's office is this way, up on the fiftieth floor. How good of you to drop by, the CEO says when I come up. How's it going? I ask. Without your work, Mr. Jørgensen, UCC would never have become the next-to-the-largest company in the organic chemistry industry in the United States, with an honorable twenty-fifth place on the Fortune 500. UCC is thus one of our nation's larger enterprises, with a leading position in both the synthetic and organic chemistry industries, as well as in plastics and industrial gases. Among our other product groups we could mention carbon (coal and graphite products, electrodes and batteries) and metal (ferro-alloys, mining and nuclear-physics products). Right! I say. The last thing you said is true, that's for sure. Another drink, Mr. Jørgensen? Won't exactly say no to that, but there's a limit for ordinary folks, too. Now, now, Mr. Jørgensen. You just relax. We really appreciate having a visit from one of our oldest and most humorous colleagues. Thanks, I tell him, if what you say ain't true, at least it's good nonsense. Because nobody's going to outdo Johan Jørgensen when it comes to speaking for himself, or making a show of himself, or having others make a show of him. Just goes to show how I am! Four months later, I wrote this letter to the editor that got printed in *Time* magazine, from the M/S *Ambjorg,* a turbine tanker belonging to Ryvarden and Imsland, Penang, while she was at anchor in Manila waiting to get a mooring at the wharf: "It's sad to hear that Lyndon Johnson thinks candidates for Vice President should be qualified to be President. The USA would have been a lot better off if John F. Kennedy had used the same criteria." In 1968 during the Olympics in Mexico, I was the guy who led the marches in and out of Aztec Stadium at the award ceremony for the winners of the women's two-hundred-meter, when Renate Stecher got the gold. You probably remember that. I did a great job, I think, stood at attention, straight and serious, when the East German national anthem by Hanns Eisler was played, and at the end of the ceremony—it was timed down to the last minute—I managed, in a firm way, but not too obvious, to lead them out in a row, the three winners, all of them so excited and waving like crazy. You remember that, don't you?

Yes, and I remember the time you scored two goals for Lovra against Fonna from Tyssedal, especially that header in the first half.

Well, like I say, I make a big show of myself, but that score I happen to remember, because it was the first and last time I pulled off the trick of steering in the ball with my fist on the referee's blind side. And the reason it was counted was that the linesman on that side was our second-string goalie, and of course he called it good for us. What th' hell, it was a fateful game after all!

Now let's go down and take a look at the engine, said Johan Jørgensen. You wouldn't think so, but way down in this old wreck there's a first-class LM Erickson rear engine. Come on, I'll show you!

Johan Jørgensen led the way, and Rasmus Høysand followed

him, a little unsteadily, out of the mess and down the ladder and through a door that opened into the enormous noise and vibration of the engine room and then down more ladders to the leaf-green cover over the motor that, with the help of mechanical ingenuity, transferred its gigantic power to the propeller, and the huge screw propeller whipped the water and the *Amanda Bakke* of Haugesund had fair winds across the North Atlantic, crossed the harsh North Sea at a speed of eighteen knots, entered the Sogne Fjord with a Norwegian coastal pilot and with her cargo deck filled with 11,000 tons of bauxite, the terra-rossa type, which had a red color and grainlike consistency and was the devil for everyone who had to work with it because it stuck to all the silos and gates, something Rasmus Høysand first saw for himself eighteen days after being picked up in the Gulf, as he stood watching the huge unloading cranes scoop up enormous loads of bauxite from the Number 2 and Number 3 hatches on the pier at the world's largest facility for discharging oxide in bulk, which belongs to the Årdal and Sunndal Works and lies on Årdal Point, and meanwhile Johan Jørgensen was busy on the ladders down in the engine room, and two seamen aft prepared to take in water as ballast in the side tanks, and a third, whom Høysand recognized as Sandefjord or Miss Johansen, wrote "Departure 20 hr." on a black sign that hung on the railing beside the gangway.

At the hatch coamings, the signalmen drew small horizontal circles in the air, some spill poured, as usual, onto the deck, down between the side of the ship and the pier, onto the pier. The fjord lay calm, the bauxite rattled sluggishly down into the silo, the clam shell closed and dropped toward the hold again, isolated dots of fog and home-loan houses clung to the mountainsides, which rose higher and higher, left the unloading dock and the ironworks behind, left the fog and houses behind, left the tree line and the power reservoirs behind, and culminated in the high, wild Falketind and Urdanostind peaks in the Jotunheim and the Hurrung Mountains and in the towering summit of Store Skagastølstind far toward the north.

Rasmus Høysand was home again.

Dawn in Norway

HAND SIGNALS

No, Rasmus Høysand was not the kind of sailor who rushed right into the Samvirkelag co-op in Årdal in Sogn and said, I want the most expensive car you've got in stock. No Rolls or Mercedes or Volvo for him. No, he didn't even buy a motorcycle or a cassette player or a radio with an FM band and a fishery band. Far from it. He barely managed to scrape together the money for the ferry from Årdals Point, and when he was supposed to pay for his ticket on the bus up from Gudvangen and over to Voss, things were really tight. The bus driver took a good long look at Høysand, who was carefully examining his pockets for more ten-øre coins and devaluated pesos, and said, This fellow obviously needs a little extra Sailors Benefits, and then he pulled out a long ribbon of ticket and gave it to his new passenger, and Høysand, whose clothing was too thin and face too tanned for this time of year, went and sat down in the very back of the bus. There he sat, tanned and alone, and looked at his hands as the half-empty bus crawled up the steep road to Stalheim, and thought, What do I know how to do?

What do I know how to do? Rasmus Høysand asked himself, looking down at his hands. They were long and narrow, and had large knuckles and light, almost invisible hair and freckles out to the middle joint. And he had frozen them on the North Sea, so in cold weather the fingers turned white like a corpse.

What do I know how to do? Rasmus Høysand asked himself again and looked down at his hands as the bus left the new

Stalheim Tourist Hotel and began rolling through the beautiful Voss district. What do I know how to do?

I can—open a skimmer so the slag runs one way and the metal the other, I know how to do that at least
—splice cables
—give Standard hand signals
—stoke in blows and add mix to a furnace (but now they probably do such things automatically from the furnace operator's control room)
—mow with a *støttorv* scythe
—speak English and Spanish and a little German
—shuffle a pack of cards in the air
—make slot-machines work by blowing in the coin slot
—tie a bowline knot
—dismantle and operate Garands, Schmeissers, and AG3s
—transport sinter
—send dispatches on the ANPRC 10 and FF 33
—start up a 81-mm BK
—be a job foreman, carpenter, lumberjack, or boatswain
—conjugate the verb *to be,* present tense, in eleven languages

The bus sped down along Oppheim Lake. They're not much good—the things I know how to do. How far can I get with them? Rasmus Høysand wondered. Don't I know how to do more things? Is this all I know how to do? Can I look forward to a rich life and a secure old age? Maybe I could start a business? Rush-cloths from RasHøy Inc. solve your dusting problems quick and easy! No. Definitely not. It wouldn't work. I'm much too kind to go into business. So does that mean I'll have to get up at six every day, except for free shifts, to go over and dig in the shit? Or put in shifts when other people don't have to work?

The bus stopped at Vinje in Voss to pick up mail and new passengers.

Midden man for the rest of my life? A line like the new moon in front of the time clock for forty years? Rooming house? And in the upper bunk at that? Oh no, oh no. What have I done to myself?

Høysand hid his head in his hands. He sat that way for the rest of the trip, not daring to think anymore. Early in the afternoon the bus arrived at Vangen. I've got to go on to Oslo, thought Rasmus Høysand, and looked up. I've got to go to Oslo and learn something useful. I've got to borrow money from the Government Loan Office for an education, and register at the university to study law. Then I can become a lawyer. Do useful work. Warm and comfortable, in an office. Guaranteed job. There will always be a fence post that's causing a dispute. Høysand had no sooner thought this than, to his great surprise, he found a five-hundred-kroner bill among the stones down by Vang Lake (where he'd been sitting and thinking and skipping small flat stones across the water: one—two—three—plop). Now Rasmus Høysand skipped a new stone. One—two—three, the stone sprouted wings, rose again, fell and rose like the wires between the telephone poles west toward Bolstadøyri and Bulken, and disappeared.

Hurray! shouted Rasmus Høysand. Hurray! Hurray! I found five hundred kroner down by Vang Lake!

Then he ran up past Fleischers Hotel and bought himself a train ticket across the mountains to Oslo, but first he had to make a trip home. It was raining, but then the weather cleared up. The rain stopped when Rasmus Høysand took the ferry from Kvanndal, and the sun came out as he rode a bus farther inland along Sør Fjord (he first had to stop briefly in Odda). This was the way it should be! There was sunshine on the Folgefonn Glacier and sunshine on the fruit trees and sunshine on the Hardanger farmers who were out shaking their apple trees before going to market, and sunshine on the cargo boat out on the fjord and fliers written in New Norwegian on all the houses telling about the dance at Hara and Lono and the European Cup Match between Odda Sports Club and Manchester United and the Cup-Winner Cup between Fonna and Milan and the poetry of Claes Gill from Odda and the strike at Norwegian Zinc and the sympathy strike at Carbide and the demonstration that blocked off the year-round highway through Tyssedal. Year-round! Yes, these Odda folks sure were a lively crew all right!

Hurray for Zinc and Roger Albertsen and Claes Gill, for Carbide and Nitrate and Cyanamide, too! Onward for the language of the Norwegian common people! Onward for a free and socialist Norway!

THE MAN WITH THE TOPCOAT

The man at the table by the window pushes his coffee cup toward the middle of the table and gets up heavily. With shuffling steps he walks across the floor over to the coat-tree. There he first takes down a red checkered scarf and wraps it loosely around his neck. Then he takes down his topcoat. He straightens out the right sleeve of his jacket and presses the outer edge against his palm with three fingers. Then he slips his arm into the right sleeve of his topcoat. He shifts his grasp and goes through the same motions with the left arm. When he has slid into both sleeves, he takes hold of the lapels with both hands and adjusts the overcoat to the shape of his body with a couple of strong jerks. He buttons four stubborn buttons. Dressed to leave, he stands looking around the room with a thoughtful gaze, as though the smoke-filled air were an imaginary mirror that reflected his impeccable image. He gives himself a shake, and his shuffling steps begin to carry him toward the stairs.

Maiquetía, says someone at a table just to his left, in a voice that sounds as though it were chewing flatbread on the word. The man does not stop, but turns his head slightly and glances in the direction of the voice. At the table nearest the stairs, two young men sit blustering, diagonally across from each other. Maybe they aren't so young after all. The man does not know them in any case, and walks on. He watches carefully where he is going, puts his left hand on the railing, and takes the first step down the stairs. Left foot first, then the right onto the same step; left—right, left—right, left—right. It goes slowly and takes time.

Maiquetía, repeats Rasmus Høysand and is vaguely aware of an old fellow struggling down the circular stairway that leads out to the street, while at the same time he notes very clearly that, diagonally across from him at the table, Arnold is dropping out of the conversation, his pupils are getting large, his eyes dark, his look distant and unfocused.

Maracaibo, Rasmus continued. Barranquilla, Panama, Buenaventura.

The next day? asks Arnold, dully and disinterestedly, as if the words were breathed through him by an invisible but living person behind his chair or at the next table.

No. It took two days of flying. I went aboard in Buenaventura on a Sunday. And that Thursday we were in Puerto Limón, where we anchored for more than two weeks.

Rasmus watches Arnold finish his drink and set his glass down on the table with a definitive movement, and in the time between when the empty glass leaves Arnold's lips and when it meets the TOU beer coaster on the table Rasmus has seen so much, thought so much, envied so much, and understood so much of what Arnold has said about the kind of man he is, that Rasmus is sure he would need a whole day to write it all down. The true story of the real life of Arnold Høysand?

Well, says Arnold. He sits with his right thigh crossed over the left one under the café table, sits awry and askew and aslant and as though he had plopped down on the café bench just accidentally and in passing, leaning forward, his left hand stuck between his thighs, the right one on the table loosely holding the glass, thumb pointing up, the way you would hold your hand if you had won at poker and were about to scoop the pot over to yourself, thought Rasmus Høysand.

Well, says Arnold again. He is a little drunk and not used to being that way, his facial expression repeats on a smaller scale his body's position at the table, the eyes that lean outward and down and seem to be trying to creep out from beneath the eyelids and in under the next table, the half-open mouth, the flabby lower part of the face that somehow looks as though it has laid itself out on the table next to the arm.

Well, says Arnold for the third time. I'd better be getting home and see if the house is standing and the wife— But he doesn't get up. A circle of foam around the edge of his empty glass sinks down slowly. The record on the jukebox has reached the refrain for the twelfth time, and Rasmus has the distinct impression that they are singing dadadadada dadtda dadadadada dadatda especially in honor of Arnold and him on this rare occasion.

And the wife is lying in bed, Arnold concludes, and gets up, breaks loose from the table like a horse from its tether. They make a lot of good records now, he adds. Then he goes down the stairs keeping his eyes in his head.

They.

Rasmus looks straight ahead. The blue checkered tablecloth, the cardboard beer coaster, the cheerless empty glass in which the ring of foam has now slid all the way down and turned into a wet blob on the bottom; the padding on the bench, which smooths out, slowly like old skin, from the impression of Arnold's body; the black slipcover with holes in it, from which yellow foam-rubber is oozing.

They, thinks Rasmus Høysand.

They. They? *They.* THEY. Always They. Who the hell are they? Where are they? Who in the hottest blackest whitest hell are they? They who make the jukebox records? They who send word of work far into the wild uplands? They who know how the world functions and why everything happens the way it does? They who choose the films at the movie theaters? They who create magazines and books? They who have started using diver phones in diving suits? They who draw the Trades with red ink through the trade-wind area? They who rhyme life with strife? They who ship brown earth from Africa and shiny metal from Norway and cars from Germany and make a profit on all of it? They who stopped learning how to listen? They who made a fortune when they robbed Peter to pay Paul. They who take the car and the house, and the wife, too, I was about to say? They who steer hurricanes in toward foreign coasts? They who are damned—damned right.

Rasmus gets no further. A man looms darkly above him. He looks up. It is Arnold.

I forgot my umbrella, says Arnold. And besides, I guess I said a lot of stupid things. I sure ran off at the mouth, didn't I?

I don't remember anything. Rasmus shrugs his shoulders.

The umbrella is hanging by its handle on the back of the bench. Arnold grabs it and disappears again.

Rasmus Høysand looks out the window. An old man who has trouble walking plods along in the rain. Arnold gets into the Anglia, white hands flutter above the steering wheel, the car pulls out from the curb and into the traffic.

Maracaibo, Buenaventura, Panama, Puerto Limón, San Pedro Sula, La Guaíra, Barranquilla, says Rasmus Høysand half under his breath, like an incantation, tentatively, as though to find out if they work after all, if these words fit in and fall into place, and they do, they exist in these streets, just like the red and green hydrant on the corner, the bakery across the street, the grocery store, the blue and white tablecloth, the black umbrella that's shaken and closed and taken along into the shoe store, the wet slate on the roof, the curb along the sidewalk, the brown smoke above the ridge of the rooftops. The rain that patters carefully in the puddles.

DAS DING AN MICH

Rasmus Høysand met Alexandra Bernadotte Victoria Voss (pronounced Fawss) for the first time at a student party in a large old apartment in Frogner (pron. Fyawngneer) in Oslo. It was one of those summer evenings in Norway after which everyone goes around the next day with hickies like large crushed strawberries on the outside of his or her throat (to mention the place visible to most people), and a few days later some of the less fortunate ones go around with blooming strains of gonococci on the inside of their throats. Høysand sat cross-legged on the floor, with a bottle of red wine and a glass and lighted candles in front of him, and listened with interest to a male student who was just concluding a lengthy commentary with these words:

So, we always need to be on the watch to be sure we demand power along with liberation, and demand liberation along with power!

Høysand looked up at the ceiling, thinking, for quite a while. Then he said:

Until these socialists discover that capital and wage-earners have developed machines that can increase a human being's power a thousandfold and electronics that can expand the capacity of the human brain a million times, the capitalists and the bosses can sleep safely in their beds at night and have no reason to shiver in their boots during the day.

There was an uncomfortable pause, as when someone has cleared his throat and the phlegm lies in his mouth. Then Alexandra Bernadotte Victoria, who was also sitting on the floor, two places to the left of Høysand, said out of inbred bourgeois tact, out of fear of "scenes" and of silence, and to rescue the situation:

Kant, you mean? Das Ding an sich?

No, replied Rasmus Høysand, who had learned good German during the six weeks he was waiting for a boat in Buenos Aires: Das Ding an mich.

Alexandra Bernadotte Victoria looked questioningly at him: I guess I don't quite understand—

Ist das Ding für dich?

With this response Rasmus Høysand's happiness began. After feverish lovemaking in the next room just half an hour later, during which the thing on Rasmus became the thing for Alexandra Bernadotte Victoria, Rasmus Høysand began to realize he was now genuinely in love (with the thin body and the blue eyes and the blonde hair and the gentle voice that expressed all the charming, minuscule variations in the nature of her home district, Akershus—Alexandra Bernadotte Victoria was from Bærum west of Oslo), and he also realized (not quite so quickly, one must add in order not to falsify history and put Rasmus Høysand in an all-too-flattering light) that until now he had been as great a danger to humanity as the Devil himself, and almost as great a danger as Leo Trotsky. Høysand soon found out, too, that the girl he had fallen in love with, and moved in with not long afterward, was not named Alexandra Bernadotte Victoria, as was written on her student card; on the contrary, she had been a particularly unfortunate victim of the unrestrained grand-bourgeois custom of giving absurd pet- or nicknames, which in her case had resulted in the everyday name of Ulla, a name that her classmates at Eiksmarka School in the eastern part

181

of Bærum had been quick to write *KN* in front of, making it a word like *fuck,* in every imaginable place—on the name tag of the schoolbag she had used ever since first grade (The teacher takes a piece of chalk and writes a letter on the blackboard. Then he turns and points at the board: This is an A! Ulla, in the first row: I don't believe it!), on her neat school books, on André Bjerke's reading book, on Øverland's blue book, yes, even on her fourth-grade report card, these scamps (every one of whom would later be civil economists and shipbrokers and revolutionary cadre leaders and big yachtsmen in the 5.5-meter class) made this brutal and baldly erotic addition. But what was more important, yes, really the *only* important thing, was that Ulla, despite her upbringing and family background, which were anything but proletarian, exhibited on many issues the same independent spirit she had shown during the attempt to teach her the alphabet. Moreover, she had grown up and was attending the university (where she studied psychology, statistics, and social economy, and got excellent grades) during a time when socialist-revolutionary ideas were strong in academic circles. Like the apt, osmotic pupil she was, Ulla appropriated these ideas within a short time and, like the clear-sighted and unsentimental young woman she also was, within a somewhat longer time she managed to make the ideas relate meaningfully to the patch of Norwegian reality surrounding her. The result was intense political activism. For example, she attended the party in the large apartment in Frogner for the single reason that she had heard that several of those who would be there were "potentially good." But then, too, here sat Rasmus Høysand on the floor, two places to her right, listening with interest to much that was said, but looking with at least as much interest at the girls around him. Rasmus Høysand, who at that time was just barely in his thirties, had seen both this and that, but his upbringing had taught him about socialism's ideas of justice and equality and freedom only through the entrepreneurial type of social democracy that had reconstructed Norway's production system in the fifties, plus he had listened to a few speeches by Stavanger Health Officer Eyvin Dahl, including one occasion on which he remembered Dahl became furious when a college student asked

182

how things were with the pacifists and the conscientious objectors in the Soviet Union. (At that time, such questions were in vogue among those who called themselves radicals.) Pacifism! Conscientious objectors! thundered Eyvin Dahl. When the worldwide reactionary movement stands ready to attack history's first peasant-and-worker state! Next question! Yes, but history books say— Yes, but history books lie! Lie, lie, lie! Bang, bang, bang on the table. Next question! And Rasmus Høysand continued to believe what the Bergen *Times* and Haugesund *News* and Stavanger *Evening News* wrote and Haakon Lie said.

He stated this very clearly, too, the first time Ulla questioned him about his social and political ideas in general, and about socialism in particular. But he had not uttered many sentences before Rasmus Høysand had entangled himself in a position that had only one way out, and that was. How many night shifts have you put in, my girl? And: How many stormy days have you stood at the helm? And: How many winter days have you worked outside? And: That's socialist, I tell you—you won't sleep with me because I'm not bourgeois enough. These were all arguments Rasmus Høysand could make with a certain authority and in a very convincing and trustworthy manner, because he still had both the appearance and behavior of a farm boy or laborer or recruit, accustomed to being treated like a dog, always on guard, that's the way life is, they whack you all the same, the sudden movements in the mess and on the orlop deck and in the bar in Takoradi; this aggression was combined with something else, something that made you feel you just had to stomp around on deck and look tough, so Høysand would jump up from what he was doing and look around with ready fists and a questioning glance to see where he could lend a hand. It was as if all that lying on his stomach or his back inside a worn-out blade wheel and tightening the screws and not being able to do it and swearing and trying to move and there's just not enough space to work inside this damn thing and they can fucking well do this themselves if this wheel is so important, was still stuck fast to the body that had lain stretched out full length and had blades jabbing into its back and sand on its neck and had not been able to use the ratchet wrench and the An tough to get at

183

and thought, Goddammit, if something starts up now! even if everything is shut off, and as though *Warning! Machine work in progress* still clung to his body, not only in the pores of his skin as old grease and silicone dust and sinter fines that had penetrated his overalls, and in his lungs as the dust of quartz and dolomite, but even more permanently, in the way he stood, for example, when waiting for Ulla to come at an appointed time (and thought: Can I love? Have I loved? Will I ever be able to love? Has anyone loved? Is there anyone? Is there a God? Is Stalin dead?), in the angle between his back and his neck and the angle at which his neck met his head and the way he stuck out his right foot when standing and the way his look questioned and the way a smile came to his face and the way he opened his mouth and began talking: Huh? No, this here, uhhhh, no that there you can keep yourself. Of course, the strange thing was that he had to go to Oslo, to meet the eyes of people who had never done the same things as he and understand how these people thought, before he could see himself this way, with the Lord's heartless, penetrating look.

But all these things helped only a little. They didn't help at all. Rasmus Høysand, who in some matters was a relatively honest man, and far from unintelligent, was driven mercilessly from bulwark to bulwark, hindered by infatuation, which slowly but surely developed into something he did not hesitate to think of as love and to run away from, but which at least always forced him back again when he did. He understood more and more clearly the rationality behind the ideas that Ulla, and gradually many others as well, developed for him, and this rationality was daily confronted with the madness that results from domination by moneyed interests or from development that's mixed up with the interests of a gang of unrestrained speculators. Ulla and the others presented their points of view calmly, easily, and nonaggressively, with secure bourgeois confidence that their demands were just and therefore obviously ought to be fulfilled at once, whereas poor Rasmus Høysand had completely different experiences with communication:

Ulla:

Secretary of Defense Harlem, what is NATO?

Well, dear Ulla, NATO is the idea of freedom and the gospel of love, which have joined forces to defend us against the ideology of hate.

Høysand:

Sergeant! 54-Høysand requests an extended evening pass. Until 0200 hours!

What! Stand at attention, you damn shit-ass homo, and shut up when you talk to me, and straighten those shoulders and request permission in hell, where you'll go when you're six feet under, and that means you're dead, and that means you can start turning in your effects!

Ulla:

Labor Union Chairman Tor Aspengren, are you really opposed to the Labor-Management Agreement, and the Labor Court, and illegal, antitariff strikes? Or is that just a mistaken impression we've gotten? Many of us feel it's time we had an answer to this question.

Dear Ulla, the task of reaching agreements is not achieved without a struggle. We in the Labor movement today cannot passively stand by and watch extremist foreign elements among the workers destroy the rights for which pioneers and veterans have fought so hard.

Høysand:

Engineer! 1168-Høysand has suffered a cerebral hemorrhage, so I can't work the night shift tonight!

What! We don't stand for that kind of whimpering in a healthy society. You can snivel blood if you want, for all I care, but you *will* be at work at eleven P.M., no matter what!

SOUL FAREWELL

Rasmus Høysand went to a study group in Marxist theory, eagerly studied the teachings of the big five (Marx, Engels, Lenin, Stalin, Mao), learned about the fundamental contradiction (between labor and capital) and what major contradictions resulted from this (between the people and monopoly capital until the spring of 1976, between the working class and the bourgeoisie thereafter), which type of contradictions were irrec-

oncilable (class contradictions) and which were The Correct
Line. (Struggle against the State and the Soviet. Yes, but isn't
this the Libertas lobby's policy? No, King Sverre was the greatest Marxist-Leninist back in his time.) Such deviations to the
right made Høysand feel like a plodding, helpless, dumb
squarehead who should have stood in a barn stall all his life and
not gotten mixed up with these beautiful and fearless folk, who
were always right, and who had discussed the debate between
Lukacs and Brecht and had discarded revisionism from the moment they stuck their heads over the edge of the crib and began
conversing with the person next to them in the nursery for
newborn babies; but despite all this, Rasmus Høysand continued to develop and improve his class views, and everything
progressed, except his studies. He became more and more self-
confident, and gradually realized that it probably was easier,
after all, to come to Oslo via San Pedro Sula than direct from
Ålvik in Hardanger. But he made no headway in his work at the
university; Høysand was as ignorant as ever about corporate law
and civil law and bankruptcy and bargaining. The political
work took too much time, agit-prop papers and fliers had to be
stenciled and handed out on the highways and byways. Høys-
and gave up law, looked around a while for something he
thought would be a cheap and easy education, and that fall
entered the National School of Library Science. Rasmus Høys-
and still lay awake at night, tossed and turned uneasily in his
bed, and sweated and thought. Was Stalin a great revolutionary?
Is the Soviet Union today a capitalistic society with fascist leaders who carry out a social-imperialistic foreign policy? Were all
the old members of the Central Committee who led the Russian
Revolution (aside from Stalin himself) bought by the capitalistic
powers and secret agents for fascism? Did they deserve to be
executed as enemies of the people? Were those who executed the
capitalistic old Bolsheviks (on behalf of Stalin) also capitalists in
disguise, who carried out a counterrevolution after Stalin's
death and introduced a fascist leadership in Russia? After Lenin
died, was there only one man in the Soviet party (Bolshevik)
leadership who stood for the proletarian line? Was there a mate-
rialistic interpretation of history? Can a fascist regime come into

186

power and then exercise that power with the help of the same government administration that carries out the dictates of the proletariat? The Party? The Central Committee? The Politburo? The Supreme Soviet? The Communist cells? The Red Army? The KGB? Høysand turned over for the last time and fell asleep, exhausted, beside Ulla.

It was early morning when Høysand awoke. He felt light and clear-headed, as on the morning after a successful drinking bout. He practically floated up from the bed. His soul had left him, lay heavy and exposed on the floor beside the bed, repulsive and harmless as a jellyfish on land. Høysand was nothing in and of himself any longer, just a cog in an objectively functioning historical machine. During the night his unconscious had answered, Yes! Yes! Yes! Yes! Yes! Yes! Yes! to all his questions. He was free! Free! FREE! For the first time! Rasmus Høysand got up immediately, observed in the mirror that his gaze had become steadier and more open, and as he walked to school he felt that his strides had become longer, his pace quicker, his manner of walking more goal-oriented, the way he remembered newly appointed bosses at the factory walking. From the very first people he met, Høysand found that he looked people straight in the eye, perceived the correct contradictions, differentiated friends of the people from enemies of the people in an alert, precise, and very consistent manner, and had important errands everywhere. At this time Rasmus Høysand is a lean man of less than average height, with a slight build and such slender wrists and ankles they could well be those of a woman. Nevertheless, he has something that Ulla's girlfriends often characterized, in whispered admiration and envy, as *proletarian radiation*. Like most people from Vestland, Høysand also is ruddy and freckled, kind and trusting, and (given even the least excuse, such as just a tiny little gleam of fantasy and flight of fancy) happy. But such excuses are always rare as long as Høysand (and other West Coast natives) have to live in Oslo or in similar places on the East Coast, in Trøndelag, at the far side of the moon, or in Sweden. Therefore, a superficial description of Rasmus Høysand's state of mind will frequently picture him as gruff, sullen, in fact gloomy. But as already stated, he is actually a happy, cheerful, generous, and often naïvely trusting soul, for which he has often paid dearly among his more cynical and calculating comrades and friends (and enemies, which, to be completely honest, he also has—and if one weren't heedlessly honest here, how would things go when one came to the dark side of life?), brothers and sisters (in spirit as well as in the far-from-weak flesh), politicos and police, sons and lovers in every land. Rasmus and Ulla, who are nearing the end of their studies, have lived together for more than a year. Now they move into an apartment complex (they were lucky, 2 rm. and kitchen, 4th fl., 650 kroner mo. + elect.) at the far side of Groruddalen in northeast Oslo, form a community action group after some months, and enthusiastically begin organizing people regarding their individual rights. Høysand felt happy. True, he had brief, but painfully clear-sighted, flashes in which he realized that in many things he would always be alone. Always. Which nobody would ever understand, which many people understood, but they didn't need to read books to understand it. Still, those areas in which Rasmus Høysand was not alone had now found their political expression. That made him feel relieved and happy. Høysand had been taught, and had always believed, that the cultural elite had the most understanding. That's what made them the cultural elite, that they had the most understanding. Otherwise, there was no use for a cultural elite, after all. Now to his alarm and great, great astonishment, Høysand discovered that precisely these people who lived so high up on their eminent knowledge, many years of education, and unsurpassed insights, were actually the most ignorant people he had ever met. The realization sent chills down Rasmus Høysand's spine. He had spent his entire childhood and boyhood and youth living among industrial workers, shop girls, public employees, seamen, and peers who had the same background as he. To say nothing of the dregs of society in all the world's seaports, whom he also had met. Except for the latter, these were all people who did hard, exhausting work, had only a few years of inferior education, and were strongly influenced by deadly, pietistic Christianity and by religious and bourgeois prejudices. Never-

188

theless, Høysand discovered, slowly and, despite everything, painfully (he was a type of intellectual himself, after all!), these people knew a lot more about themselves and about the country and the world in which they lived, and above all, had a far more precise understanding of what they lived from (expressed through many different social and political morphologies) than did the professional opinion-cultivators who spent their added value as publishers, university teachers, theater people, critics, radio broadcasters, culture writers, journalists. It amazed Høysand how all these people formed a homogeneous and tightly organized social network, agreeing on most things, always on speaking terms, without money problems, without worries about how to manage, without concrete nouns, without the least idea about industrialists and union men such as, for example, Sigurd Kloumann, Ole O. Lian, William Henry Sneath, Halfdan Jønsson, Bjarne Ericksen, Karsten Torkildsen, Per Blidensol, Anker Nordvedt (though there are statues or streets bearing names from the employers' side throughout the country's industrial towns), whereas they were very familiar with writers like Gunnar Heiberg and Sigurd Hoel, with Kjetil Bang-Hansen and Knut Faldbakken; without even knowing who played center-half on the national soccer team at some particular time or other, without (to tell the truth, and as the great moralist Georg Johannesen said) any knowledge of the land in which they lived other than The Mountains (where they went skiing at Easter and during winter vacations) and The Country (where they regarded it as completely obvious and natural that they should lie around for two months each summer playing croquet and writing novels):

THE COURAGE OF DESPAIR

Chpt. 1
A group of young people from Slemdal near Oslo lie around each summer for two months at the family's summer house in the south of Norway playing croquet and discussing the tensions that arise among members of the group as time goes on.

Chpt. 2

The group consists of: the handsome young doctor, Karl, who has socialist sympathies; Benedictine, his divorced sister; Frida, who used to be engaged to Ronald, a yachtsman who is studying theology and raises the eternal question, Is there a God, oh Lord? and receives the answer of our times: I will be a friend of the people; the refined author, Sigurd; the three radical Bull brothers; and the mysterious Ayra, whose origins nobody knows (she is fictitious) and who rows out to sea in an open boat at sunset with the wind in her flowing amber-colored hair.

Chpt. 3

Confound it! said Alf, and wiped his perspiring brow as the green ball sneaked, simply sneaked, outside the wicket.

   Awfully annoying indeed, said Vera, and lightly pressed his hand.

Chpt. 4

Ronald travels to Sandefjord after a clash with Valentin. Frida prays for him, but is surprised by Alf. Ronald misses the train he had planned to take. It is two hours before the next train will leave. Ronald collapses on the platform.

Chpt. 5

Old Magdalon the postman does not bring the *Daily News* when he delivers the mail at eleven o'clock. Johan tries to understand what Magdalon says, but must simply give up. Magdalon pedals off on his bicycle. What has happened? The tension mounts. The group gathers in the sitting room. Both of her daughters are Marxist-Leninist.

Chpt. 6

Alf dives from the three-meter. Ayra is still nowhere to be seen. The three radical Bull boys read old copies of the *Daily News* on the floor in the dining room. Evening falls.

Chpt. 7

Tension arises between Thomas and Evelyn, between Christian and Ayra, between Jacob and Evelyn, who has come over from her father's summer place, between Thomas and Jacob. The unpleasantness spreads. Rain beats against the windowpane. Alf is silent.

Chpt. 8

With trembling hands Carl Henrik opens the telegram. He holds it up to the light. The heavens are silent. Must deliver manuscript to publisher latest medio–August stop Ronald still willing to be consultant stop. Ragnar comes up from the cellar. Wilfred leaves. The tension is slowly discharged.

Chpt. 9

Trine looks at the smooth, bare, sloping rocks that come to the surface of the sea like the round shoulders of a young girl.

Is everything, then, barren petrification? she wonders, and shudders.

His eyes follow the ferries, they pass each other. He murmurs: No, there is a meaning.

Chpt. 10

Frida raises her eyes from the green ball with an irritated look, and stares over toward the camping ground on the other side of the bay.

Actually, I don't think it *is* so awful about the camping ground, she says. When one realizes that many people who didn't have the opportunity before, now have a chance to get out in the country . . .

Nicolay adjusts his grip on the croquet mallet.

You are kind, he says quietly, and knocks the blue ball against the post so it sings.

GALGEBERG STADIUM

Rasmus Høysand was happy. As happy as it was possible to be under a late stage of capitalism. But the soccer fields were a problem. Why was there no playing field, no main stadium (in fact, not even a miserable first-run movie theater) on the east side? Ulleval was terrible, had never been a soccer stadium. Bislett was all right for some things, skating World Championships, frostbitten toes and higher mathematics, but in soccer you didn't often get up into double-digit scores, even when

Norway played international matches, and anyway, why did the players and trainers and spectators for the Vålerenga and Skeid teams have to take the streetcar around half the city, into the heart of the petit bourgeois areas, Ila, St. Hanshaugen, Bislett, Fagerborg, even when Vålerenga played home games against the petit bourgeois in Frigg? To say nothing of the grand bourgeois in Lyn? Could there be a clearer example of lack of self-interest on the part of the Norwegian working class? Self-sacrifice? Cooperation between the classes? On the middle class's terms? No, there should have been a small playing field, for instance, at Daehlenenga, where "Yea, Frigg!" was forbidden and a large stadium at Galgeberg, instead of Bajern and the new Grønland Police Station (yes, there's Jordal Amfi, but what's Jordal Amfi? And Norwegian ice hockey has few social consequences and offers experiences that are at about the same level as Norwegian films). Galgeberg Stadium, with fifty thousand seats and where even the feeblest "Yea, Lyn!" would lead to certain death, in fact where even "Yea, Norway!" would seem a little suspect. Think what this could have meant for the city of Oslo, for the atmosphere in that sprawling capital city without any identity. It could have lightened a little the heavy cowl over this low, shapeless, thinly populated, sparsely inhabited mixture of Fritz Lang's Dusseldorf and a Nordic Los Angeles, this distant province in the national consciousness that has never forgiven the rest of the country for changing its name from Christiania to Kristiania and depriving the city of the aristocratic *Ch* and which every single day regards its newest name, Oslo, as an active, nonlocalized cancerous tumor deep within its broad sportsmanlike breast. A foreign land, which borders on Denmark and two tennis courts, with the Bergen School of Business on the fourth side. Rasmus Høysand stood on the corner of Mauritz Hansen Street and Pile Street looking at the trolley tracks, Frydenlunds Brewery, Bislett Stadium and Bolteløkka, and suddenly thought about something Emile Durkheim had said in 1897 in his book *Suicide:*

"Social fact is materialized at times to such a high degree that it becomes part of the environment. A particular type of architecture, for example, is a social phenomenon. And to an equal extent it is partially incarnated in houses, in all types of buildings which, once they are built, have a separate reality, dependent upon individuals. It is the same with communication methods and means of transportation, with instruments and machines used in industry or private life that express the state of technology at each point in history; it is the same with written language—and so on. The life of society is crystallized, as it were, and attached to material carriers. It has thereby been externalized, and has an inner effect on us from the outside." Right— not the text, but the texture, thought Høysand, and passed the counting machines as he went in to the Standing Room Only bleachers at Bislett Stadium.

OUT WITH THE WORDS!

The years went by. Twice, both times late in the evening, Rasmus Høysand was tempted to write his autobiography. Not because he dreamed of success and literary fame, no, he altruistically thought the working class ought to be able to learn something from all his exciting experiences and waywardness, and besides the question did not exist, because now his own private interests had merged completely with the objective interests of the working class as a whole. Høysand dreamed vaguely of a brilliant career as the reliable interpreter of industrial Norway, or as the working boy who became clown and poet in order to tell about the secret strength of the working people and about the ravages of capitalism and about the baseness of the high and mighty. The first attempt started with Rasmus Høysand trying to hitch a ride on a highway across Luneburger Heide in northern Germany, and it began like this: "On the highway in front of me, the cars swished past like the brightly polished blades of a huge guillotine that was carrying out a mass execution." In the second version, which started out several years earlier in his life, Rasmus Høysand stood at the top of Nonskilje Mountain between the Kvann and Grønstøl valleys (that is, on the side facing Kvannskår Peak) one stormy fall day after the sheep had been rounded up, and began his story with these words: "The air trembled in a feverish northeasterly gale, and sweated snow in large flakes." But this was as far as he got with either version. For a long time afterward, Rasmus Høysand was in the same situation as that described by Ivar Aasen, the great founder of the New Norwegian written language, in a letter to Georg Grieg on June 25th, 1868: "I sit here immured in a mass of fifty thousand words, and still I am always at a loss for ignition words when necessity demands. It is like a merchant who has received a large cargo of wares, but never can find time to organize them and put them on the shelves. When customers come and request some item or other, he says he surely must have it, but he never knows where it is. And it may even be that he does not know himself what he has."

But all good things come in threes. The third attempt began: "She plants her heels on the concrete and stands." And that beginning satisfied Høysand. Everything went along fine. He was happy. He went running every day and felt he was getting in shape. He sped through Lillomarka woodlands at the edge of Oslo every evening, light and eager, as if he were running in History and it was the revolution, not good physical shape, that would follow. Living together with Ulla went well, they tried to find a balance between two-sided introspection (turning oneself inward toward the other) and what Ulla called outrospection. After two years, Høysand took his final examinations and became a librarian at the university library, where he specialized in picaresque literature and nearly every day had the pleasure of holding endless discussions about where, in what genre, important works of Mateo Alemán, Quevedo (now the Spanish from Buenaventura was put to good use!), Thomas Nashe, Defoe, Fielding, Tobias Smollett, Grimmelshausen, and Holberg should be placed. And Rabelais should also come in here somewhere, shouldn't he? And what about Laurence Sterne? The life story and thoughts of Tristram Shandy, gentleman, were probably not exactly a picaresque tale, but Høysand thought he saw parallels nevertheless, and defended this viewpoint in countless lunch breaks. At the same time, he did not forget to fight toward getting the university librarians who worked picaresque literature, the baroque, and surrealism to organize their own association and demand a raise of at least fifty wage levels with cost-of-living increases to level sixty-nine on the government wage scale, and he tried his best to see this demand, which so clearly was at odds with bourgeois rationality, as it related to other short-term political demands and the course of the People's War.

One evening when he came home late from a meeting, Ulla was still up and she looked at him for a long time with big eyes and chapped lips as he sliced some bread and made a sandwich.

Rasmus?

Yes.

Do you notice anything different?

Different?

About me.

No.

Silence. Slice of bread in the mouth, teeth against cucumber and liverwurst, and press together. Women are never as sentimental as men.

So what is it, Ulla? Out with the words!

Rasmus, I'm pregnant.

They decided to get married (they hadn't felt the need to do it before, but this was a good opportunity to dispense with that kind of radical-culture deadweight), and then they had to have a larger apartment, and then they had to have money.

Rasmus?

Yes.

You could go and meet my family. It's about time. My father is disgustingly rich. And disgustingly reactionary. Politically, he stands to the right of Ivan the Terrible. Quisling. He was even a collaborator during the war.

He can change.

He'd have to be born again.

And why not?

Because our congregation has rejected the Virgin Birth.

But so have our Christian theologians, like Origenes, for instance, who believed in Satan's eventual conversion.

We really love each other. That's the awful thing.

Then let's go and talk with him.

A big party was held at the luxurious house in Bærum, with many speeches, and Ulla herself announced her engagement to Rasmus Høysand, in an unpretentious and straightforward way. Then Høysand carefully tapped his glass with his knife, stood up, blinked nervously out across the guests in formal attire that glittered with St. Olav and Storkors medals, cleared his throat, and said:

SUPPORT

When wild and far my wanderings have led
And night is black as six feet underground
I know a place with upland heaths to tread
Where heather, grass, and foxglove still abound
And parsley fern and rushes grow and spread
And pipelines go down to a shining Sound
Where folk with honor, country ways, and toil
Built farms and factories and tilled the soil

They tunnelled rock with blasts of dynamite
They tamed the mighty waterfalls' wild roar
Into electric current which flames white
Makes shining metal out of smelted ore
And lights up schoolbooks in the dark of night
And warms us from the winter cold outdoors
Where shifts take turns and show their unity
No traitor's part of the community

They stand there when a ship sets sail anew
A load of solid force for steel it brings
For wrenches, sledges, sights for rifles, too
And slender, secret strength for airplane wings
They stay there, yet they have a whole-world view
Of toil, relating, and creating things
And when the ocean heaves and crests, I'm sure
Their davits hold my lifeboat still secure

In Vestland's Valley money now holds sway
And leads our land with heavy-handed schemes
So we must battle capital today
Must be invisible as volts it seems

Then, like a sudden blaze, flame up and say
We have demands, and we have daring dreams
And ask you for support, to choose up sides en masse
For honest toil, the Party, and the working class!

THE RIGHT OF REVERSION

Everyone clapped heartily, and there were scattered shouts of Bravo! from the gala-dressed crowd. Høysand, flushed and per-spiring and proud, bowed and smiled, Thank you, thank you, and Mrs. Voss, his pale, anemic table companion, held his arm and whispered words of praise into his ear. After dinner, Mr. Voss himself came over and offered cognac and a cigar and lay his tuxedo-clad arm in a father-in-law manner on Høysand's shoulder.

Thank you for the excellent speech, he said. I must admit that toward the end there were a number of ideas that are at odds with my ideals of a free society, but we'll just let that be for now. In fact, I know a little myself about the milieu you just described so excellently. With all modesty I must tell you, in fact, that I know a little about those particular places myself. Rather de-pressing, I must say, many of them. A great deal of inbreeding, at least in earlier times. But be that as it may! You could find many peasant girls who looked like princesses, Lichtenberg was right about that, they're certainly to be found! I myself spent several years during the war at a place called Lovre, and under somewhat unfortunate circumstances, I must say, although I was not to blame in the least for the problems that arose. But then, let bygones be bygones, I'm not going to allow bitterness to spoil my old age. At any rate, I worked for A/S Nor-Dag, an important German-controlled firm which, I might note in pa-rentheses and in all modesty, founded the Norwegian alumi-num industry in fact. I myself, it's true, had the misfortune of being put in charge of, first, developing Lovre Falls and, later, building Lovre Factories, which, unfortunately, were razed to the ground after the war because a handful of ignorant popularly elected officials managed to force through the order. My life work was destroyed. The same thing happened, of course, with Nor-Dag's aluminum-oxide plant in Saudesjøen. So today Lovre is just a memory, but I must confess that in my solitary moments I often think back on that time. As I said, I'm not bitter, even if I might have good reason to be, and even if it consumed my entire youth. Thirty years! A whole generation ago. That's a long time. A lifetime. My lifetime. Oh well, one mustn't get sentimental and bury oneself in the past. We've got to look ahead. Even in that difficult time I realized this. Fortunately, it turned out that I was put in charge of liquidating the barracks buildings that remained after the work at Lovre I, and I did such a good job of it that I more or less could see a bright future ahead of me when I left Lovre. Not with unmitigated joy, I must say. Not with unmitigated joy. Not at all. In many ways, I was attached to the place and to the people who lived there. At that time, of course, I was still a bachelor, and I certainly had my small digressions, it's true. But they were beautiful girls. Incidentally, they had some baroque names in those parts. Durdei, I remember one was called. Yes, just simply Durdei as a forename. I baptize you Durdei. Think of that! Incidentally, the situation with Durdei was a little delicate. She got pregnant; but people overlooked that, of course, and she, and most likely the child, too, for that matter, is probably still living her simple life there, as they have done since Arild's time.

At that moment Rasmus Høysand heard Ulla's voice behind him.

Splitting up into factions already, are you? she said cheerfully. You mustn't keep Rasmus to yourself the whole time, you know. He's got other social duties as well, now that he's meeting the family at last.

That's no doubt true, but we men still need to be allowed to have some secrets, even if they're about women and revolution and I don't know what all. You're welcome to join us, though.

Oh, said Rasmus Høysand, and began to cough violently. When the worst had subsided, he signaled a toast and drank his glass of cognac. Then he turned to Ulla.

Høysand and Ulla exchanged a few words before Høysand

198

left the house unobserved and walked down to the garden gate without looking back. He closed the gate quietly behind him, waved to Ulla, and continued on down the fashionable street, a thin, slightly lopsided figure with reddish-blond hair in a light tropical suit. Nothing special about him. Ulla waved back, and remained standing in the doorway with a thoughtful expression on her face. What will become of Rasmus Høysand now? she asked herself. Will he ever understand that he can never reach true freedom, success, and happiness for himself alone? And what's more important: will those to whom I'll tell this whole pathetic story of Rasmus Høysand understand the emptiness and futility in his lonely search for happiness, and learn that in this gray void, in the classless limbo outside history, one finds only unhappiness and destruction? Because this is the most important thing to know.

She got no further in her thinking. A red truck with the name of a company painted on the side of it drove into the driveway, and a man in overalls jumped out.

WHS, said the man, and began pulling wrenches and hammers out of the back of the truck.

WHS? We Had Success?

Water, Heat, Sanitation. You've been having some leaking here?

Noooo, Ulla replied absent-mindedly.

Oh, it's plugged?

Plugged?

The drain?

The preoccupied expression on Ulla's face turned to mild irritation. She said decidedly, and a little sharply:

No, everything's just as it always is here!

The man shrugged, a wrench in each hand:

Okay, okay, okay, okay! Then it must be at the house next door.

He tossed the tools back in the truck, got in behind the wheel, and backed out onto the street. Then he was gone.

So was Rasmus Høysand when Ulla looked for him again. But it doesn't really matter, she thought. I'm sure he'll manage.

Then she turned abruptly on her heel and went back into the house. I'm sure he'll manage, Ulla said aloud to herself. Rasmus Høysand is an unsuccessful opportunist, and when all is said and done, and now all *is* said and done, that's the decisive test of high moral (social, aesthetic, political, etc.) character.

I stand here in my long-time Prison and look out through the Grate and ponder how all Things the cruel Winter did imprison are now once more loosed and liberated and made fresh by mild Summer. The Sun and all the Beauties of the heavenly Firmament do now praise their Lord and Creator Who hath banished the thick and dark and heavy and unkind and woeful winter Clouds with their snow, their cold, their damp, and their oppressiveness! The Earth hath joyfully put on a splendid green Garment and doth bedeck and adorn herself with all Manner of colorful Flowers, which do offer a lively Fragrance and Incense to the Lord in Thanksgiving that His Blessed Majesty hath brought them out of the cold and stifling Prison of Winter! The great Lakes and delightful Streams, the running Brooks and rich Seas flow and well forth and gush in rushing Currents and do praise the Lord Who hath taken from them the cold and hard and heavy Ice. The Birds beneath the Heavens do praise the Lord early and late upon the green Branches; and the Animals of the Field rejoice in the Valley, to the Glory of God; and the Fish of the Deep offer to the Lord a thankful Breath for He hath given them Space to breathe and Warmth above; and the great Whales and Ocean Wonders gambol and frolic in the Sea to the Glory of God and each in its own Way doth proclaim His great Mercy. The Ships on the Sea unfurl their Flags and praise the Lord with Trumpets and Shouts of Joy for He hath led them out of their Prison unharmed by Ice and Snow, and the Seagulls with great Delight do glide on and off the Waves. All fertile Fields and Vineyards, Meadows, Forests, and Valleys laud and praise the Lord that now have they been released from the Custody of Winter and can multiply and bear Fruit according to their Powers to the Glory of God and for the Nourishment and Benefit of Mankind.

I stand here in my Prison and look out through the hard iron Grate and think how the unreasoning Beasts that this Winter have been imprisoned, away from the Frost and Cold, are now loosed, and do run and dance and rejoice in the Fields to the Glory, Laud, and Honor of the Lord. I see how Men lead out the young Horses that through the long Winter have been standing still, and do revive them with riding and jumping, and refresh their stiff Legs in running Water. In summa, I see People, high and low, rich and poor, young and old, large and small, going to and fro, strolling and rejoicing in the mild Summer that hath rescued them from the Prison of cold Winter; and therefore do they praise the Lord their God and Savior. I stand and think how People on Land and Water are now filled with Gladness and do go about their common Rounds, each one according to his own Purpose. I stand and think how His Royal Majesty, our most merciful King and Lord, and all his Cavalry and lawful Soldiers now do revel and rejoice out in the Field and do smite their Enemies with ready Will and heroic Manliness. His Trumpets sound, his Drums reverberate with Glory for the Lord out in the Forests, Mountains, and Valleys; and his Kettle Drums, Tabors, Pipes, Musketeers, and Field Sergeant do ring and run and thunder and praise the Lord for He hath given them Victory over their Enemies. I stand and think how all His Royal Majesty's honest and vigorous and loyal and sincere and manly Servants and Soldiers do willingly offer their Blood and Soul to the Lord, with stout Courage and Gladness, for the Honor of God's Name, the Protection of the Christian Throne, and the Pleasure, Piety, and Benefit of the King and all Christians. Yea, do I stand here and think, and believe that all Things which Life and Freedom hath, must now most surely revel and rejoice! But I, unhappy Person, though desiring and wishing to serve, to serve for the Honor, Pleasure, Piety, and Benefit of God and the King and my Fatherland (which Service can also, and of Necessity, be without these Walls in this tumultuous Season), I must, alas, in Sorrow remain imprisoned in Land after Land, and from Year to Year, all due only to a Danish Lass, and must henceforth be destroyed in Prison and thereby afford mine Enemies and Foes the greatest Pleasure; ah yes, I know the Danes do likely say that already I am fallen into Ruin, albeit they well know that I wish them no Harm. But I entrust myself to God and give thanks to Him, and to His Royal Majesty who through the Intermediation of Your Grace and Highness doth grant the lawful Right to defend myself against mine Enemies, that still I am not subjugated to their evil Intent and Desire. I now further beseech Your Grace and Highness to deign, for the Sake of God, mercifully to mitigate my long and wearisome Imprisonment, that I fall not entirely into Ruin. My Misery in regard of Body and Clothing and Health and Vitality dare I not express, but address such Concerns to God, that He alone may know them.

Should I still with such Injustice be imprisoned when the Autumn cometh, then will I, alas, be more a Beggar than a healthy and useful Servant. I do assure Your Grace and Highness that I shall present myself wheresoever and whensoever it be commanded. Thanks be to God, I know my Crime is not so great that my Life can be in any Danger; and I would also that Your Grace consider how I did willingly return to my Home here in Stockholm and since that Time have made my Defense in an open and an able Manner; and I do hope there will be found against me no Complaint other than that which a faithful Swede doth owe his Fatherland. I shall, moreover, take particular Heed lest my Perseverance give to Your Grace any Reason for Concern. Now may Almighty God protect me and harken to my Misery and move the Hearts of those that hold the Power, that they with merciful Eyes regard me and do not suffer my Destruction according to the Desire of mine Enemies.

—Laurentius Wivallius, "Petition to the Imperial Council," May, 1632 (National Archives of Sweden)